BOOKS BY SUZA KATES

The Savannah Coven Series

Whisper of a Witch
Conviction of a Witch
Binding of a Witch
Haunting of a Witch
Possession of a Witch
Deception of a Witch
Suffering of a Witch
Vengeance of a Witch
Sacrifice of a Witch

The Sisters' Grimoire Trilogy

The Sisters' Grimoire
Winter Fae
Chosen Blood
Brit

The She Series

She Who is Hidden

Single Titles

Hallowed Eve
The Penance Stone

RETURN OF A WITCH
THE SAVANNAH COVEN SERIES

SUZA KATES

ICASM PRESS

SAVANNAH

Published by Icasm Publishing LLC
5710 Ogeechee Rd. Suite 200 #278, Savannah, GA 31405
www.icasmpress.com

Library of Congress Cataloging-in-Publication Data

Kates, Suza
Return of a Witch / Suza Kates
    p. cm.

ISBN-13:978-0-942318-39-2
ISBN-13:978-0-942318-40-8 (ebook)
I. Title

Printed and bound in the United States of America

10 9 8 7 6 5 4 3 2 1

Acknowledgments

I have to give a super-huge thank you to the editing and beta-reading team that stuck with me through the final and very hectic days of this book. To Mandi Cranson, Sharyn Cerniglia, Donna Wood, Dorothy Beecher, and Stella Racicot—THANK YOU for sticking with the crazy lady once again.

I also want give special thanks to my street team, the Advo-Kates. You guys keep it fun every day! And this go-round, I need to show my appreciation to Laura Molina, who stepped in to help me with Lucia's Spanish.

To the readers who've waited very patiently for this book, I hope you enjoy the story as much as I did. Your love for the coven made the series a success, and for that I am truly grateful.

Lastly, to my husband David. My writing ups and downs have put him through the ringer the last few years but, amazingly, he is still by my side. Thank you for your patience and continued support, because I wouldn't make it without you.

All my love to every reader out there, and I'll see you the next time around! ~~ Suza

THE COVEN

Anna St. Germaine
Hair: Long, straight, sable brown
Eyes: Sapphire blue
Color: Sapphire blue
Cat: "Ivy" gray female with lime green eyes

Anna sees visions of past, present, and future. She is the coven's head witch and is a descendant of the three women who originally banished the demon Bastraal three centuries ago. Her ancestral home is on an island off the coast of Savannah, Georgia and now serves as coven central.

Claudia Grant
Hair: Straight, long, flaming red
Eyes: River green
Color: Coral
Cat: "Rowan Von Ashbi" coloring of an American Wirehair with yellow eyes

Claudia is a history professor who only needs to touch an object to sense its past and previous surroundings.

Hayden Wells
Hair: Brownish red "caramel"
Eyes: Golden brown
Color: Pale pink
Cat: "Daisy" black tortoiseshell with yellow eyes

Hayden is a medium from San Francisco who sees and talks to spirits/ghosts.

Kylie Worthington
Hair: Long, wavy golden-blonde
Eyes: Hazel
Color: Yellow
Cat: Sassafras "Sassy" also a long-haired blonde but with bright yellow eyes

Kylie is a college student who's "on a break" to do her part for the coven and is able to control electricity in any form.

Lucia Ruiz
Hair: Long, wavy deep brown
Eyes: Brown
Color: Red
Cat: "Iris" black Persian with blue eyes

Lucia was born to privileged wealth in Spain and has the ability to find anything that is lost. She is an adventurer, world-traveler, and renowned relic-hunter.

Paige Reilley
Hair: Shoulder-length, white-blonde with ragged bangs
Eyes: Turquoise blue
Color: Turquoise
Cat: Tiger Lily "Tiger" brown and gray with white chest and belly, bright green eyes

Recently discharged from the military, Paige is a soldier in every way with the added abilities of super-strength and speed.

Shauni Miller
Hair: Long, straight, black
Eyes: Emerald green
Color: Green
Cat: "Cuileann" black short-hair with green eyes

Shauni is a nature-loving biologist from Colorado and communicates with animals telepathically.

Viv Sakurai
Hair: Shoulder-length, black, angled bangs
Eyes: Gray
Color: Purple
Cat: Kikoku "Kiko" orange tabby with yellow-green eyes and a grumpy disposition.

Relocated from Chicago, Viv is a physicist searching for an explanation for her own special power of telekinesis.

Willyn Brousseau
Hair: Wavy, shoulder-length, light blonde
Eyes: Pale blue
Color: White/cream
Cat: "Snowball" pure white with golden eyes

Willyn is a nurse, a mother, and a Christian. Raised in Alabama, she uses her healing powers to help those in need. She came to Savannah with an additional package, her young son, Tadd.

THE GUYS

Dr. Michael Black   *Whisper of a Witch*

This tall handsome veterinarian fell in love with Shauni in the first book of the series. He has dark blonde hair and gray eyes and is able to read a person's aura. He's a pretty calm guy until someone messes with his witch.

Dare Forster   *Conviction of a Witch*

Dark and handsome with deep blue eyes, this male witch came to the coven's island with his own plan. He wanted to partner with one of the women, but he never expected to fall in love. Especially with a gentle, Christian soul like Willyn. Now married, the two have made a family with Willyn's small son, Tadd.

Nick Reagan   *Binding of a Witch*

The coven likes to hang out in their favorite pub, and the owner of the bar always liked looking at Viv. His eyes are the color of the whiskey he sells, and his past is one of struggle. One night Nick finally got the nerve to approach the Asian beauty, but he got a lot more than he bargained for. The demon Bastraal had been destroyed once before, and his remains had been buried. Beneath Nick's very own pub.

Trevor Roch *Haunting of a Witch*

One of Savannah's finest, this homicide detective clashes hard with the coven's ghost whisperer, convinced she's a con artist. Hayden has no choice but to work with the annoying man and find a serial killer who's working with the Amara. Staying true to form and following the coven's pattern, the two fall for each other. Against their better judgment.

Ethan Drake *Possession of a Witch*

This demon hunter is well-acquainted with evil and has been chasing his own monster since childhood. When he offers to help the coven with their demon infestation, he has no idea he's about to be taken on the adventure of a lifetime. Lucia Ruiz is hard to resist, and is the one woman who might be able to save him.

Cole Lonergan *Deception of a Witch*

As Trevor's police partner, Cole has been introduced to the coven and all of their secrets. While he admires the women and considers them all good friends, he never expects to feel anything more. But Claudia Grant is a long-legged-wicked-smart witch, and much like his favorite candies, Cole finds himself wanting to take a bite.

Quinn St. Germaine   *Suffering of a Witch*

Quinn is the younger brother of the coven's head witch, Anna. With sable hair and cobalt eyes, he is the masculine and handsome version of the siblings. His knowledge runs to occult history and magickal languages. He assists the coven in all things, and though he has his eye on a particular witch, he does his best to deny it.

Chris Decker   *Vengeance of a Witch*

An Army Ranger recently discharged, Chris was first introduced to the coven and their demon issues during a bachelor party gone wrong in the e-novella "Boys' Night out." Blonde-haired and blue-eyed, he's pretty laid back and easy going. Which is a good thing, since he's blessed with super-strength and speed, and has fallen in love with a rather temperamental witch.

Ian Keller   *Sacrifice of a Witch*

A tall, blonde, hot "Viking," Ian is the reincarnation of Ronja's long-dead brother Vanir. As lawyer for Ronja, he was introduced to the coven in previous books. Once he started to fall for Anna, Ian began to look to the future. While a dark past and vengeful "sister" wanted to drag him back to the dark side.

1

The time had come.

In a dark and distant part of the world, a raven stared down at a fire burning wild. Hungry red and gold flames devoured the shadows, a bright and lethal rage within the once-peaceful woods.

Perched high above, the raven cried out before lifting away into the midnight sky. Now was the time to begin its journey, to carry warning to those in need. Both man and beast faced great peril.

For soon the fire would spread.

Determined and bold, the bird followed the stars, a seemingly endless river of diamonds. They flowed from this world and on to the next, guiding the raven to its fate. A destiny set by the gods of old.

With tireless wings and unwavering resolve, the creature kept its sight on the distant mountains. Their monstrous peaks stood in dark silhouette, a craggy fortress rising from the earth.

Thrusting harder now, the raven soared high, cresting the summit with the first light of dawn. A shimmering line lit the horizon. Then an explosion, the sun bursting free. And the black water turned to a deep, perfect blue.

Hope stirred in the bird's breast as the ocean gave way, and grasses and trees spread far afield. The life-affirming green offered promise for the future.

But one keenly balanced on a razor's sharp edge.

Veering south, the raven dared not stop, its mind on the intended goal. Until at last, its destination drew near. An isolated place.

A lone island in the sea.

The bird's sleek body skimmed over tall oaks, traveling inland, black eyes on the ground.

Then there she was, dark-haired and barefoot, a woman standing on an emerald lawn. Her sheer white gown ruffled in the breeze, and with a smile of welcome—a flourish of magick—Anna St. Germaine opened her arms.

Eager now, the raven rode the wind, but a sudden fierce gust blew it off course.

Anna took a step forward. She reached higher.

Spirit surging, the bird homed in on her outstretched hand. It was almost to safety. Almost there.

But infernos still raged in the world left behind, vicious fires that wouldn't let go.

Engulfed by the heat, the raven closed its eyes.

And burst into a cloud of fiery black feathers.

Anna lurched out to catch what remained, but her hands grasped only smoke and cinder.

She heard her own voice rising on the air. "Ashes to ashes."

The ground below her shuddered in response.

"Fire to fire."

Anna shook her head. *The words aren't right.* But she couldn't think clearly. The stench of scorched feathers grew into a smog, smothering her breath and stinging her eyes.

Harsh light washed over her, and she jerked her arm up in defense.

Ashes to ashes.

"Anna." Her name whispered from the dark, echoing from a place she could not see. Too blinded by the angry sun.

Fire to fire.

"Anna." Another quake rattled the world around her.

"Anna, wake up."

This time, the motion pulled her to the surface. She followed Ian's voice away from chaos, and out into the soft light of morning.

Fingertips pressed to her forehead, she released a long breath and let the tension flood from her body. "Ian," she said, sighing his name in relief. She turned her head and touched his cheek, comforted by the blond stubble beneath her palm.

"You were talking in your sleep this time," he said, picking up a strand of her sable-brown hair to rub between his fingers, a sweet morning ritual of his. "You kept repeating something, but I couldn't make it out."

Remnants of the dream taunted her, images of a bird and fire floating in her mind. In search of security, she snuggled under Ian's arm. "It was just a dream."

Though when in her life had they ever been *just* dreams?

She couldn't banish the strange words from her head. They revolved inside her, seeking release.

"Ashes to ashes." Anna rolled to her back and glanced out the window, where mossy oaks swayed and shivered in the breeze. She shivered along with them as she whispered, "Fire to fire."

"That sounds right." Ian stroked her arm. "What did it mean?"

Anna shrugged. As a clairvoyant, her dreams often held clues to solving problems she faced, offering simple information like where she'd left her gardening shears or reminders of upcoming appointments she shouldn't miss.

But sometimes, though rare, the premonitions were urgent, with ominous symbols. Warnings of danger.

She flipped through the sequence of the dream one more time. Why did a chill crawl in her bones? Why did her neck prickle with expectation? She didn't feel threatened. Not exactly. But without question, the vision held an aura of dread.

So she basked in Ian's warmth. She inhaled his scent.

Voice low and tender, he stroked her hair. "Do you want to tell me about it?"

His touch grounded her, smoothing away the rough edges of doubt. "I can't make much sense of what I saw, but someone I know is returning to Savannah."

He chuckled and gave her a squeeze. "I hate to second-guess a psychic, but we do have a house full of out-of-town guests. All of whom fit that description."

The casual humor and plain logic helped Anna relax. As Ian had likely intended. After two years, he'd grown accustomed to her waking up in various moods. Moods often affected by the messages she received in her sleep.

Curling her leg around his, Anna gazed up into steady gray eyes flecked with blue. "You're probably right." She pressed her lips to his for a brief kiss and settled back against her pillow. "But still . . ."

"Tell me." He propped on his elbow, giving her his full attention. "You always feel better when you talk it out."

With a nod and a sigh, Anna spoke to the ceiling. She told him of the raven fleeing from a fire, how it crossed the ocean and came to her. "When the bird flew toward me," she said at last, "it seemed somehow familiar. I was happy to see it."

And frightened when the bird had vanished into flame.

Anna controlled the shudder that wanted to rise. "Then it disappeared," she said simply, choosing to keep the worrisome ending to herself. This was supposed to be one of the happiest times of her life. And Ian's too.

So she refused to let one of her cryptic visions ruin it for either of them.

Besides, she knew better than anyone how confusing dreams could be. Nocturnal wanderings of the mind could be interpreted many ways, especially those of a witch attuned to the mystical world.

Determined to push it all from her mind, she shrugged off

any remaining shivers and rolled on top of Ian. This time the kiss she gave him held more than easy affection.

"No more talk of dreams, because I'm wide awake now." She arched her spine as he traced his fingers down her back, then dropped to nip the corner of his jaw. "I can think of much more interesting activities to occupy my mind." Like making early-morning love to the gorgeous man beneath her.

The man who would be her husband in four days' time.

Brushing aside the strap of her gown, Ian dipped a kiss to her bare shoulder. "What about our guests?" He worked his way up her neck, stopping at the special spot that still made her heart flutter. Every. Single. Time.

Anna tossed back her hair and let him have his way. "We don't need to worry about the girls." A touch on her thigh and Anna grew breathless. "I think they know their way around."

~~~

An exceedingly pleasant hour later, Anna ran her hand along the mahogany bannister, admiring her nails painted a hot Lava Red. Halfway down the stairs, a sudden cry carried down the corridor. The sound brought a smile to her lips, and she paused mid-step, turning to follow the carpeted walkway on the third floor.

The wails grew louder as she neared a closed bedroom door and knocked lightly. From inside, a harried male voice called out, "Come in." Then lower, "*Please*, come in."

Anna entered to find the source of the outraged screams. A tiny terror named Tori, currently red-faced and furious, thrummed her fists and feet in the air while in her father's arms.

Unable to help herself, Anna crossed her arms and grinned. "She gets that temper from you, you know."

"Ha. Ha." Dare made a kissy face at the baby and continued

to make soft shushing noises. They had zero effect. Despite the high decibels that surely battered his eardrums, he all but shone with adoration as he gazed down at his baby girl.

He angled toward Anna and, still cooing, gently began to sway. "This will be her second breakfast. Guess she gets that from me too." The little bundle he held had a tuft of hair, dark like his, but the sky-blue eyes of her sweet-natured mother.

And right on cue, Willyn rushed inside shaking a bottle. "Okay. Okay." She breezed past Anna and handed the formula to her husband. As soon as Dare offered it, Tori latched on and fell into blissful silence.

Tucking her hair behind her ears, Willyn blew out a breath. "I forgot what these early months are like." She leaned over, touched her daughter's pink cheek, and made a humming sound. "But I also forgot how amazing they can be."

Anna took in the pretty scene, her childhood friend standing beside her sister of the heart, their heads close together as they lost themselves in the wonder they'd created. With a light touch on Willyn's arm, she said, "I'll leave you to it."

Dare glanced up. "You two go ahead. I've got this." He spoke again to Tori. "Now that the little hunger-monster has been appeased."

"Thanks, sweetheart." Willyn kissed him twice on the cheek and pivoted to Anna. "I'll take that deal, because I'm starving myself. And the breakfast fairy is already hard at work."

"What's she making?" Anna asked, referring to Mrs. Attinger, the woman who cared for the island estate and all its inhabitants, and had long served as honorary mother to Anna and her brother Quinn.

"She had eggs and plenty of colorful ingredients laid out on the counter." Willyn rubbed her palms together as they hurried down two more levels. "And did I mention the scent of baking cinnamon rolls?"

"You so did *not*." Anna rubbed her stomach. "Those are my

favorite."

As they reached the slate flooring of the grand hall, Willyn came to a halt and took Anna's hand between hers and gave a light squeeze. "That's as it should be. This week is about you, and should be filled with all of your favorite things. And Ian's, too," she added. "Though I don't think the guys will have nearly as much fun as we will."

As if spontaneous joy took hold of her, she wrapped Anna in a hug and rotated back and forth. "Oh, I'm so, so excited, and no one deserves happiness more."

Misty-eyed, Anna squeezed her back. She'd missed the female camaraderie of her coven even more than she'd realized. "It means so much to have all of you here for the wedding."

I just wish you could stay.

But she didn't say that. It wouldn't be fair.

Her coven had done their part in fulfilling the prophecy—defeating a powerful demon, an immortal witch, and their hellish followers here on earth. Her friends had earned whatever lives they wanted to live. *Wherever* they wanted to live them.

But that didn't mean a small but selfish part of her didn't want to keep them close. That she wouldn't give anything for them all to be back in Savannah.

"Of course we're here," Willyn said. "We wouldn't miss seeing you walk down that aisle." She pivoted to wave a hand at the green velvet couch. The comfy piece faced a huge painting that slid to one side to reveal an equally large television. "And, of course, we *have* to have a girls' night in our favorite room."

Many days and nights had been spent in the grand hall—nine women planning, arguing, bonding, and turning into what they had always been meant to be. Not only a coven, but a sisterhood.

One big, fire-throwing, spell-casting, ass-kicking family.

Overwhelmed by nostalgia, Anna took Willyn's hand. "A

movie night is definitely on the itinerary. One for girls only."

"Yes." Willyn dragged out the word and squeezed her fists to her chest. "But we can't let Kylie and Paige force those horror movies on us. At least, not the super-gore." Her face morphed into an expression of revulsion, just as the excited sounds of chatter carried from the kitchen.

"Someone else is up," Anna said.

"Let's go defend the cinnamon rolls." Willyn raced toward the voices with Anna right behind her. They came to a stop at the doorway and stumbled into each other.

Giggling like schoolgirls, they righted themselves to see Kylie with her head bent sideways, watching a dark stream of coffee pouring into a cup.

"Quinn and I have had espresso in Italy, true matcha tea at a Zen monastery, and Bordeaux wine in . . . well, Bordeaux." Long blonde curls tied back in a tail, Kylie stood upright, bounced once on her toes, and retrieved her steaming mug. "But I still love this magic coffee machine."

She moved to the crescent-shaped island in the center of the room. "Good morning, sleepyheads," she said to Anna and Willyn, saluting them with her cup before taking a long drink. She blinked slowly and sighed. "Mm-mm-mm. So nice to be back home."

Hearing the younger woman call the island estate "home" made Anna's heart swell to three times its size. Her bookish brother had met his match in the vivacious blonde, often calling Kylie his sunshine girl. Even though it was lightning she conjured from the air.

A silver amulet hung from her neck, the stone a cheery yellow, as suited her personality. But in typical Kylie fashion, she'd paired the centuries-old talisman with black workout clothes. She'd likely run the length of the island before anyone else had even opened their eyes.

Except for Mrs. Attinger, the spry woman with short silver

hair who stood near the counter whipping the eggs and other ingredients. She usually rose with the sun most days, then directed it where and how to shine.

Willyn walked to join Kylie at the island. "I know what you mean," she said, pulling out one of the wrought-iron stools and sliding onto the burgundy cushion. "I don't miss the reason we were all summoned together, but I do miss the never-ending slumber party."

With a sentimental grin, Willyn tilted her head and took her own amulet between her fingers. Hers was an almost identical version of Kylie's, eight small stones of various colors nestled in a pattern of silver whorls. The jewels encircled a more prominent stone, but where Kylie's reflected the color of the sun, Willyn's was clear as a diamond and rested just below a small silver cross.

Anna would swear the rich blue stone of her own necklace grew warmer in the presence of her sister-witches, as if it too were happy to have the coven reunited. "Slumber-party meets magick camp," she said with a laugh. "And I never thought I'd say this, not after everything we went through, but after you all left, this place was far too quiet. Only one cat. One witch—"

"And one new man," Kylie said with a wiggle of brows. "I bet you and Ian made plenty of noise."

Mrs. Attinger made a tsking sound and sent Kylie a look of rebuke.

Kylie smiled back, unabashed.

With a harrumph for extra measure, the older woman returned her attention to the bowl in her hands. But not before Anna saw her lips curve up.

"*Buenos días.*" A sleepy voice with a thick Spanish accent rolled in to join the conversation. Wavy brown hair in a tangle down her back and a red silk robe that hit mid-thigh, Lucia Ruiz looked bed-rumpled, half-asleep . . . and absolutely stunning.

"Good morning," the group of women responded, almost in

unison.

"Kylie, *mi hermana*, make me a coffee, *por favor*." Lucia bee-lined to the counter and all but crashed onto a stool. "I am still on Bangkok time and had trouble falling asleep."

"Bangkok. That's right," Anna said. "Did you find the golden statue you were after?"

Lucia could find anything that was lost and, when not helping others find sentimental or important objects, she preferred playing treasure hunter.

Lucia shook her head. "I didn't get a sense for it. If the statue was ever in the waters of the Chao Phraya, someone else already found it. But," she added, perking up, "Ethan did help a family rid their small son of a rather annoying demon."

Kylie snapped her fingers. "And just like that, we're back to the good old days. Demonologists, lost artifacts, and witches in the kitchen."

"Very true," Willyn said.

"Don't you mean, tru dat?" Kylie shot back, plugging a little plastic cup into the machine and hitting the brew button.

But Willyn had no time to reply as her son Tadd ran into the room waving a child-sized golf club. "Mom! Mom! Guess what I'm going to do?"

"Hmm." Willyn pretended to be confused, rubbing her chin for extra measure. "I can't imagine."

"Golf! Dare said I'm big enough now, and he even got me this." He held out the putter. "I get to knock my ball in the hole, but only after all the guys have their turn."

Willyn beamed and ran her hand over his sunny cap of hair. "Playing golf with the men." She pursed her lips. "Will you please stop growing up so fast?"

"Nuh-uh." He shook his head. "And I might get to drive the cart, Dare said. But you wanna know the best part?"

"What's the best part?"

"All the quiet." Tadd's smile took on a hint of mischief.

"Because no chatty females."

"Oh, really?" Willyn's brow winged up as she sent a sidelong glance to Anna. No eight-year-old came up with a phrase like that.

Quinn chose that moment to enter the kitchen. And every pair of female eyes landed on him at once.

Kylie cocked a hip and her head as she stared down her boyfriend. "All ready for your nice, *quiet* game?"

Quinn had the grace to cringe before joining Kylie at the counter. He kissed her cheek and whispered something secret in her ear.

Judging by the expression that warmed Kylie's eyes, Anna knew her brother had been forgiven.

Ian swooped into the kitchen and gestured to Quinn. "We all set?"

"Yep. Ethan and Mr. Attinger are loading the gear now."

"And tomorrow, we're all going fishing!" Tadd leaped and threw his little fist in the air.

"That's right, little man." Quinn dropped his hand for a low-five from the boy. "Let the games begin."

"Golfing. Fishing. Fairly safe adventures." Ian met Anna's gaze. "After hearing about Michael's bachelor party, I decided it best to stay away from the pubs."

"Right." Quinn pulled his mouth to one side. "No chasing any . . ." he caught himself in time, "*minions* through the streets."

When Tadd was present, "minions" was the code word they used for demons or any other supernatural creatures the coven had faced.

But the moment was ruined when Tadd hiked one blonde brow—the very image of his mother—and looked up at Quinn. "You guys are always talking about minions. You do know they're just cartoons, right?"

With no way to answer, Quinn could do nothing but shrug. "What can I say? I love cartoons." He sniffed the air. "And cinnamon buns." At the oven he bent to peer inside, grabbed the handle, and jumped when Mrs. Attinger swatted him with her towel.

"They'll be ready when the timer goes off. Not a minute before."

Prepping for another snap, the older woman wound up the towel like a locker room bully.

Quinn wisely raised his hands and backed away.

Behind Anna, Ian wrapped his arms around her waist and pressed his cheek to her temple. "Happy?" he asked.

"Very," she said, watching her friends talk and tease. Only those who'd traveled from out of town were staying here on the island, but the commotion in the kitchen did her heart good. Quinn was telling Tadd all about Mulligans, while Lucia and Kylie compared notes on shopping in Europe.

Anna leaned back into Ian's chest. "You're right, Kylie. This *is* just like the old days."

Kylie inclined her head, eyes sparkling. "Only better."

The timer dinged just as Quinn and Willyn burst out laughing. Blessedly content, Anna put her hand over Ian's and silently agreed. *So much better.*

2

In the peaceful stillness of early morning hours, Arik Mansur entered his library. He crossed the wide expanse of gothic tile flooring and made his way to an elaborate desk. There he paused, drinking from the cup of black coffee in his hand. He opened the journal atop the dark leather blotter, flipped to the next blank page, and scrawled the date across the top right corner.

Just as he did every morning.

As his father before him had done. Every morning.

Sunbeams slanted through diamond-paned windows, but shadows still gathered to huddle in corners. Arik pulled the cord on the bronze desk lamp, shining light on the papers he'd examined last night. Written circa 1720, the unbound letters were correspondence between a woman in New Orleans and her sister in Boston.

While the sisters held no interest for Arik, the lady in the South had been engaged to a man. A man made reckless by his newfound romance who'd spilled confessions across his lover's pillow.

Confessions he never should have shared, even as whispers in the dark.

Arik, however, was grateful for the indiscretions, since they provided him with a brand new lead. He gathered the letters into a thick folder and strode toward one of the two flights of stairs. Curved staircases mirrored each other from opposite sides of the room, winging up to a mezzanine where additional shelves lined the walls.

The house had been built in the late eighteen-hundreds, a structure described by many as a brick Goliath, even among the sprawling mansions of Savannah's historic downtown. Most of the rooms were large and high-ceilinged, normal for the Victorian age, but the library outshone them all, the prize jewel of the Queen Anne-style home.

In addition to books, the upper level housed periodicals, codices, and all manner of research documents, including several illuminated texts acquired over many decades. Once on the landing, he punched a code into a small panel and waited for the familiar *clunk* and *hiss,* telling him the mechanical lock and pressure seal had both disengaged.

With a slight rush of air, an entire section of bookshelves swung open, revealing the hidden climate-controlled storeroom where he kept the oldest and most fragile documents. The three-hundred-year-old letters qualified due to age and, more importantly, for the minimal yet crucial information they contained.

One tiny piece of a much larger puzzle. A single word.

Huktai.

The writer of the letter hadn't known what it meant, only that the man she loved had whispered it in his sleep during their last night together. Before he'd left for Savannah, and never come back.

Arik didn't grasp the full history of the Huktai, but over the years he'd compiled enough data to surmise they were a group who used codes and cryptic languages to guard an ancient secret.

A secret cloaked in danger.

After his father's passing, Arik had razed the library, hoping to understand all the things left unexplained. He'd scoured his father's wealth of journals searching for clues, but each presented its own mystery, inscribed with bizarre and unintelligible writings.

The entries consisted of Sanskrit and Persian intermixed with an unknown language. Now, years later, Arik spoke the first two fluently—as well as Italian and a passable form of French—but had made no headway with the strange scripts.

If some type of cipher for the language existed, his father had taken its location to the grave.

Inside the storeroom, Arik inhaled, swearing the scent of cigar smoke still lingered. That his father's voice whispered from each page of every book. *This room holds our family's legacy. My life's work. But by my hand and the grace of God, this duty, this burden, will never be yours.*

The words weren't the last his father had spoken to Arik. But they were the ones that haunted him.

As memories assaulted, he clenched the folder, shoving the letters into the open slot. And instantly regretted the abuse of such fragile documents.

He closed his eyes and inhaled, trying to quell the frustration before it took over. Still, the questions rolled through his mind. Questions he'd asked himself a thousand times before. What was the truth behind his family's legacy, this poisoned inheritance now passed on to him? What was the dark secret of the Huktai? How was the ancient group related to his father's tragic death?

And his poor mother . . .

No. I can't go there. With another deep breath, Arik raked a hand through his dark blonde hair.

After years of dedication to this one pursuit, the answers remained elusive, leaving him to fumble his way toward the truth. His father had done a damned fine job of keeping his own secrets, hiding every scrap and detail from his only son.

If this was a family legacy, his father should have told him more, especially once he'd reached adulthood. He should have taught Arik the language in the journals, no matter the danger. Maybe if he'd been with his parents that night, the outcome could have been different.

But the questions and what-ifs were as useless as the anger still thrumming through his veins. He would never have the chance to ask his father, and brooding over that fact was a distraction he didn't need, not if he intended to make any progress today. The best way to push his frustration aside was to focus on his search, to lose himself among the people and stories of centuries past.

Calm and steady-handed again, he exited the storage area and secured it behind him. He scanned the shelves and pulled the genealogy book he needed to trace hereditary lines. If the sleep-talking man had been a member of the Huktai, then he should have connections to people and places Arik had already identified. So that's where he'd focus next.

With his mind on the possibility of forging new links, Arik descended the stairs. He froze when a sudden banging interrupted his thoughts. Head cocked, he stood still and waited.

The knocking resumed, louder and more insistent. Who could it be at this time of day?

He set the genealogy book on a credenza and left the library, making his way through the maze of corridors to the wide foyer. Once there, he could hear shouting from outside.

"I know you're in there, boy, so you might as well open up!"

He recognized the hoarse voice but had never heard it so fraught with distress. Yanking open the door, Arik found a frazzled-looking woman, strands of white curling hair escaping the patterned red scarf on her head. "Mahalia," he said, "what the devil?"

She slapped an aged brown hand to his chest. "Oh, let's hope not, boy. Let's hope not." She pushed past him, swishing by in one of her signature broom skirts, today's choice a rich crimson to match her scarf. She patted the old-fashioned doctor's bag she had tucked under one arm. "We've got work to do." She waved for him to come with her as she marched down the hallway in the opposite direction of the library.

"Wait a minute," Arik said, but she ignored him, hoofing her way around the corner and out of sight.

He had an idea where she was headed and caught up to her in the dining room, just as she was reaching for a large floral centerpiece. He stabbed a finger at her. "Not on the dining table."

He expected her to argue about needing more room, but she surprised him by giving him a reluctant nod before barging through the swinging door that led to the kitchen. "Come on, come on. We need to hurry." Her voice projected each time the door swung open.

Reaching deep for patience, Arik entered after her. "Mahalia, you should have called first. You know I don't like surprise visits, and I've got a lot of—"

"Work to do. Yes, yes." She finished his sentence and shook her head, pawing through the physician's bag she'd laid on the large butcher's block island. "Believe me, I know. Research, study, seek. It's the Mansur way."

Before he had time to consider being offended, she paused to look up, eyes gleaming like brown topaz. "But I'd lay odds that today you'll learn more in one throw than from a week's worth of reading." She slapped her palms on the flat surface. "I had a vision. An omen."

Arik expelled a breath and rubbed his forehead. Known locally as a root doctor, Mahalia worked in voodoo, a little hoodoo, and dabbled in whatever occult practice suited her needs. She rarely used the word omen, however, and since she had, he knew there'd be no putting her off. The sooner she completed whatever juju she'd come to perform, the sooner he could get back to work.

So he consoled himself by pouring a cup of coffee to replace the one he'd left in the library. Leaning against the sink, he watched as she unrolled a brown leather mat. He couldn't be certain, but it looked like her favorite, the one made from opossum hide. He hiked a brow. *This must be serious.*

With a small smile, Arik shook his head, filled with vexation, amusement, and affection. The usual sentiments Mahalia inspired.

Though the first time she'd barged in on his life, he hadn't been quite as accommodating. The day after his parents' *incident*, Mahalia had shown up on his stoop, eyes red and swollen from crying.

Arik had thought her crazy, of course, with her wild clothes and desolate expression, but her suffering had been obvious, and the only thing that had kept him from slamming the door. Though he'd offered, she'd refused to come inside, speaking only of grief and the anguish they now shared.

What a pair they'd made, the bereaved voodoo woman and the angry young man. But she'd insisted they were bound together, and that as time unfolded, he would see her again.

And so he had. Many times. Since Mahalia tended to show up unannounced, whenever and wherever suited her whims. Despite her eccentricities and his obsession with the past, an odd yet sturdy friendship had formed. Sometimes he would go months without hearing from her. Other times she simply materialized on his doorstep, as she had today. Though usually with a little less fanfare.

He'd let his gaze drift to the floor, but now he shifted his attention back to Mahalia. From the doctor's bag, she retrieved a small suede pouch and a wooden bowl, items Arik had seen before. "Look," he said, holding up a hand in a halting gesture, "is this really necessary? I don't have much time."

"No," she snapped, "you *don't* have time. Why else would I be here at the crack of dawn?"

The sun had been up for an hour, but he felt it unwise to say so. Mahalia was not herself today, almost vibrating with an urgency that was starting to worry him.

She held out the pouch and shook it. "Now do as I say."

"Fine." Keeping his face and demeanor blank, he accepted the small bag with one hand but remained leaning against the counter. He took a casual sip of his drink. "What did you mean before? Tell me about your vision."

She gestured to the mat. "I'll tell you after you throw."

"I'll throw after you tell me."

She threw up her hands. "Lord save us from stubborn men! Didn't I just say there's no time?"

Arik lifted a shoulder and took another slow drink. "Then you'd better talk fast."

"I had a dream." Mahalia planted her fists on her hips as if ready to do battle. Brown eyes sharp on his as she leaned forward and rasped, "I dreamed of buttons."

For a moment, he didn't move or speak, wondering if she expected him to know the significance of this. "Buttons?" He cast his gaze toward the mat and her bag. "All of this is about buttons? I thought you had learned something about my father."

She rolled her eyes. "The buttons were *bull's-eyes*."

Exasperated, Arik set down his coffee with a clunk, hard enough to slosh a few drops onto the counter. "Is this going to make sense sometime today?"

Mahalia bristled. "Listen up, boy. Not everything in life can be found between the pages of someone else's sorry old books." She crossed her arms and straightened her spine. "Sometimes you gotta' look at what's being shown to you, or else you'll never see."

Mirroring her move, he crossed his arms. "I assure you that I *don't* see."

She huffed and narrowed one eye at him. "Buttons," she

began slowly, as if speaking to a child, "represent a joining together of two things. The bull's-eye is a symbol of a goal."

Stepping closer, she lifted both hands as if offering Arik an invisible book. "I'm certain these were a symbol of *your* goal."

Arik might wonder over some of Mahalia's strange ways, but he'd witnessed enough to know she possessed certain capabilities. He dropped his arms to his sides. "All right. I'm listening."

"The buttons were scattered across your desk, beside an old clock. One thing was very specific. The clock read 7:44, and I believe it meant today. *This morning.*"

Arik glanced at the numbers on the microwave, flashing a bright blue 7:40. "That's four minutes from now." If there were any validity to her claim, he'd be a fool to brush her off. "What exactly is supposed to happen?"

"Well . . ." For the first time, she seemed unsure, shifting her gaze to the side before she muttered, "Your eyes shine gold."

"My eyes—" He broke off. "Is that another representation of something? Another symbol?"

"I don't know. That's why I need you to throw!"

Silence filled the kitchen, dust motes in a sunbeam the only movement in the kitchen as they stared hard at one another.

Finally, she drew a ragged breath and stepped to him. Her fingers curled around his wrist like a living manacle. "For once, listen to me." Her voice dropped to a whisper. "Arik, please, just throw the bones."

A chill shot down his spine and straight to his heart.

She never used his name.

Without a word, he moved around the island, turning so that they faced each other across the animal hide. He opened the small suede pouch and poured out its contents. Tiny animal bones clinked dully as they tumbled into the wooden bowl.

At her nod, he tossed the tiny bones onto the hide mat.

Mahalia leaned over the table, squinting as she studied the

scattered remains. "Hmm," she murmured, turning her head this way and that. Still bent forward, she flicked her gaze up to his. "Changes are coming."

Arik lowered his voice to match hers. "What did you see?"

She shook her head, brushing aside his question to look at the microwave. Already the numbers had morphed to read 7:41. "We've got to get back to your books, back to the library. That's where it happens."

"Then why are we still here?" He pivoted and slammed his palms against the swinging door, overcome with a sudden need to see if her dream was going to come true. If it did, if she was right about what he might learn . . .

He fell into a fast clip, leaving Mahalia scurrying to keep up with his longer stride. Together they hastened from one side of the great house to the other. Arik thrust open the library door and strode to the center of the room.

Mahalia put a hand to her ribs as if winded. "Now quick, go stand behind your desk."

Arik did as she said. Without hesitation. His phone sat charging on his desk, so he checked the time. Then he and Mahalia stared at each other in silence. For two solid minutes.

When the display on the screen changed to 7:44, Arik sucked in a breath, more on edge than he would have expected. He turned in a full circle, searching, waiting—hoping.

But nothing happened.

He blew out a breath. Another false hope. Another dead end.

There was real research to be done, yet here he was, standing behind his dead father's desk, watching the seconds tick by on a clock.

Because a dream and some squirrel bones said he should.

Too defeated to feel angry, he pinched the bridge of his nose, pushing back against a headache pounding like war drums. "This is crazy. I can't do this right now."

"Arik."

"No. No more. I need to focus on—"

"Arik!" Mahalia said his name again, impatience tightening her voice.

Both the tone and the use of his name finally registered. He opened his eyes to see Mahalia pointing across the room. "*Look.*"

Only then did Arik notice the glow emanating from behind him on the right. He moved only his head, turning slowly until he located the source of the brilliant light.

Situated between a window and the carved marble fireplace, a globe with old-world cartography spun slowly in its hardwood base. Not only was the orb spinning of its own accord, but illumination seeped from inside. As the globe rotated, a gilded line streamed from continent to continent, outlining certain areas on the map.

Arik blinked against the bright light, and had no doubt his eyes reflected the gleam.

No doubt they shone with gold.

His lungs froze but his heart sped up. A chilling excitement took over his body, filling his chest until the air lodged inside of him expelled in a rush.

How could this happen? What source of energy had activated the globe? The thing was at least three centuries old, so it had no plug. It held no batteries.

And yet it spun and glowed from within.

While his rational mind fought to make sense of what he was seeing, Mahalia spoke. "That belonged to your father." It wasn't a question.

Arik could only nod, his heartbeats still pounding in rapid-fire succession.

On halting steps, she came to stand beside him, transfixed by the unnatural phenomenon. "What does it mean?" she asked.

"You tell me." Dragging his gaze from the radiant sphere, he studied her profile, her mouth parting slightly as she stared.

"Tell me, Mahalia, what you saw, what you know. Tell me *everything*."

"Changes. Big changes. I knew once you threw the bones."

"You said that before." Arik turned to her, his brow creasing. "What else?"

Hands clasped together, she faced him fully, a frown pulling at her lips. "Pain will return. Yours . . . or another's. I can't be sure."

"I don't understand."

She swallowed loudly. "The buttons, you see, the rejoining. It's people who will be brought back together." She paused as if searching for the best way to tell him, then her gaze tracked past him to the globe. "I suspect the time was important." She looked back to Arik. "And if I'm not mistaken, the exact time that her plane touched down."

The first tendrils of alarm unfurled in Arik. "*Whose* plane?"

Mahalia placed a hand to her chest and whispered, "The heart you wounded. It draws near again."

Arik's own heart clenched and his mind exploded with denial. *No. Not her.*

"This time, you must see her."

He shook his head and backed away, as if his actions could alter Mahalia's decree. His hands fisted at his sides. "You know why I won't do that. Why I *can't*."

"You have no choice, boy." Her expression held a mix of sympathy and support. "You've always known this thing wouldn't end easily. That you'd have to face danger to find your answers."

"The answers." He ground his teeth and glanced back to the revolving globe. *Always the answers.* The search for them ruled Arik, just as it had ruled his father.

And look at what that pursuit had caused, the destruction it had rained on their family.

He advanced on the globe, daring to reach out and graze

his fingers across the gently turning surface. Was this magick? Not a metaphor from one of his books, but real magick? Active, alive, and here inside his home?

More than ever he needed the truth, but how much would he be willing to risk?

He'd have to make that choice. And soon. Though Mahalia's words filled him with dread.

There was only one person who Arik had hurt. Only one heart he'd ever wounded.

And if Mahalia was right, she'd just come home.

3

Anna and her friends followed the path up from the docks and over jewel-green grass, their four sets of high-heels click-clacking on the winding flagstones. A quick boat trip from the St. Germaine island had carried them to the mainland house. On her first night day in Savannah, Shauni had dubbed the color lemon frosting, but to the women of the coven, it was known simply, and affectionately, as "the yellow house."

Kylie hurried ahead to open the door. "After you," she said to Anna, bowing at the waist with a flourish of her arm.

"Kylie." Anna rolled her eyes. "It's a shower, not a coronation." But she had to admit she was enjoying the pampering in the week leading up to her big day. A day made all the more special by the presence of her dearest friends and loved ones.

She passed through a pristine mudroom and entered the bright, airy space of the kitchen. A woman stood at the counter, arranging petits fours on a tiered silver dessert stand. She shone with the beauty of her African and Cherokee heritage with full lips, chiseled cheekbones, and glowing bronze skin.

Claire and her husband Joe oversaw the mainland home and, along with the Attingers, had stepped in to care for the orphaned Anna and Quinn. And though Anna dearly missed her mother and father, especially now during such an important occasion, her surrogate parents had been a true blessing.

Claire turned when Anna stepped into the room and, in perfect key, sang out, "Here comes the bride."

Cheeks heating with a blush, Anna shook her head and moved to give her a one-armed hug, not wanting to mess up the beautiful little cakes adorned with sugar flowers. "You constantly amaze me, Claire." She studied a pale pink square with white petals. "I've always known you were a master chef, but these are impressive."

Claire tilted her head back to touch her temple to Anna's. "Anything for my girl." She sniffed suspiciously. "I just can't believe you're getting married."

Anna's throat tightened as emotions rose. She kissed Claire's soft cheek and whispered. "I love you, and I hope you know how much this means to me."

"Sweet child." Claire drew a ragged breath. Then she quickly cleared her throat and nudged Anna with her hip. "Now go on before you make me cry and melt these little flowers."

"Yes, ma'am." Anna gave her another squeeze and backed away, just as Lucia edged up to the counter to admire Claire's work. "*Vale. Son tan bonitos que da pena comerlos,*" she said, and translated, "They are so pretty it seems a shame to eat them."

Claire shot her a wink. "Thank you, sweetheart. But I'll be upset if you don't."

Lucia rubbed her stomach. "You know how much I appreciate food."

"That looks like it will need at least two people to carry," Kylie said as she and Willyn eyed the tiered platter. "Can we give you a hand?"

"You can give me one." This from Shauni as she entered from the far side of the room. The biologist and animal whisperer was usually most at home in cargo pants and a T-shirt, but she wore a sweet white dress for the ladies' luncheon. Her raven hair was in a long braid, and other than a wedding ring, the only jewelry she wore was her coven amulet, the center stone a brilliant green that matched her eyes.

She opened the refrigerator and pulled out a pre-arranged silver tray with mini-caprese bites, passing it to Kylie who waited with her hands out. Shauni then retrieved a second tray filled with crackers and what looked like dill-speckled salmon and tiny chunks of white cheese.

Anna's mouth watered and her stomach rumbled. She recognized Mrs. Attinger's handiwork, the older woman having come over earlier to start preparations. She and Claire both cooked like angels, but when they combined their talents? *Yum*.

"The girls are all here," Shauni said, stopping in the doorway on her way out again. "We're just waiting on a few more of the other guests." She glanced to Claire. "Any word from Joseph and Sylvie?"

Still placing the petits fours in perfect rings, Claire sighed. "Yes, and I'm sorry to say they're running late. Joseph had to record data for one of his experiments this morning. Something about the sounds plants make after stimuli are applied to . . . something, something." She tossed a look over her shoulder that told exactly how much she understood her son's plant physiology studies. "There's traffic on 75 South, as usual, so they'll be stuck for a good while."

"Oh, no." Anna frowned. "I hope they get here in time for Sylvie to enjoy some of the party. Atlanta's not a short drive." And she was looking forward to spending time with Joseph's wife, a fact that sometimes still amused her.

Once a member of the Amara and a coven enemy, Sylvie had been bloodthirsty and fierce, using her hoodoo craft in the practice of dark arts. Until falling victim herself to the strongest spell of them all. Love.

Fast-forward a few years and she and Joseph were married, making her an honorary sister-in-law to Anna. So instead of trading magick-fueled blows, they now swapped cookie recipes and gardening tips.

Hands on her hips, Claire stood back and admired her work.

"There. All done." She turned to Anna. "Ian's mother made a dash to the store for some last-minute items, so we've got everything covered. All you have to do is kick back and enjoy yourself." She puckered her lips and blew a kiss.

Anna pretended to pluck it from the air before curling her fingers and pressing them to her cheek. "You know what? I think I just might do that." With a soft laugh, she turned to follow Shauni and Kylie down the hall, leaving Lucia and Willyn chatting with Claire.

Here in the yellow house, dark wood floors contrasted exotically with creamy walls, a much more modern style than in the island mansion, but home to Anna just the same.

As she walked, she contemplated Claire's words and decided to take a wise woman's advice. This really was the start of Anna and Ian's happy ending, and after all they'd gone through—all they'd sacrificed—she would focus solely on the joy in her life.

Starting right now.

All morning, pieces of her dream kept wheedling their way in, doing their best to ruin this bright day. But her closest friends and family surrounded her now, and the last dregs of the nightmare faded at last.

No dread weighed heavy in her stomach. No chills of warning crawled on her skin. So she cast aside the notion that her friends were in danger. And wouldn't she know by now? With all of them here in close proximity?

She had yet to pick up on the slightest bad vibe and predicted nothing but fellowship, fun, and food.

Just what the witch doctor ordered.

She let relief spread through her and bring a smile to her lips as she skirted through the foyer and into the parlor. Once there, she spotted three women standing around a kentia palm tree. With their heads close together, they created a pretty palette of fiery-red, black, and white-blonde hair. The two brainiacs—Claudia and Viv—seemed to be getting a gardening lesson from Paige, the coven warrior-turned-nursery owner.

In fact, the riot of bright blooms on the curved stairs and porch out front were courtesy of Paige. Large planters all but sang with a chorus of purple hydrangea, cheerful lilies, and the pinkest tulips Anna had ever seen.

Anna let her gaze travel around the room, moving from Paige, Viv, and Claudia to where Shauni and Hayden sat on a French-style settee, both laughing at whatever outrageous comment Kylie had just made. Like the flowers, her coven's true beauty came from the union of such different yet complementary personalities.

A touch on her arm brought Anna's attention to Lucia, just as Willyn walked up on her other side. A familiar vibration filled the air. The sweet connection of nine hearts. Nine witches.

Nine sisters.

All conversation in the room stopped and, one by one, the women glanced around at each other, smiles lighting up every face as if someone had flipped a switch.

"Well, the girls are back together again." Holding her arms up as if basking in the sensation, Viv drew a deep breath that raised her shoulders. When she dropped them again, she said, "I just wish I could figure out how to measure the wavelength." The physicist brushed aside black bangs to reveal gorgeous Asian eyes crinkling at the corners from her grin.

"Hey, that's our signature hum you're talking about." Kylie shook a scolding finger at her. "No recording or sharing coven secrets."

Viv quirked her mouth to the side. "Even in the name of science, brat?"

Kylie scurried over in her favored kitten heels—today the color of cherries—grabbed Viv's hands, and shook them playfully. "I've missed your insults, and that quizzical little wrinkle. The one you get between your brows when you're intellectualizing. Or being stubborn. Like now."

Viv let her head fall back and released a velvety chuckle. "I've missed our verbal sparring matches, too."

Though polar opposites in character, looks, and—almost everything—the serious scientist and bubbly coed had clicked almost instantly.

The hum leveled out and softened, as it usually did once the initial bond was made, and Anna linked her arm through Willyn's. "Can you believe it's been over four years since you all first came to Savannah?"

"I really can't," Willyn said. "And I wouldn't trade our time together for anything in the world. The nine of us learning about magick, learning to fight—"

"And learning to love one another as true *familia*," Lucia ended with a sappy smile. "I'm just sorry you spent your whole life preparing without us. A centuries-old prophecy was a lot of weight for your young shoulders."

"Yes," Anna agreed. "I can admit that now." She took Lucia's hand and surveyed the other women in the room. "And the fulfillment demanded more of us than I had ever imagined, but we beat Ronja. And Bastraal."

A feat she never could have managed without each of these wonderful, loyal, and fearless women.

Her throat tightened and her eyes began to sting. "By the goddess," she said, "I just love you all so much."

"Oh, Anna." Willyn sniffed and put her head on Anna's shoulder. "No crying allowed. I can hear the tears in your voice, and if you start, so will I. Then Shauni and Hayden will join in because they're so empathetic."

"Nope. Uh-uh. That's not going to happen." Paige crossed her arms mutinously. "I already got a haircut, and I'm wearing a dress. And heels—*heels*—for the love of Pete. So I'll be damned if we're all going to start blubbering too."

"But what lovely heels they are," Claudia said, sliding over for closer inspection. "And this dress. Caribbean blue is your color after all. Is this a Talia Monahan? That new SCAD graduate who's taking Atlanta by storm?"

Paige pulled back her head and looked at Claudia as if she'd offered her a dose of bubonic plague. "Do you think I know who you're talking about or if this dress has a name?"

"Chris bought it," Hayden called out from the couch, blinking her golden-brown eyes with false innocence. "Or was I not supposed to tell?"

Paige only shrugged. "It's not like anyone here would be surprised."

"That your hot, ex-Ranger husband knows more about fashion than you?" Kylie tilted her head. "No. Not surprised."

Hayden stood up from the couch and walked toward Paige. "But I am surprised you didn't have a wedding. Yes, even you," she added before Paige could protest. "You and Chris ran down to St. Augustine to elope, and I had to hear about it secondhand. From a ghost."

"That's why it's called eloping. You're not supposed to tell anybody." Now Paige actually looked a little shamefaced. "I just didn't want all the fuss. No offense," she said immediately to Anna.

Anna winked back. "Never any taken." Paige might sell plants for a living, but her exterior was still a tough-as-hell shell.

"Did you at least take pictures?" Willyn's expression grew sentimental. "What did you wear? Did you have something old, borrowed, and blue?"

Paige blushed, prompting Claudia to say, "Oh, someone grab their phone and take a picture. I think pink just might be your new color."

"Anyone takes a picture of me right now, and their color will be blood red."

Using her telekinesis, Viv lifted her phone from her purse across the room and danced it through the air to hover over

Paige's head. "Come on. Just one. Pretty in pink."

"Stop teasing her," Hayden said. Behind her Shauni nodded, the two of them always ready to play peace-makers.

And just like that, Anna's eyes flooded in earnest. She rushed for a handily located box of tissue, sending silent thanks to Claire and Mrs. Attinger. They'd clearly been expecting the tears from today's reunion.

She dabbed at her cheeks and eyes, careful not to smear her makeup.

"Let me help," Lucia said, taking the tissue to gently wipe her eyelid. "The bride-to-be can't have spider-leg eyes."

"I'm sorry. I'm sorry. It's just . . ."

"We all get it, Anna." Willyn reached for a tissue herself. "Today's the first time we've all been in the same room since . . ."

"Since we all said good-bye." Shauni stepped closer.

"And I just love seeing all of your faces again." Anna pressed her palm to her heart. "Your being here is the best present I could ever ask for. Sometimes it's still hard to believe what we went through. And that it's really over."

"I feel the same way," Shauni said. "I'll be helping Michael at the clinic or making dinner, and then out of the blue, it just hits me. I look over my shoulder, expecting to see one of you standing there."

"Because we always had each other's backs," Paige said. "And we always will. No matter where we are."

"Look. We even formed a circle without trying." Kylie took Viv's hand on one side and Hayden's on the other. "All we need now are those amazing dresses Mrs. A. made for us. Remember the amulet-choosing ceremony?"

"You mean when they flew through the air and chose us?" Claudia touched the peach-colored stone of her necklace. "How could we forget?"

"Magick chose us," Hayden said. "Magick brought us

together. It made us the nine." She linked her fingers with Shauni's, extending the connection. The rest of them touched hand-to-shoulder or hooked elbows, forming a complete circuit. A never-ending bond.

"I just wish we could do this more often," Anna said. Then promptly bit her lip. "I'm sorry. I told myself I wouldn't say anything. What I want more than anything is for you all to be happy. And I know for some of you," she glanced at Kylie and Lucia, "that means traveling far away, searching for adventure, new experiences, new friends."

An odd expression fell over Lucia's face before she slid a sly gaze over to Willyn. The two shared a moment.

"What?" Anna asked. "What does that look mean?"

Lucia raised her brows as if asking a question.

Willyn nodded in response and said, "It's your week, Anna. We didn't want to steal your thunder."

Heart pounding, Anna went perfectly still. "Why would you? What do you mean?"

Lucia spread her arms wide in a *ta-da!* gesture. "Willyn and I are both moving back to Savannah!"

Anna squealed like a little girl and clapped her hands, then performed a happy dance amidst excited cries from the rest of the women. When she finally calmed down, she began firing questions. "Is this really true? When? Where? How did it happen without my knowing?"

Caught in a crushing hug from Paige, Willyn emitted a choked-off giggle. "I don't know. Maybe your third eye was too busy looking at bouquets and wedding cakes to notice what we were planning." She pulled free of Paige and caught her breath before adding, "Dare and I are going to start looking soon, but Lucia and Ethan have already bought a house."

"No," Anna gasped.

Lucia lifted her shoulders in a shrug. "We wanted to surprise you."

"Yeah, well. Mission accomplished." Viv raised a champagne flute containing a frothy orange mimosa, did a little dance of her own.

"Talk about stealing someone's thunder." Kylie put one hand on a hip and conjured a miniature bolt of lightning in her other palm. "No pun intended." Her pink painted lips curved and mischief danced behind her eyes. "Quinn and I have traveled a lot. We've seen amazing places and met inspiring people from all walks of life. But . . ."

"Kylie?" Anna asked, her voice coming out as a whisper. She clutched a shining ray of hope in both hands while one fat tear escaped down her cheek.

Kylie gave a quick little bob of her head. "We're ready to settle down for a while. We're coming back home."

Anna and Kylie leapt into each other's open arms, and the other women followed suit. Hugs and kisses abounded, creating one bouncing, laughing mass of elated females.

After a moment, Shauni broke free, retrieving more mimosas and handing them out. "This means we'll be living together again. Okay," she amended, "not under the same roof, but hey," she lifted her glass, "who's complaining?"

"There's plenty of room under Lucia's new roof." Willyn spread her hands. "It's huge! Not as big as the St. Germaine castle but still mind-boggling."

"Yes, you must all come to take the tour," Lucia insisted. "Though, I warn you, we have no furniture yet."

"I'll bring camp chairs," Shauni joked, clinking glasses with Viv and Claudia.

"Hold on. Hold on." Per the norm, Paige's hard-edged voice sliced right through the excited babbling. "Does anyone else remember the last time we all just happened to relocate to Savannah? At the exact same time?"

"That was different." Kylie gave her a soft elbow to the ribs. "Don't kill the buzz."

"Yeah. We did our part. All the bad guys and bad demons are dead and gone." Hayden's brow furrowed. "Right, Anna? You haven't seen anything, have you? No signs or omens? No dreams?"

Anna sucked in a breath and could actually feel the blood drain from her face. Her friends noticed, and the cheerful mood flattened as if someone had stuck a pin in their balloon.

She saw herself reaching for the bird.

She remembered the flames.

"I'm not—" She began but choked off when the doorbell chimed. To her ears, the soft, crystalline bells sounded unusually sharp.

Mrs. Attinger appeared and bustled through the foyer. "I'll get it," she called out in a sing-song manner.

"Wait!" Anna said, more harshly than intended.

The older woman stuttered to a halt.

Hands clasped together, Anna went to Mrs. Attinger. "Please, let me," she said softly, receiving a worried look from the older woman. An expression of concern that reflected those of her coven.

And likely her own.

Because a ball of lead now sat in her gut, and the jitters she'd defeated had come back in full force. She walked to the front door, stopped, and took a moment to rub the bumps on her arms. The chills and prickles of premonition.

She conjured a bright smile of welcome. Opened the door. And found Emma Scott holding a large box wrapped in silver and white paper.

Anna's shoulders lowered in relief. Emma was a friend from her youth and had been expected. But more importantly, she was also a local. She certainly hadn't traveled over land and sea.

She beamed at the absolute sweetheart of a woman she had known since childhood. "Emma, I'm so glad you could make it."

Emma usually radiated warmth and kindness, but today she all but sparkled. "Let me tell you, I am equally glad to be attending your wedding. Maybe there's hope for our crew of difficult women yet." She chuckled, gave Anna a wink, and held up the box. "As you can see, I have a present."

Eyes gleaming, she stepped back and angled her body to the side. "But I also have a surprise."

Caught off guard, Anna stepped out and followed Emma's line of sight. It was her turn to stumble to a halt as her heart swelled and her stomach flipped.

Emma's sister stood on the porch, surrounded by Paige's colorful blooms. Long brown hair hanging free, she stood with one hip cocked, wearing an air of confidence as casually as the black knit dress that showcased sexily-toned arms and legs.

Anna blinked as memories burst like flashbangs, each haloed in the light of nostalgia. Schoolyard games. First sip of beer. Moonlight rituals.

And so quickly it seemed, the tears of heartbreak.

"Rae," she said on a breath, rushing forward but stopping just shy of the other woman. Hand shaking, she held out two fingers. Rae mimicked the gesture and pressed her own fingers against Anna's.

Then they both kissed the tips and tapped them to their hearts, a secret childhood greeting they'd never outgrown.

They'd never forgotten.

"Hey, girl," Rae whispered, the two little words carrying a wealth of emotion.

Inside Anna, joy rose up. But was held in check by fear.

Because now she knew. Now she was certain.

"Rae," she said again, pulling her into a tight embrace. "You're my raven."

4

Rae released a pent-up sigh that felt years in the making and returned Anna's embrace. "I have missed you *so* much," she said, giving her friend one more squeeze before ending the hug. She quirked a brow. "And did you just call me a raven?"

With a little laugh-and-shrug combo, Anna said, "Oh, you know how I am about symbols." She waved her hand to dismiss the subject, but a shadow skittered behind her bold blue gaze.

Rae angled her head and studied her friend. "I know you too well, Anna, and there's something you're not telling me."

Anna huffed. "There is. I'm not sure what to make of it, but I had a—"

"Dream?" Rae said, completing the statement. How many times had she seen Anna worked up over something she'd seen in her sleep. "Still peering into the ether realm, are you?"

Anna's tense expression was replaced by a broad grin. "I can't believe we used to say that. The *ether realm*. We were so dramatic back then."

"Maybe a little," Rae agreed. "We did what we could to lighten things up." Considering the very heavy burden Anna had been born to carry.

"So . . . how serious was this dream?" She was intrigued by the raven comment, but more concerned about Anna dealing with any stress during her wedding week.

Again, Anna shrugged it off. "How about we meet for lunch? We can talk about my overactive imagination then." She wrinkled her brow. "How long are you staying?"

This time. Rae could sense the unspoken words. "I promise I'll be here for the big day," she said, and meant it. Because she owed Anna at least that much.

"Thank you, Rae. That means so much to me, especially since I know how hard it is . . ."

"Well, I think I can squeeze you into my schedule," Rae teased, but also took the opportunity to steer them back to more cheerful topics. "I can do lunch whenever you want. Your place, my family's, or I can take you somewhere special."

Anna looped her arm through hers. "How about tomorrow at your family's house? I haven't sat in those gardens in so long."

"It's a date." Using a finger, Rae crossed her heart.

"But first," still holding on to her, Anna tugged Rae toward the door and ushered her into the house, "I want you to meet the girls."

"Absolutely." Rae smiled and went along. She'd come to expect the odd heaviness in her belly whenever she returned to town, but at the mention of Anna's other friends, nerves fluttered to life right beside the weight.

At long last, she was about to meet the coven.

As Anna's friend, Rae had grown up knowing all about the St. Germaine prophecy and the long-anticipated Savannah Coven. And after three centuries passing without so much as a glimmer of evil, Fate—the fickle bitch—had decided to set her sights on Anna.

All of her life, Anna had waited, worried, studied, prepared. And when the demon had risen from the darkest depths, she and her coven had defeated him, along with his legions of followers. She and eight other women had fought, bled. And even died for that victory.

Or so Rae had heard.

Because when her oldest, closest friend had needed her most, Rae hadn't been there.

Though her skills in the Craft were nowhere near the level of Anna's natural magick, she still kicked herself for not coming back. For not visiting to at least toss in moral support. Like any decent friend would have done.

When guilt reached up to grab at her throat, she tightened her jaw and clamped down. She refused to dwell on regret and risk spoiling this happy day.

Too often, she made a habit of failing the ones she loved, but damned if that was going to be Anna. Not this time.

Not again.

So instead she focused on Anna's radiant smile and met it with one of her own. Together they stepped inside and walked to the open doors leading into the parlor where her sister, all bubbly laughter and smiles, was already in deep discussion with a pretty Asian woman and a sleek redhead in a killer dress.

But that was Emma. She never met a stranger.

Rae, on the other hand, felt glued to the spot, as one by one, the group turned to look at her. Did they know who she was? Did they know how close she and Anna had once been? Would they judge her?

She rolled her shoulders and started to inch forward but skidded to a halt when someone behind her said, "Hold it right there." The familiar voice and accompanying scent of vanilla caused a rush of nostalgia as Rae turned to find a pair of sharp blue eyes twinkling at her.

"Rae." Mrs. Attinger spread her arms. "You come right over here and give me a hug." The silver-haired woman who'd corralled her and Anna for so many years made a soft motherly sound as she pulled Rae close and smacked a kiss on her forehead. "How have you been, my little dancing queen?"

The laughter that rolled from Rae's gut was unexpected and unstoppable. "Please, no, Mrs. A. I'd like to at least try to make a good impression on Anna's friends." She held up a finger.

"You are *forbidden* to tell that story."

"Hmm. We'll see." Mrs. Attinger pinched her chin gently. "If you behave."

"You always did drive a hard bargain." Rae leaned into her, overwhelmed by the sense of comfort and protection Mrs. Attinger provided. As she always had.

With one arm around Rae's waist and the other on Anna's, Mrs. Attinger walked them both into the parlor.

Despite the elegant decorations and lovely refreshment tables adorned with pink peonies, Rae drew a long, bolstering breath. The entire room was watching, and she still didn't know what her welcome would be.

But she received only friendly expressions of interest. Even from the fearsome blonde who had to be descended from the Amazons. *Must be the infamous Paige.*

And what a relief that one didn't want to tear a strip from her hide.

Rae studied the group of women, trying to pair the appropriate names with the descriptions provided in Anna's emails.

"I see Emma's introduced herself," Mrs. Attinger said to the room.

From behind the punch bowl, Emma waved back with wiggly fingers.

"And this is her sister, Rae," Anna said. "I know I've mentioned the Scott girls before, two of my oldest and dearest friends."

Mrs. Attinger cackled. "What she really means is the two she got into the most trouble with. Before any of you came along, that is. These two, especially." She indicated Anna and Rae. "Thick as thieves."

"And wicked as witches," Anna murmured, reaching behind Mrs. Attinger to poke Rae in the back.

The old inside joke created a cascade of warmth that soothed the last of Rae's fluttering nerves. She gave Anna a poke in return and wondered how she'd let herself get so churned up. She'd redirected her own shame and self-admonishment, allowing it to color the way she thought others would see her.

The effects of spending so much time alone in the wild. She made a mental note to brush up on her social skills.

Heart lighter and smile brighter, she said, "We never got much past you, Mrs. Attinger."

"No. Unless you stayed at your house on the mainland. Too far for even me to know your every move." The older woman cocked her head and sent Rae such a tender look that she had to gulp down a rise of emotion.

Having already stepped in to help raise the orphaned Anna and Quinn, Mrs. Attinger had also taken Rae under her stern but loving wing when her mother passed away.

The soft-hearted Mrs. Attinger must have been feeling the same rush of sentiment, because she touched Rae's cheek before clearing her throat and rushing on in a playful voice, "But you girls don't have to worry today. I didn't put ambrosia on the menu."

"Mrs. A!" Anna and Emma cried at the same time, while Rae burst out laughing again.

"Wait. Ambrosia? The food of the gods?" This from the flame-haired Claudia.

Anna shook her head. "Hardly. But you don't want to hear all that." She held out her palm in a halting motion, but her friends wouldn't be put off.

A flurry of voices assailed them at once, the charge led by a talkative woman with a wealth of sunny curls who rushed over to take Rae's hands. "I've heard so many stories from Quinn, I feel like I know you already." Then she winked. "So you can tell me anything."

"You must be Kylie." Good job, Quinn, Rae thought, thinking fondly of the studious boy she'd watched grow up. "You tell that boyfriend of yours to watch it, because I know a few of his secrets, too."

"Ooh. Ooh. Do tell."

"Give her a minute, Kylie." A blonde with a gentle Southern accent shot a disarming two-dimple smile at Rae. "This group can be a bit overwhelming. Believe me, I know. I'm Willyn, by the way. And don't worry if you can't keep us all straight."

"Come on. Spill." Kylie pleaded with her eyes. "Since Mrs. Attinger brought it up and you all reacted that way, it's got to be good."

"More like embarrassing," Rae said under her breath.

"Even better." Kylie hiked a thumb over her shoulder to Emma. "Besides, I have a feeling she'll tell us if you won't."

"Okay, okay." Anna looked to the ceiling and heaved a sigh. "When we were teenagers, we had a slumber party at the Scott house."

"And Bell was there," Rae said, before explaining to the gathering group, "a good friend of Emma's."

"Right," Anna nodded. "She's the one who brought the ambrosia." She looked at Rae and they both shuddered.

"Which is disgusting enough all by itself," Rae said. "But then *somebody*," she peered over Willyn's shoulder to stare at her sister, "had the brilliant idea to break out the sherry."

"How was I supposed to know?" Emma held up her hands. "All the fancy people on TV seemed to drink it."

"Not *cooking* sherry." Anna shivered and made a face. "Ugh. I still get queasy just thinking about that night."

Emma had to stifle her laughter. "We all got sick as dogs and went outside hoping Dad wouldn't hear. We threw up sherry and pink marshmallows all over the azaleas."

"So the evidence would be disguised." Rae hooted and clutched her midsection. Then she turned to Mrs. Attinger. "But how did you find out?"

Mrs. Attinger crossed her arms. "Your father found the

evidence the next morning—unwashed glasses along with newly decorated shrubbery. It wasn't hard to piece together, and he called me to discuss suitable punishment. I told him to wake you all up and serve a greasy breakfast."

"That was you?" Anna's jaw dropped.

With a smug expression, Mrs. Attinger shrugged.

"Pink marshmallows?" The Spanish vixen named Lucia crinkled her nose.

"Fruit, nuts, whipped cream, among other things. And *marshmallows*," Mrs. Attinger confirmed. "Ambrosia. I'll give you the recipe."

"No, no. Please don't." Lucia sipped her drink and closed her eyes as if warding off the very idea.

Willyn eyeballed the mimosa. "I want one of those so badly," she said. Then shocked Rae by grabbing her own breasts. "But for every drink I have, I can't nurse for at least two hours."

As if realizing what she was doing, she made an oh-shape of her mouth and dropped her hands. "I am so sorry. I blame sleep deprivation."

"No worries," Rae said, genuinely charmed.

"Any more of that and I'll start filming." Kylie slipped behind Willyn to pop her on the butt. "We'll call it Witches Gone Wild."

"I'd buy that," Emma called out. She appeared to be fitting right in, with a champagne flute in one hand and a petit four in the other.

A woman with hair the color of caramel—Hayden, Rae remembered—slipped closer and said, "Any conversation that makes Willyn fondle herself is one I want to be in on."

"No. Stop." Willyn covered her face.

"It is such a pleasure to meet you." Hayden offered her hand. "Any friend of Anna's is one of ours."

"That means a lot." Rae shook her hand, and a tingle of power spread across her palm. She'd grown accustomed to that happening on occasion with Anna, but this shiver of magick jolted her. She glanced up, but Hayden hadn't seemed to notice her reaction.

She'd been around the Craft all her life, but never around such abilities. Eight witches, eight women, all of whom had helped Anna fulfill her family prophecy. In truth, they'd probably saved Anna's life, and for that Rae was forever in their debt.

As the rest of the group gathered close enough to hear, she decided not to waste the opportunity presented by having them all in the same place. "Ladies," she began, raising her glass slightly to draw their attention, "I'd like to say something, and I know we've only just met."

She shifted her gaze to Anna first, then skipped back to Hayden, Willyn, Kylie, and every one of the women in Anna's coven. "I just want to tell you how happy—no, how truly *grateful* I am—that all of you came into Anna's life. That you answered the call. And that you were there to give her your friendship and support."

Especially since I wasn't.

Ignoring the lump in her throat, Rae hoisted her glass higher. "So cheers to you, the Savannah Coven," she slid a glance to Anna, "for taking care of my friend."

"Here, here," Mrs. Attinger said, having found a glass of her own for the toast.

"Cheers," Emma said from her spot near the table.

Anna remained silent, but her eyes told Rae she appreciated her words.

"That is so nice of you to say." Hayden tilted her head. "And she took care of us, too." Then she and Anna shared a moment of communion, of camaraderie.

One that Rae would always be a stranger to.

"I sense tears coming on," Paige said. "So. Change of topic. Rae," she said, aqua-blue eyes locking onto her, "where do you live?"

She opened her mouth to reply, but it was Emma who said, "Nowhere. Everywhere." Her doe eyes rolled to the ceiling. "That's my sister's motto."

"Uh . . ." Rae stuttered, returning her attention to Paige, "I've been in Peru the last few weeks, but I'll be heading to Tibet soon."

"Is travel a part of your job?" Claudia asked.

With a nod, she explained. "It all started with my love for photography. In the beginning, I tried to be a travel-writer, but it turned out that I enjoyed being off-grid too much and never got my articles in on time, back before data-capable cell phones could connect to towers and the web. But it's worked out well, since I can focus now on getting good shots."

"You mean outrageous shots." Anna shuddered and told the others, "The highest mountains, the thickest jungles." This time the smile she sent to Rae was filled with pride. "She specializes in the hard-to-get pictures." Anna sighed. "It takes her far away, but . . ."

Without warning, regret returned, leaving an acrid taste in Rae's mouth. Anna said she understood, she knew why Rae had gone—the main reason, at least—but she couldn't quite hide her sadness.

Rae hated being away so much. She hated being away from friends and family.

But that wouldn't stop her from leaving them behind once again, just as soon as Anna said "I do."

Latching on to the idea, Rae said, "So, let's talk wedding." Her lips curved up as she hip-bumped Anna. "When do I get to meet this Viking warrior who stole your heart?"

"Viking warrior?" Anna asked, then they both glanced across the room and said, "Emma," at the same time.

"My sister is a romantic with a flair for drama."

"She's a darling," Anna said just as the doorbell rang. "Oh, that will be more guests. Why don't you go back to the kitchen and say hi to Claire? Just make sure she isn't carrying anything she can't afford to drop. She's going to die when she sees you."

"I'll peek in before I surprise her."

"Ohhhh." Anna wiggled. "I'm so happy you're here for the wedding. Now it's exactly as I always dreamed it would be." She gave Rae one more quick hug before whirling around to go answer the door, so clearly ecstatic her steps barely touched the ground.

Before heading back to the kitchen, Rae watched her friend for a moment longer, and felt a pang just below her heart. As much as she adored Anna, Emma, and all of her family, this visit would be another of the short and bittersweet variety.

She'd do as she'd promised and stay a few days. Just long enough to attend the wedding.

But then she had to get the hell out of Savannah.

5

She woke to a world of darkness and pain.

Alone, naked, curled in a fetal position. And colder than should have been humanly possible. Just as she had a thousand other times, waking in a panic, her body entombed by what felt like mud. But smelled like death.

Putrid sludge filled her nose and mouth, burning her eyes if she dared crack them open. Stifling and revolting, the slime pressed in from all sides, like a rotten womb that refused to give her up.

Every other time she'd found her way to consciousness, she'd been met by a complete and terrible absence of sound, even her own heart seeming silent and still.

But this time was different.

Listening intently, she picked up on a soft scraping, like the legs of insects crawling across silk. A faint and distant *esh-esh-esh* barely registered to her ears, but as she focused, as she concentrated, a pattern began to emerge.

Not random scratches, but low voices, rasping the same sounds in repetition.

She strained to make out the words, but the mire suddenly clutched around her, crushing inward while shoving up from beneath. As the pressure under her steadily increased, she sensed herself rising, the mud sliding over her flesh.

Nausea churned as the speed increased, thrusting her higher until she broke free and felt the frozen sting of air.

Too many sensations flooded her at once. Space, sound, touch—stimuli she hadn't felt in so long. Too long. The endless void of the pit had erased all measurement of time.

Beneath her the sludge solidified, and she found herself lying naked on the ground.

Now she could hear harsh, guttural whispers filling the air, chanting in a language she didn't recognize. A multitude of voices surrounded her, the heavy drone shooting a chill down her already-frozen spine. The intonation sounded ominous. Ancient.

Angry.

She tried to move, but her muscles cramped and screamed. She felt like a corpse in rigor mortis. Still, she needed to see. She needed to know.

Slowly, she rolled onto her back. The change in position sent a rush of pain to the back of her head, a splitting throb as if someone were prying her skull open from behind. She collapsed with a groan, and the menacing whispers fell silent.

All but one.

Khnyokk.

The sound jolted into her, raping her brain with an icy stab. But despite this new torture, questions trampled through her aching mind. Who had spoken? What had they said? She opened her eyes and blinked to clear the slime. Had they called her name?

If they had, she wouldn't know. Because her name was something she no longer remembered.

Khnyokk.

Again the word penetrated, a jagged blade piercing bone. She clapped her hands to her temples and pressed against the pain, then with great effort rolled up to her knees. She tried to stand but couldn't make it, her legs far too limp and unstable.

How long since she'd last been on her feet? How long trapped in the rotting ground?

She opened her mouth to beg, to cry out for help, but her throat was clogged. The first attempt at speech caused a fit of coughing and sent her stomach muscles into spasms. Abdomen clenching over and over, she finally disgorged a stream of oily sludge. Greenish black, the bile tasted of acid and smelled of rot.

She vomited again.

After emptying her stomach, she used a trembling hand to wipe her mouth, then raised her head to study the surroundings. She was inside a large dark chamber, perhaps a cavern, a black expanse far above. Was it a ceiling? A sky? She couldn't tell.

She glanced around in search of whoever had spoken. Pillars lined the area, creating a huge rectangle. The design reminded her of the Greek Parthenon, but the columns here stood alone, supporting no cover or roof.

Just the opening overhead and a view of the abyss, its depths deeper, darker, and farther than Hell.

She wiped away more of the filth from her eyes and, at length, her vision crystallized. Bizarre lights flickered through the pillars, crimson flames burning trails along the walls. But even the minimal light scorched her eyes, unused for so long.

She could barely see the shadows lingering among the columns, but at first glance, they seemed wrong somehow. She squinted, trying to get a better look. A patch of black shifted. It eased away from the pillars.

Terror sank claws into her heart.

Not a shadow, but a figure. They all were. Huge, looming bodies disguised by darkness, despite the red glow of flames. Inky vapors obscured their forms, creating the illusion of shadow.

As one, they began to advance, stealing closer until they loomed around her. Even at close range, their shapes remained dark, their features hidden.

Again her chest clenched with fear. "Please," she rasped.

A sharp *crack!* filled the air and a gash opened on her arm, as if she'd been lashed by an invisible whip. Agony ripped a scream from her throat.

Another wound opened on her thigh.

"Stop!" she pleaded, reaching out in entreaty.

The next hot, bloody slice appeared on her stomach, and her back bowed in response. Labored breaths coming in rapid bursts, she clamped a hand to her thigh, the other to her stomach. The slime still covering her skin pressed into the gaping flesh. Burning. Infecting.

Her head wheeled with confusion as nausea and pain made her entire body quake. Keeping her eyes on the ground, she raked in her breaths until she regained control. "Who are you?" she whispered.

Another strike, this time on her neck.

With a wail, she dropped her head back. "What do you want?"

A sharp lash on her forehead, cutting too close to the corner of one eye. Her breath lodged in her lungs, and when it broke loose, she inhaled for another scream.

But realization struck, and she bit down on her lip, hard enough to draw her own blood.

Don't scream. Don't speak. Her eyes rolled wildly as she studied the tall creatures. She didn't understand their power, but every time she spoke they cut her. Every time she screamed, another slice.

They didn't want her to make a sound. But why? Why bring her out of the pit only to do this? Why the confusion? Just another form of torture?

She'd long ago stopped wondering where she was or who she was, accepting that her life now consisted of pain and misery. An existence she feared would be eternal.

A whimper escaped from her lips. And a second mark crisscrossed the one on her stomach.

She sucked on her tongue and ground her jaws together. No

sound passed. Not a single moan.

After too many strikes, she'd learned her lesson. She'd learned to be quiet.

Jha na.

The voice pierced her brain again, and it took every ounce of her will to remain silent. She could only hope the sound of her ragged breaths through her nostrils didn't bring more punishment.

Because that's exactly what it was. Punishment for a crime she didn't remember. Whatever her offense, she was now at the mercy of these beasts—these monsters—who demanded her respect. Her *deference*.

Terrified to move or make the slightest noise, she kept her head lowered and remained on her knees. Painfully still, she waited. What felt like minutes passed as the dark ones moved closer. Watching her. Studying her. Staring at her brutalized body.

Finally, another one spoke. The guttural words still hurt her head, still pierced her mind, but after enduring the stench and suffocation of the pit, she could endure a few jarring sounds.

A rustling drew her attention to the pillars again, where other forms suddenly appeared en masse. Unlike the devils who tormented her, these new beings had pale gray skin, almost translucent, and they wore no clothing to cover their long-limbed bodies.

They slunk closer, eyes fully white and unblinking, only bloody red lines where their eyelids should have been. They bowed their heads when they passed the dark ones, carefully avoiding any contact.

They neared, and she could see their mouths had been sewn shut. With rusty wire.

Had they once been human? Once like her?

Was this to be her fate?

She clapped her gaze onto the ground again, too horrified

by the notion to risk angering the masters. For there was no longer any question who held command.

The shadows mastered all in this forsaken place.

She closed her eyes and tried to quell her trembling. She pitied the pale creatures, the ghouls whose lives must be anguish, but they seemed to have been summoned to the chamber.

And they continued to close in on her.

Barely a foot away, they halted as if barred by an unseen force. They waited. She waited. She held her breath.

Goern fak. Another order rasped out in the peculiar language.

And the ghouls fell on her like a pack of wolves. Muttering and whining, they grabbed her with three-fingered hands. The spindly digits latched on to her arms, legs, head, and torso, cocooning her until she was all but paralyzed.

She struggled. She fought. Yet all the while, she crammed her teeth together, willing her vocal cords to remain mute. The lesson of silence was still too fresh.

Once she'd been fully subdued, the pack picked her up and began to carry her, their hands squeezing like vises. Not to maintain their grip, but to cause pain.

One of the ghouls dug its fingers into her breast. Another slipped his inside her mouth. Then one of the creatures assaulted her in another way—the worst way—and panic finally won out.

Wrenching her face to the side, she freed her mouth and drew in a breath. But another hand clamped over her lips before she could scream.

Unh-unh. A ghoul grunted in her ear. Trying to threaten her? Keeping her silent for her own good? Or for theirs? They too, apparently, had their orders.

She didn't want to think about what the monsters had planned. Couldn't bear to imagine where they might be taking her, or what would happen when they arrived.

A kind of numbness stole over her body, as if her subconscious were taking control. Taking her under. *Please, let it be so.*

But her eyes stayed open and her mind alert, giving her no reprieve from whatever was to come. They took her through the columns and toward a high wall beyond, into a cave-like opening and a twisting tunnel.

Bound tightly, she couldn't look behind her, but she sensed the dark beings following the mob. Felt the coldness of their presence on her bare skin.

After several turns, the ghouls halted abruptly and dropped her to her feet. Two of them still held her arms, detaining her yet also providing support. She was so cursedly weak.

Before she knew what was happening, one of them gripped her jaw and forced open her mouth, while another shoved something wet and gelatinous inside. The texture almost made her gag again, but since the substance had no scent, she was able to choke it down.

Almost instantly, her blood flashed with renewed energy.

The beasts had fed her.

The coldness of the dark ones drew near, watching as the ghouls guided her around a stone edifice and into a chamber. The room held an all too human appearance, and the sudden disorientation almost made her faint.

She steadied herself and took a closer look. This time her knees gave out, but the ghouls held her up.

A long wooden table stood in the center, shackles on both ends and dark, grisly stains mottling the surface. Along the stone wall hung gruesome tools—chains, hooks, blades, and more of the iron cuffs.

She didn't know how it was possible—here in this underworld—but they'd brought her to a medieval torture chamber.

Using her burst of strength from the feeding, she threw off the hands on her right arm, but where two ghouls had restrained her before, four moved in to overpower once more.

One of the shadowy masters eased across the room, stopping before an upright metal casket with a horrendous screaming face at the top. The master lifted his arm and a ghoul rushed forth, opening the device to reveal a hollow interior.

Hollow. Except for the spikes.

A hand slapped over her lips, another wrapped around her throat, as her pale-skinned captors shoved her the remaining distance to the device. A device known as an iron maiden. They released her only to throw her inside, impaling the back side of her body from head to heel.

Stunned by the pain, she froze, too petrified to even draw a breath. Then the ghouls slammed the door, stabbing her body from the front as well.

She'd learned her lesson. She'd learned to be silent. But all fear of punishment fell away to madness.

As her mind snapped, she screamed. And screamed.

6

"The ladies' luncheon was lovely, and it's been such a nice day." Emma pulled into the curving brick drive near Emmet Park and jerked her car to a stop. "Why do you have to ruin it by coming here?"

Outside, people strolled along the sidewalk, green grass and fountains on one side and the buildings of Factor's Row on the other, all under the canopy of towering oaks drenched in Spanish moss.

Rae let her head fall back against the seat and shut her eyes. "I knew I should have asked you to drop me off at the Pirate House."

"What difference does it make where I drop you?" Lips pressed firmly together, Emma stared forward out the windshield but shook her head, loose brown curls swaying. "I would have known. You always end up here."

"Then why have this same pointless argument?" Rae grabbed the door handle, but she paused at Emma's sharp tone.

"You want to talk about pointless?" In a rare show of temper, Emma turned quickly in her seat to face Rae, her normally-smiling eyes brittle with anger, and a healthy dose of accusation. "You hardly ever come home. You spend most of your time far away from here, away from your family, and supposedly it's to avoid the pain this place causes you."

"Emma—"

"No. I'll have my say this time, because it's gone on long

enough. You've missed so much over the years, birthdays, celebrations." She gave Rae a pointed look. "Bryn's graduation."

Oh, that one hit hard. "You know I tried to get back," Rae objected, feeling itchy and restless from the fingers of guilt squeezing the back of her neck.

"I'm sure you did, but it's hard to get back from Timbuktu in a timely manner. So, yes, there *is* a point, Rae." Releasing a sigh, Emma said, "It's not right that you use old wounds as an excuse to stay gone, then as soon as you do come back, you head straight here to torture yourself. You purposely expose yourself to the very thing you say you want to escape. It's not right. It's frustrating to all of us."

Emma's lip quivered. "And it hurts."

Now those fingers of shame wrapped around Rae's throat and all but choked her. "I know. I know. It's not fair. I can see why you don't get it, but . . . it's complicated. And you know I'd never upset you if I could help it."

Emma was right, Rae thought, I *am* ruining this day. "Look, I miss you too, Em. You and Dad." She pushed her palms into the seat, gripping the edges until her knuckles stung. "And Bryn."

Hanging her head, she blew out a breath, unable to vocalize all the meaningful things in her niece's life she'd missed out on. "Believe me. I hate it, too."

"Then why, Rae? Why can't you stay? You don't have to come here." Emma laid a hand on her arm. "Maybe if you didn't, things wouldn't be so hard."

Rae only shrugged.

"I'm telling you this now, because I don't know when I'll get another chance. But you can't lose any more time with us. We're your family, and I would think we were just as important as . . ." Emma trailed off.

Rae knew she'd stopped out of consideration. She didn't say his name.

"It's just not healthy, and it can't go on forever." Emma took her hand away. "No matter how good a reason you think you have."

Not just one reason. Rae placed a hand to her stomach. She had a second and equally compelling reason to get gone and stay gone. But what was she supposed to tell her sister? That coming home literally made her sick?

The churning in her gut wasn't nausea. Not exactly. More like a pit that formed in her stomach, an intense gravity constantly pulling and twisting.

But only when she returned to Savannah.

She chalked it up to nerves and painful memories, each time swearing she'd be stronger the next. But as soon as she set foot on the Georgia ground, the same black hole opened up inside of her.

On the first day, she'd be mildly uncomfortable, but as the hours added up, discomfort turned to misery. The weight became an intense and unrelenting pain, one she could only bear for a short time.

A doctor had ruled out physical ailments years ago, suggesting her symptoms were psychosomatic.

Or in other words—she was totally bat shit.

Rae studied Emma's disappointed visage. Maybe having her family think she was crazy was better than their thinking she just didn't care. Because she did care, so much, and it tore her up when she had to say goodbye.

"You're right, Emma." Rae met her sister's sad, baffled gaze. "I'll try to do better."

"Okay, then how long are you staying?" Emma countered, firming her jaw as if determined not to back down, to hold Rae accountable. She didn't often play the role of enforcer and was much better suited to nurture and tend.

Just one of the reasons Rae loved her so much.

"I'll definitely stay through the wedding," she said, hoping that would be the end of it.

Of course, it wasn't. "And then?" Emma asked.

"And then we'll see." Rae grabbed the handle again, but this time she opened the door and put one foot out. "I'll see you at home, okay?"

Emma's expression went flat. "Sure." She swiveled around and put her hands on the steering wheel. "See you."

Rae wanted to say more, to say she was sorry. But until she could tell her sister what she wanted to hear, her words would be empty. Useless.

Pointless.

She opted for the false safety of silence, got out, and shut the door. Then turned so she wouldn't have to watch Emma drive away.

She tossed a glance to the Old Harbor Light and studied the huge anchors scattered over the lawn. As children, she, Emma, and their brother, Sam, had made a game of the area, crawling under and leaping over the anchors, a child-sized obstacle course.

But that was a long time ago, and the nostalgia of those days was no longer quite as sweet.

With a sigh, she started down the winding cobblestone street that led to the river, bobbled in her high heels, and righted herself before continuing on with more caution. She'd navigated Huayna Picchu with less trouble than the uneven cobbles of her hometown.

Even the historic steps of hewn stone along the outside of the park's retaining wall would be preferable, but for safety's sake the city had locked the gate to the steep, slick stairs.

Once around the bend, she reached the bottom, giving silent thanks for the perfectly flat sidewalk as she passed behind the statue of the Waving Girl.

Then she laid eyes on the row of crepe myrtles, blooming their springtime pink, and her mood took a long, deep dive.

The old wooden bench still sat beneath the cypress tree, in front of the stone wall sprouting lush ferns and moss. An image rose unbidden to her mind, but she forced herself to acknowledge the memory. To remember the two of them together in this place.

On *their* bench. Under *their* tree.

In their special spot.

Though heartache overwhelmed her, she moved to the bench and sat. So much time had passed, yet she couldn't shake the feelings this place inspired. More than anything, she wanted to forget her past, to move beyond the memories that held so much power over her.

Emma had been dead right. Things were unbalanced. So just how much did Rae have to endure? How long before she just womaned-up and got the hell over it?

But her sister didn't understand—and Rae didn't tell her—that the desire to move beyond the pain was exactly why she kept coming back to this particular spot. No matter how long she stayed away, the anguish was still waiting for her when she returned.

So she did the only other thing she knew to do to help herself. She used this private little nook as a type of test, each visit serving as exposure therapy. She immersed herself in the past, reliving it again, hoping to become desensitized.

Maybe then she'd enjoy being home. Maybe then her stomach would stop tearing her in two.

Maybe then she wouldn't think of Arik.

But no, she thought, closing her eyes to block his handsome face. He was always there, always with her, like her own personal phantom. His power was at its strongest here, where they'd once shared hopes, dreams, and the purest of true love.

Something inside of her pinched, so she released a low moan and collapsed against the back of the bench. Staring out over the water, she let herself remember. She let herself ache. And prayed that this time she'd begin to heal.

A ship sounded off and snapped her from the daze. With no idea how long she'd been sitting there in silence, she glanced upriver. The sun now hung lower in the sky, painting the clouds in soft amber and lilac.

The foghorn boomed across the water again, prompting Rae to stand. Her experiment was over. And again had failed. Coming here had done no good. In fact, the only thing worse than the pit in her stomach was the fresh, raw wound in her heart.

The scent of pralines drifted down River Street, so she followed the enticing smell. Imagining the sweet pecan crunch dissolving in her mouth, she gave up on fighting, and gave in to indulgence.

Like her grandmother always used to say—no better cure for what ails you, than butter and sugar.

Right now, she'd take any-and-all comfort at her disposal, certain she couldn't feel any worse.

"Rae."

The sound of his voice struck her from behind, like a crashing wave that stole her breath. Staggered, she lurched to a stop, blood rushing and roaring in her head, pounding the cadence of her erratic heart.

This can't be happening. He can't be here. Shocked and slightly horrified, she dug deep for calm and slowly turned around.

Not an illusion. Not a figment of her imagination, but a ghost standing before her as if summoned by her thoughts. *Arik.*

The years hadn't changed him, or so it seemed. His eyes still burned a rich, smoldering brown above the oh-so-kissable mouth set in serious lines. The style of his hair had changed but maintained the rich gold, as if gilded by angels.

She used to call him her warrior scholar—always ruminating but ready for a fight.

As brutally handsome as ever, he stood in a relaxed stance, arms hanging loose at his sides. Long legs, wide shoulders, all toned and muscled. No doubt he still worked out daily, sparring and practicing the katas taught to him by his father.

She felt her lips part in surprise, but no sound escaped.

Arik took it upon himself to speak again. "How are you?" he asked, the low, delicious stroke of his voice stirring the embers of the love she'd once felt.

And the desire.

The sudden and desperate attraction was like a punch to the gut. And she reacted in kind, protecting herself from the threat. She took all of the pain, all of the longing, and transformed them into an impenetrable shield of detachment.

Oh, she wanted to ball her fists and vent her fury. She wanted to tell him where to go. But that would only show how much he still affected her, and though he dared behave as if nothing had ever happened, dared to approach her—*here*, of all places—she wouldn't let him see how much she still hurt.

She wouldn't give him that satisfaction.

Offering him a watered-down smile, she inclined her head. "Arik," she said, her tone silky and smooth, a queen addressing her subject. "I'm well, and you?"

"Fine, thanks," he said automatically, but then he shook his head. "No, actually that's not true. I'm not sure how I am." He drew a heavy breath. "I realize this is unexpected, but . . . Do you have a minute?"

Like hell. Rae kept the smile plastered to her lips. "I'm afraid I was just leaving. Maybe another time." *Or maybe never.*

"I really need to talk to you."

"No." She eased back. "You really don't." Her façade was breaking down, allowing anger to drip-drip-drip through the cracks. "I have to go," she muttered and started to turn, a maelstrom of emotion warring within.

"It's about what happened to my parents."

Rae froze in place. Bitterness continued to seep, but he'd said the one thing that could stop the flow. In an instant, she lowered her guard, remembering how much he'd suffered. How lost and confused he'd been during that time.

After that night.

~~~

Arik hadn't anticipated this cool and aloof version of Rae. He'd fully expected her to lash out, to blast him with temper, and he'd come prepared to offer penance.

So when she didn't reject him, argue, or slap at him with insults, the speech he'd so carefully crafted simply crumbled to the ground.

He hazarded a step closer.

She took one in retreat.

Easy, he told himself. Rae might be acting poised and self-assured, but the expression she wore was haunted, suspicion and distrust darkening her amazing eyes.

Eyes the color of bottled honey, that he'd seen in his dreams far too often for peace of mind.

Shaking off the effect she had on him, he held out both hands and did his best to appear harmless, even going so far as to edge away from her. To give her some space.

And as he did, he took advantage of the moment to study her, and the face he'd always considered one of nature's works of art. Carved cheekbones, straight brows, and full, lush lips to balance out a strong jaw—features both feminine and bold.

She'd been a striking young woman when he'd known her, and the years had only enhanced her beauty, adding layers of polish and sophistication.

Arik couldn't stop looking at her.

"What about your parents?" she asked, snapping him back to attention. Beneath the hesitation, he could hear the concern in her voice. "Is your mother all right? Has she—"

"No, no. She's . . . the same." He didn't elaborate, but the mention of his mother got him back on track. "But something's happened, and my mother *is* part of why I'm here."

As if puzzled, Rae furrowed her brows and gave a slight shake of her head.

"It's a long and convoluted story, but after my parents' accident, I discovered some things about my father. Incredible and troubling things." Arik could hear himself and knew he wasn't making a lot of sense. Still, he barreled on. "I think it's all connected, and if I can find the last missing pieces, I may be able to help her."

"Your mother?" She reached across her body, clutching the strap of the small black purse hanging from her shoulder, a subtle yet defensive move. "I don't understand why you're here telling me this. What does it have to do with me?"

"I don't . . . know." He stumbled over the admission. "But when you came back today, it *triggered* something."

"I have no idea what you're talking about. I didn't trigger anything." Disbelief stamped on her face, Rae ran a hand through her long, dark hair. Then she went abruptly still. She whipped her head toward him and narrowed her eyes. "How did you even know I was back? Better yet, how did you know to find me here?"

Arik shifted on his feet and slid his hands into his pockets. This was where things got sticky. "Someone told me."

"That's not possible. No one knew I'd be here." Her brows shot up. "Emma?"

"No. Not Emma. Someone else knew where I could find you." Mahalia had known. Because she had *seen*. After the globe had put on its supernatural light show, she'd returned to the kitchen to throw the bones for herself.

Arik had cursed when she'd directed him here, the worst possible place to reach out to Rae. The woman he'd hurt. The heart he'd wounded.

He steeled his body but exuded calm. "Do you remember when I told you about a woman coming to see me the day after my father died?"

"Yes. And?"

"Over the years, I've gotten to know her better. She's become a friend and an advisor of sorts." The more he talked, the less she seemed convinced. So he threw it all out there. "She's a voodoo practitioner who's been gifted with unique abilities. She told me when and where to find you."

When Rae simply gaped at him, he rushed on. "Look, this is a lot to process, and here really isn't the place for us to have a conversation. Why don't we go somewhere quiet?" Somewhere that wasn't saturated with torturous memories.

"Hmm. No." Rae scoffed. "I don't think I need to hear anymore of," she circled her hand, "whatever this is. We haven't spoken since—" She broke off and looked out to the river, her brow wrinkled.

Then her gaze slammed into his. "Look, Arik, we haven't spoken in a very long time. We don't know each other now." She spoke in a steady monotone, void of all emotion. "And I think it's best to keep it that way."

As he watched, the rage he'd expected sparked to life. And how could he blame her after what he'd done? "Rae," he began, his tone mild and rational, "I know this all sounds—"

"Crazy? Far-fetched?" She lifted her chin. "*Obsessive?*"

The intended dagger struck home. Rae had been the first person to point out his fixation on the mysterious family legacy. That he'd started down the same endless path his father had taken.

Fixated. Consumed. Obsessed. All descriptions she'd used. All of them true.

And that was *before* he'd found his father's journals.

He could feel the situation slipping from his control, and he needed her to listen. "I get it. I do. Why don't you come with me to see Mahalia? Maybe if you meet her, talk to her, she can get a read off of you and explain things better."

"A read?" Rae's eyes popped into incredulous discs. "That's why you came? After all these years? You sought me out *here*," she stabbed a finger at the ground, "so you could take me to a voodoo woman and get *a read* on me?"

Well, when she put it that way. "Rae, listen."

"Stop." She thrust out her palm. "Just stop. I'm sorry for what happened to your parents, you know I am. And if I knew how to help your mother, I would. But whatever you and this woman are doing, I cannot be involved." She drew a ragged breath and stumbled back. "I just can't."

When she whirled around and stalked down the sidewalk, Arik contained the urge to run after her. He'd shocked her, caught her off guard, and he knew her well enough not to push. Not now.

But he would have to see her again before she left. He had no choice. He hated tormenting her, but some things couldn't be changed. They couldn't be undone.

As she walked away, he looked up, watching purple clouds drift across the sky. *I'm sorry, Rae.* Sorrier than she would ever know.

And despite her refusal, despite his wish that things were different, Rae would have to talk to him, she'd have to hear him out.

Because like it or not, she was already involved.

7

Arik exited his car amid thick stands of trees and blooming shrubbery sheltering a slender three-story home. Pale yellow paint and white gingerbread porches on each level lent the house a cottage appeal. But the real whimsy, he'd always thought, lay with the treehouse perched high in the limbs of an ancient oak.

Panels of stained glass hung from beneath the golden wood, like banners declaring the owner's eccentricity. In daylight the colors would shine like gemstones, but now the glass glinted darkly under moonlight and swayed in the gentle wind.

Arik's steps crunched over dirt and gravel as he passed the red and white camper parked in the drive and entered through a picket fence. Before he even made it to the front steps, the door opened.

"Come on in, boy." Mahalia's silhouette filled a rectangle of orange light. When Arik reached the porch, she pulled the door wider, loosing a savory scent that made his mouth water. And his anxiety spike.

Mahalia was baking herb bread. Never a good sign.

"What's got you worried, Mahalia?" He sniffed the air and leveled her with a stare.

With a harrumph and a grin, she swatted his arm. "You know me too well." She stuck her head forward and whispered, "Made some baked ziti, too."

One of Arik's favorites. Now he was truly concerned. "You've been expecting me." And had made comfort food for them both. Clearly, an important discussion was planned.

Mahalia's only reply was to crook her hand, indicating he should follow her to the kitchen. He trailed her down the hallway over shining hardwood planks, most likely original to the house, and into a room that managed to feel spacious and cozy at the same time.

Arik took a seat at the round table on one side of the room, noting that it was already set for two, and looked out the windows. In back, a lawn banked by more thick foliage stretched out before feeding into marshlands.

Taking in the scenery, he waited for his hostess, knowing better than to offer assistance. Mahalia would never hear of a guest doing work, no matter how often that guest visited or how close the friendship.

A few minutes later, she put out a dish of ziti covered with cheese and red sauce, along with a basket holding freshly sliced bread. She poured them both some sweet tea, sat across from him, and said grace.

Prayer complete, she filled his plate and hers before finally broaching the subject he'd come to discuss. "How'd it go with the girl?"

A piece of bread halfway to his mouth, Arik paused and shook his head. "As well as you might expect."

"That good, eh?" Mahalia stabbed her pasta with a fork and held it up to cool. "How much did you tell her?"

"Humph. I got as far as the voodoo woman who'd located her by looking into a crystal ball." His laugh was dry and humorless. "The conversation derailed after that."

"I don't use a crystal ball." Mahalia tried for levity, hitching up one side of her mouth in a crooked grin, but when it failed to cheer either of them she quickly turned solemn and looked down at her plate. "It may be hard, but you've got to find a way to get through to her. You've got to make her listen."

"I'm afraid it's too late for that."

Mahalia's head jerked up. "She's already gone?"

"No." Arik shook his head. "It's too late for *us*. She doesn't want to hear anything I have to say, especially after how I handled things today. If possible, I alienated her even more than she already was."

"Well then, you've got to get back into the game. I don't think we have much time, so you have to make her see what's at stake."

"Hell, I don't—"

"Language." She cut him off, one brow jerking upward.

Grinding his teeth, Arik slowly expelled the breath from his body. No cursing at the dinner table, a hard and fast rule. "Fine," he said, "but there's a problem, since I don't know what *is* at stake."

He gestured with his butter knife. "And neither do you. We're both still operating in the dark, trying to find our way. And every time we turn a corner, we find more questions than answers."

"It's a shadowy maze, for sure. But," she waved her finger, "we do have one answer, and that's Rae. We just need her to be more receptive. To open up. Maybe . . ." Mahalia let the sentence hang, pausing to sip her tea. "Maybe it's time you opened up to her. Time you told her the truth."

Arik looked at his plate, then out the windows, anywhere but into Mahalia's keen gaze. "What truth?"

She tsked and pursed her lips. "Don't pretend to be dense, boy. You know what you're holding back from her, what you've always held back."

Arik knew exactly what she meant, and the irony of his current dilemma wasn't lost on him. He'd once cut Rae out of his life, trying to protect her from his deadly family legacy.

Now, if he ever hoped to understand that legacy, he needed Rae's help.

"You both have to move forward, to move beyond your histories." Mahalia prodded, refusing to let the subject drop. "More than that, she deserves to know why you broke her heart."

"No." Arik didn't want to imagine that conversation or the pain it would dredge up. "She's moved on with her life, so why open old wounds? Why cause her that trouble?"

"Because we've got bigger trouble stomping right toward us!" Mahalia exploded, thumping the table with an open hand. "And whether you like it or not, she's part of this. She's the catalyst."

"Catalyst to what?" Arik asked, barely containing his own annoyance. Frustration strained his voice and tensed his body, eager for release.

He cut some loose and dropped his fork on the plate with a clatter. "Why Rae? Why her, of all people? I keep thinking this must be some terrible coincidence, some sick cosmic joke. If this is Karma's work, then she's a master manipulator and a spiteful—" He stopped himself, reining in the anger before he cursed again.

"Listen to me, boy," Mahalia said when he raked a hand through his hair. "You aren't being punished." She spread her hands. "This is just your destiny. And so it's also your obligation. All you can do is follow the signs you've been given."

Like his father's globe burning like the sun to announce Rae's return. A pretty hard sign to ignore.

"Okay, but why now?" Arik asked. "Why not back then?" If this had happened years ago, he might never have hurt her. He might never have caused the irreparable rift between them. "And how can I ask for help if I don't know even what I need?"

"You'll figure that out as you go, but none of that matters if she doesn't hear you out. First thing, you've got to make her listen. And you've got to make her stay here in Savannah."

Arik scoffed. "That's not going to happen." No one *made* Rae do anything.

"You'd better make it happen. Tell her whatever it takes to get the job done."

Arik's fingers tightened around his glass as irritation burgeoned anew. He gently put the tea on the table. "Like you've always done to me?"

Mahalia put a fist to her mouth and coughed, but her ploy of avoidance didn't work any better than his had.

"You tell me just enough to keep me listening. Just enough to have me do what you want." Elbows on the table, Arik leaned forward. "You talk about my truth and how it's the key to changing Rae's mind. But what about *your* truth?"

"You know I'll tell you—"

"When the time comes. So you've said." A vein throbbed in his temple. "Well it's here, Mahalia. The time is now."

Eyes cast downward, she smoothed her wrinkled hand across the glossy wood. "I know it, boy. I know." She'd grown so quiet he could barely make her out. "But not here. Not at this table."

Her gaze lifted then to clash with his. "It's a hard story, and not one I can tell in this house."

With an expression of defeat, she gestured to his food. "Go on and eat what you can. Give me a few more minutes to gather my thoughts." She forked up another bite for herself. "I promise we'll talk. After."

The way she pursed her lips told Arik the subject was closed, so he did as she asked and waited.

He waited for her to finish her meal. He waited for her to clear the table. He waited for her to wash, dry, and put away every single dish.

At last, she hung her dish towel on the oven handle and faced him. After one slow nod of acceptance, she stepped out to the back yard and left the door ajar. His signal to follow.

She walked down the porch steps and out into the grass. Anguish creased her face as she halted to look up at the fat white moon.

Arik eased up beside her, troubled by her distress yet still determined. "You know what I want to ask," he said.

A night bird cried out in echo.

Mahalia shivered and pulled her black shawl tighter around her shoulders. "About my loss." Moonlight reflected in her eyes as she slid them to his. "And how my suffering is entangled with yours."

"Yes," Arik whispered, afraid to say too much, afraid to push too hard. This subject had always been forbidden, and he didn't want to give her any reason to continue her secrecy.

"Bad things came before. They're coming again."

"Before?" he asked. "When my parents were attacked?"

"Then and before. And before and before."

Arik tensed, worried she would digress to the incoherent and cryptic speech she sometimes used to deflect. He gritted his teeth and remained silent, until his patience paid off.

"One night your parents left your home, slipping away in secrecy." Mahalia's fingers clutched the shawl. "And on that very night, my mother did the same."

Chills marched across the back of Arik's neck. "Your mother?"

As if he'd never spoken, Mahalia continued. "I have no idea where she went or what she did. And believe me," she added with a frown, "I've looked. I've used every means available, but in all these years, I haven't found a clue. All I know is what she told me before."

She stared off toward the distant marsh. "And how she was when she came back. Abused," Mahalia whispered. "*Altered*."

"What happened?" Arik asked softly, feeling a new kinship with the woman who'd hidden so much behind her mask of fortitude. All this time, they'd had more in common than he'd ever realized.

The breath she took next was deep and ragged. "I don't know who she was going to meet, but I'm sure she had no choice, that she was being coerced." She inclined her head as if confirming to herself. "Before Mama left, she told me she had to keep a promise. That she had to do *one thing*, and then we'd be safe."

A shudder racked Mahalia's shoulders. "The next time I saw her, she was in the emergency room at Candler Hospital. Her tongue cut out." She choked off a sob. "Her hands cut off."

"Mahalia," Arik said, staggered by the gruesome images. Who committed such violent acts? Particularly on a woman who had to have been near sixty years old at the time?

He would have touched her shoulder in sympathy, but she waved him off. "There's more." She leveled him with a stare. "She'd been found that way, floating in water. At Daffin Park."

"Daffin Park," Arik repeated, the name setting off alarms and filling him with dread. "My mother was found on Victory Drive, trying to crawl along the sidewalk. Near Daffin Park." He spoke in a perfunctory manner, as if the words had to be drawn from him one by one.

The connection exploded with jagged clarity. "Our mothers were victims of the same attacker." He curled his hands into fists. "The same bastard who killed my father." Though what remained of his body had taken days to be discovered.

Arik had thought he was calm. He'd believed he was ready. But Mahalia's revelation raised a slew of new questions. And concerns for the people involved, the people he cared about— his mother, Mahalia . . .

Rae.

A long-buried fear resurged, sending cold, dark terror pulsing through his veins. How could he drag her into this? The risk was too great. The danger too monstrous.

Suddenly dizzy, he walked several yards away, allowing the cool breeze to whisper over his face, calming his shock and clearing his head.

At length, he whirled to face Mahalia. "What the hell is all of this? How can my father's research be related to your mother?"

"I don't know, but the connection they shared has been passed down to us. Because whatever evil hurt them isn't gone. It isn't done with us yet."

"Which is why you should have told me," he said, unable to disguise the accusation in his voice.

"Maybe." She shrugged. "But I couldn't be sure how you would react or if you would push me out. I just knew you needed me in your life." She covered her heart with her hand. "And I needed you."

He crossed his arms and frowned, even as a part of him gentled.

"That night, I talked to a paramedic in the ER," she said. "He let it slip that another woman had been found near the park. He said what a coincidence it was."

Arik shifted his feet. "But you knew different."

"I knew the two things had to be related, so after I sat with my mama the whole night—crying, raging—" Mahalia wiped at the ghosts of those tears. "I learned your mother's name, and the next day, I hovered near her room. When I saw you leave, I followed you home."

"And decided to knock on my door." To tell him of a bond forged by sorrow. One Arik could feel now, like a line of blue pain tied tight around them both.

"Yes," she said. "I had to know what you knew. I had to find out why my mother was tortured and left to die. Although death might have been better than what she went through. She couldn't speak. She had no hands. No way to do for herself or to communicate."

Curling her own hands into a ball and pressing them to her stomach, Mahalia glanced back to the house, as if seeing memories played on a reel. "When she was well enough, I brought her home. She kept trying to write, to tell me what happened, but she could only draw messy lines. A bunch of gibberish."

She turned back to Arik. "She lived for another two weeks, in constant terror. Eyes wide and darting when awake, tormented by night terrors when she tried to sleep. Two full weeks lying in bed. And gradually losing her mind."

Mahalia sighed. "In the end, it was too much for her. I found her one morning. She was gone."

"Mahalia, I'm so sorry." Arik's chest ached for his friend. "For her, and for you."

Taking three slow steps, she moved toward him. "You're the only one who knows what I feel."

"I know exactly. And that's why there can be no more secrets between us." Arik softened his expression. "You were right before. We do need each other."

"And you need Rae."

Hearing her name was like a slap, but as Mahalia had pointed out, he couldn't ignore the signs. "Yes, it's all connected—your mother, my parents, the legacy, the globe. Here he paused and closed his eyes. "And Rae."

When he looked to Mahalia again, his body was stiff and rigid. "If I were to give up and end it all here, I might never know what happened to my parents or if there's a way to help my mother. But if I go drag Rae into this, I put her at risk."

In the short beat of silence that followed, Arik felt pressure in his chest, the crush of the inevitable. "That's one hell of a choice."

Mahalia reached out and, in a show of affection, she took his hand. "I'm afraid the fates have already cast the die, boy. And the choice is no longer yours."

8

Lured by the aroma of freshly brewed coffee, Rae wound her way down the floating staircase of her family home. Once her feet touched bottom, she took a moment to indulge in a habit held over from childhood—a stretch, a yawn, and a backward tilt of her head, the last allowing her to look through the center of the spiral and up to the stained-glass dome on the roof.

Situated in the center of the house, the feature had been designed to channel the Southern summer heat upward to be released via small vents. The original architect had possessed a head for practicality and an eye for beauty, a fact Rae greatly appreciated.

Once done, she padded across diamond tiles of black and beige and veered toward the kitchen in search of a java fix. When she found her niece, Bryn, staring at the coffee maker and tapping her foot, Rae lit up inside and gave a broad smile. "Hey, kid."

Bryn whipped her head to the side and grinned back. "I thought I heard the dead rising upstairs." She turned to lean her hip against the marble. "Decided I'd be kind enough to brew you a wake-up potion."

"Very kind. And very anticipatory." Rae scratched her head and yawned again. "If that's a word." She went to Bryn and tousled the hair falling in dark waves to just above her niece's shoulders. Then she enveloped her in a bear of a hug.

Bryn squeezed Rae in return and lifted her off her feet,

squeezing a laugh out of her. "All right, all right. Don't make me wet my pants before I've even had my coffee."

"Yuck." Bryn dropped her instantly. "That did it." She pointed to the table by a spread of windows overlooking the back gardens. "Go sit," she ordered. "You still take it black?"

"As black as my heart." Rae padded over and took a seat, but instead of surveying the flowers and fountain out back, she studied the kitchen instead. Little had changed over the years. Cabinets remained white, as did the marble counters, and the wallpaper was still French country in a pattern of blue.

Wherever Rae went, that particular shade always made her think of this room. And of her mother, who'd adored the wallpaper and sworn she'd never change it.

Which is probably why the rest of family never had either, preferring to keep the sweet reminder of the woman who'd been the heart of the family, and in many ways still was.

Rae could catch a glimpse of her mother in Bryn whenever she smiled, flashing that single dimple on her right cheek. Just the sight of it warmed her and plucked her heartstrings to play a tune of remembrance.

"I tried to wait up for you and Dad last night," Rae said when Bryn brought over a steaming mug. "Sorry I didn't quite make it."

"No worries. Jet lag will do that to you." Bryn sat and stretched out her legs to cross them at the ankles.

"So did you take gold?" Rae asked, referring to the karate tournament her niece had competed in the day before.

"I placed first in my division in traditional sparring but only took third in combat weapons."

"Slacker," Rae teased, tossing a sly grin over the rim of her mug before she sipped.

Bryn flashed her dimple in return.

Rae considered her niece as she leaned back and enjoyed the bright, sunny day through the wall of windows. A born fighter, Bryn had learned to be tough at a young age, and then had blossomed into an accomplished and self-sufficient young woman. She was driven, practical, and most of all, resilient, the product of being raised by a loving and supportive family.

Yet one without her parents.

Rae felt a small twinge of resentment, as she often did when she thought of her brother. Like her, Sam had been a wanderer, taking off after college to explore the world and taste all it had to offer. Then one day he'd shown up without notice, surprising them all with his baby daughter.

Two days later he'd gone again. But without little Bryn.

He'd left no word, no apologies, and no mention of his child's mother. All they knew of the woman was that she probably carried Asian blood, considering the slight lift at the corners of Bryn's beautiful brown eyes.

"I started to make you some eggs," Bryn said suddenly, tapping the table with her finger to draw Rae's attention, "but Emma said you'd be having lunch with Anna soon."

"Hmm?" Rae glanced to the wall clock. "It's after eleven? Wow. I really did sleep." She ran a taming hand through her hair. "Where is Emma, anyway?"

As if on cue, a clamor arose from the far end the house, carrying down the large entrance hallway that ran front to back. Rae heard the voices of her sister and father, along with the unmistakable sound of claws tapping over floor tiles.

Rae set her coffee on the table and swung her legs to the side. She clapped her hands. "Beau! Here, boy!" She was rewarded with an enthusiastic scrabble of clickety-clicks that barreled closer before an elated and bug-eyed dog bulleted into the kitchen and straight up into her lap.

"Hey, Beau. Hey, boy." She scratched his neck and back between tight hugs and kisses to the flat of his nose. "I've missed you, too. Yes, I have." She cooed and fussed as the dog smiled up at her, tongue lolling to one side.

Beauregard Ambrose the Curious—so named due to his habit of getting strange objects stuck on his puppy head after sticking his nose in too far—was the most recent in a long line of family pets. Usually, at least two rescue mutts resided in the Scott home, but after the loss of Rae's mother's favorite—Arrabella Jane the Loyal—they simply hadn't had the heart to replace her yet.

"There's my girl," her father's voice boomed.

Rae rubbed Beau one more time and let him slide off her legs. She stood and moved to meet her father in the middle of the room, where he swept her off her feet in a crushing hug.

Again, the laughter rolled forth. "Put me down," Rae begged, ticklish in the ribs. As her father well knew. "It's bad enough to get it from you, but why did you have to teach Bryn to greet that way?" Despite the chastisement, she gazed up at him in adoration.

A few inches over six feet, her father looked back at her with light-brown eyes just like her own. "She picked that up by herself." He set Rae down and gave her a head-to-toe inspection before declaring, "Too skinny." He sandwiched her face in his palms. "Good thing we got some food."

"Dad." Rae rolled her eyes and picked back at him with a flick to the hair at his temples. "And I think I see more silver than the last time I was here." Though, as with most men, the streaks only enhanced his black hair and rugged charm.

When he quirked his mouth and shook his head, she peered around him to watch Emma unload two large white bags. "What's all that?"

"Lunch for you and Anna," Emma said, offering a shy smile. "Bryn's friend has a French café down at Factor's Row. Something a little different I thought you'd both enjoy."

Recognizing the gesture of truce from her sister, Rae joined her at the counter and helped her unbag a plastic container of ham and Swiss croissants drizzled with honey. "Thanks, Em," she said.

And that's all that was needed.

They'd weathered too many emotional storms to let any disagreement, large or small, stand between them for very long. When their mother had died, they'd stepped in to help raise Bryn, two turbulent adjustments in a very short time, especially for teenage girls.

But the tragic loss and new responsibilities had brought them closer, making very clear what mattered most in this life. Family, health, home—and all of the people they cared about.

Another twinge just below Rae's sternum, but this time it was melancholy. She wished she could be here more often and for longer stretches. But her stomach clenched at the very idea, and she grimaced.

"You okay?" Emma said, pausing to send her a sidelong glance. She looked down to Rae's hand resting on her belly. "Are you sick?"

"Uh-uh. Just hungry." Rae sloughed off the concern by peeking into the second bag. "Salads, quiche, and ooh, I love you, big sister." She wiggled her brows at Emma. "Macarons."

"*Oui, oui,*" Emma said in a terrible French accent. Then she jumped and jerked her bare leg to the side. "Beau, stop that." The dog licked her leg again, sat on his haunches, and whined.

"Sorry, buddy. Emma's soft heart won't help you now." Rae bent to scratch his head. This is *my* food. And on that note, I'm off to shower before Anna gets here."

She surveyed the kitchen, from dog to food to family, and lastly, to the sun shining on her mother's blue wallpaper.

A warm thrill simply bubbled up inside of her. *This is going to be a perfect day.*

Thirty minutes later, with her hair still slightly damp, Rae hurried down the stairs to find Anna being hoisted off of her feet by her father. "Dad, for the love of Pete," Rae called, stopping on the bottom step to place both hands on her hips.

"Don't scare her away."

Her father's expression was skeptical. "I don't think anything scares this one."

"True enough." Rae waved for Anna to come with her as she began easing toward the back. "We're all set up in the garden. Tea is still good for you?"

"You know it. And since it's my wedding week, I'll even take it sweet." Anna caught up with Rae as she stepped out to the veranda. Then she stumbled to a halt and clapped both hands over her heart. "Oh, I forgot how glorious it is here."

Taking a moment to appreciate the view with her friend, Rae scanned the courtyard walls and carriage house enclosing the vast gardens, each covered in trailing vines. Springtime was in full blossom, filling the air with the scent of magnolias and providing a colorful array of flowers. In the middle of it all sat a sunken patio and fountain, a black wrought-iron table prepared for two near the burbling water.

"The azaleas are *huge*." Anna gaped and slowly made her way down the porch steps, then the ones leading to the fountain. She fingered a magenta-hued bud as big as a baby's fist.

"Dad and Emma have kept things up beautifully," Rae said.

"But not Bryn?" Anna's sly grin told Rae she already knew the answer to that.

"Ha. No." Rae chuckled and sat at the table. "That girl can forecast what an unknown and unheard of stock will do three days out, but don't expect her to remember to water a plant."

"I heard that." Bryn placed a silver tray arranged with croissants and macarons on the table. She hiked a brow at Rae before leaning over to hug Anna. "It's good to see you."

"You, too." Anna gently squeezed Bryn's upper arm. "Still at it, I see. Good for you."

"A fight a day keeps boredom away." Bryn waggled her fingers goodbye and sauntered away just as Emma set salads in front of Rae and Anna.

She gestured to Rae. "Just so you know, we don't usually treat her like the prodigal daughter." She patted Anna's cheek. "All of the service today is just for you."

"Gee, thanks," Rae murmured. Then she tried to evade, but Emma succeeded in patting her cheek as well. "Ow. That had a little bit of slap in it."

"Oops." Emma shrugged, turned, and went back inside the house.

With a laugh, Anna picked up her fork to stab some lettuce. "I'm so happy to be here, and it's nice to see some things never change. Like you and Emma," she added with a grin before popping the bite into her mouth.

Rae stirred the romaine, vinaigrette, and pecans around her bowl. "No matter how long I'm gone, as soon as I step through the front door things settle into place. Like I'd never left at all."

"That's good," Anna said between chews. "Kind of like us, a friendship that just *is*. Solid and sure enough to not need tending. One hour or ten years, it will always be here when you come back."

Rae raised her gaze to Anna's. "Thanks for that."

"I'm only half of the equation." Eyes of cerulean sparkled at Rae. "So thank you, too. Thanks for coming home." Anna's tone fell to a heartfelt whisper. "And stop that right now."

Rae jolted and held up her hand in query. "Stop what?"

Now those blue eyes homed in and held fast. "Stop beating yourself up."

9

Anna could see the guilt weighing on Rae's shoulders, a self-blame wholly undeserved and one she planned to put an end to right now. "Rae, I know you're sorry you weren't here when the prophecy finally came into being."

Rae sipped her coffee, but Anna noticed her troubled gaze skimming the courtyard. Sweet and brilliant with spring, the hidden gardens echoed with birdsong as Asian jasmine flowed along the stone paths and purple wisteria fluttered in the breeze.

The scents and sounds of new life always cheered Anna, but clouds of worry hung over her friend.

"I thought I was hiding it pretty well," Rae said at length. "Guess I should know better than to try to fool you."

"Yes, you should. We've been friends too long for that to work. For either of us."

"I just wish—"

"Don't," Anna said firmly. "Just don't. You know I understand what happens when you come home." Rae had filled her in a long time ago, telling her not only of the emotional anguish but the physical discomfort that plagued her when she returned.

So, of course, Anna didn't resent her absence. She was far more concerned that both issues persisted.

"I appreciate that, Anna. I really do. But the fact remains that you had to battle a demon, a thousand-year-old-witch, and an entire army of hellish beasts." Rae gestured wildly with her mug. "While my happy ass was out on safari."

"That's your job." Anna leaned in and purposely let impatience creep into her tone. "You think you didn't do your part? That you didn't do what you were meant to in the grand scheme of it all? Rae, all those years, you were my sounding board. When I couldn't talk to Claire or Mrs. Attinger, and I didn't *want* to talk to Quinn, you were the only one I had. The only one who could settle me down, calm my fears, and give me hard, straight advice."

Anna sat back and kicked up one side of her mouth. "One smart-ass witch to another. As you used to put it."

Chuckling, Rae shook her head. "I remember. I do. But in comparison, that was the easy part. It's not like I stood beside you in battle."

"That depends on your definition of battle. Don't you remember the time I got it in my head to leave Savannah, certain that the prophecy would skip me by if I just wasn't here for it to find me? Who rode with me all the way to Charleston? *Nagged* me all the way."

Anna let her head fall back and hooted. "I swear, I was so sick of hearing you babble on about responsibility and destiny that I actually turned the car around and chose to face an ancient evil instead of listening to you."

Rae joined in the laughter. "You didn't speak to me for a week after we got home."

"I was brooding."

"You were sulking."

Anna smirked. "That, too."

The expression on Rae's face seemed genuinely relieved. "Okay. You've made your point. I'll try to go easier on myself."

"Please do."

Rae cut into her quiche. "I did burn a fire for you, though."

When Anna sent her a quizzical look, she explained, "That Halloween. Emma made sure I knew it was happening, so I sat outside my tent in the Serengeti and burned a bonfire. I pulled out sage, amethyst, and a white candle I'd carried over three continents, saved for that particular moment. I worked a spell written just for you and the coven and sent every bit of positive energy I had riding with the sparks. I willed it up to the stars, and all the way to Savannah."

"I felt it," Anna said. "And it mattered."

The two of them shared a meaningful look before easing into an amiable silence, a peaceful few minutes to appreciate the tasty food and soothing ambience.

But while the mood relaxed, Anna's mind churned. The mention of Rae's practice in the Craft had veered her thoughts in a new direction, forging links between her friend's inexplicable stomach pain and the one possibility they'd never considered.

No medical condition she'd ever heard of relied on a person's location. And even heartbreak—even the devastating loss of true love—should have been alleviated by now. Those paths her mind wandered began to circle, leading Anna back to the facts she possessed, and the sinister omens she dared not ignore. Which is why her concern for Rae was greater than ever.

And why she had to tell her about the dream.

Between wedding plans and Rae's short visits, time was at a premium, so the conversation needed to happen now. She hated to wreck this glorious day, to darken it with tales of fire and ash.

But whether the nightmare had been a vague hint or literal warning, the sooner she found out, the better.

Cutting straight to the point, Anna gripped her hands in her lap beneath the table. "How are you doing, by the way? Any pain yet?"

Rae pursed her lips and wiggled her head a little in a gesture implying it wasn't a big deal. "No. It's fine."

Anna saw through the ploy but continued on in a casual tone. "Have you ever wondered if the discomfort you feel is somehow related to magick?"

Rae froze in the act of reaching for a croissant. "Um . . . not really." She wrinkled her forehead. "What made you think of that?"

"A few things. As you know, Savannah is a hotbed when it comes to the supernatural. Hauntings, strange phenomena and, as I can attest, a history of demonic infestations. My grandmother had a theory and used to talk about mystical lines running throughout the earth. She believed the places they intersected were vortices of power, gathering places for magickal energy."

"A whirlpool of magick," Rae quipped. "No wonder this place makes me ill."

Anna tried to work up a smile but the attempt failed and it slid off her face. "Since you're here, maybe we should look into it further."

"I really don't see the need." Rae gave a careless shrug. "What would magick suddenly want with me, and why such an adverse and harsh effect? No." She shook her head. "I just don't see it."

"You have innate skills," Anna pressed.

"Please, girl. I'm in the witchcraft baby pool while you're swimming the English Channel. Besides," she fluttered her hand, "I'm here for a joyous occasion. This week should be all about you, Ian, and an orange blossom special."

A grin tugged at Anna. "You always did try to make me laugh."

"Good. You should laugh. You should be ecstatic. And not worry about anything other than connubial bliss." Rae winked and stretched her arm across the table. "This is *your* time, Anna, and I can't tell you how happy that makes me."

"Thank you," Anna whispered, reaching to take Rae's hand in hers.

And when she did, a flurry of images besieged her. Not foggy or cryptic but clear as water—the curve of river, a wooden bench, and Rae in the dress she'd worn yesterday. Standing toe-to-toe with a very intense-looking Arik.

"You saw Arik," she blurted, the scene fading from sight.

"As I said," Rae sighed, "I just can't fool you." She slapped her palms to her thighs. "Yes, I did see him, and I spoke with him. I spoke with Arik. There." She tossed up her hands. "I said his name."

"What happened? And why didn't you say anything?"

"I thought about it." Rae pulled away and sat back in her seat. "But like I keep trying to tell you, I don't want to distract from your wedding."

"Well, you have my permission. *Please,* distract me." For a moment, Anna's focus relocated from one issue to another. "I want to hear all about something as momentous as this. How long has it been since you've spoken? Eight years?"

"Nine." Releasing another long breath, Rae rubbed her arms as if suddenly chilled. "A long time for two people who'd once shared everything to go without speaking." Her honey-brown eyes flared as if she'd just caught sight of an enemy. "And somehow that makes me angrier."

"What do you mean?"

"He sought me out yesterday, finally wanted to say something, and do you know what he wanted to talk about? His father's never-ending research. Apparently, Arik's caught the same disease." She made a derisive sound. "He's even recruited a voodoo woman to aid his cause."

"Wait. What? Okay, this calls for sugar." Anna skipped the quiche and snagged two macarons, one yellow and one mint-green. "Now start from the beginning."

"I don't know much more than that, and he wasn't making a whole lot of sense. He said he'd discovered something about his father and implied I had something to do with all of that."

"The family legacy?" Anna asked, recalling bits and pieces

from what Rae had told her when she and Arik had been dating.

"I guess. Who knows?" Rae ripped her croissant in two with more force than necessary. "He said my coming home *triggered* something."

Anna stopped mid-chew and swallowed the second macaron whole. After a small, choking cough, she grabbed her tea and gulped some down.

Rae leaned forward. "Are you all right?"

"Mm-hm." Anna made sure her throat was clear before she spoke. "What did he mean by that? That's an odd choice of words. What did you trigger?" Her dream. Arik's bizarre declaration. This couldn't be coincidence.

"I have no idea." Rae grew solemn. "Honestly, I think Arik's become obsessed. Just like his father. Actually, that makes me a little sad." She hugged herself. "And afraid."

Anna recalled the details of the tragedy and a shudder coursed through her. It made her afraid, too. "Rae, I need to talk to you about something. I don't want you to be alarmed, because I don't know what it all means, but—"

"But I'm your raven?" Rae nodded. "Yeah. That stuck with me for some reason, and I assumed you'd bring it up if it was important. So," she picked up her coffee and held it as if warming her fingers. "What did you dream?"

Bolstering herself, Anna relayed the nightmare, telling of a black bird traveling across land and sea. How she'd felt a familiarity, a kinship, opening her arms in welcome. And how the raven had burst into flames.

"Now, you know I can't be positive," she said quickly to allay any dread, "but I do think it was about your return to Savannah. The raven flew to me, because you came for my wedding. The rest is still up for interpretation, but added to your encounter with Arik . . ."

"Right." Rae repositioned in her chair. "Do you think I should be worried? No, scratch that. Are *you* worried?"

"I'm . . . curious. And yes, I'm unsettled. But you know how this goes," she rushed on, hoping to console her friend. "It may be as simple as a kitchen fire you need to watch out for, or only a symbolic warning that you aren't going to complete a task."

"Because I go up in flames?" Rae's laugh was thin and tight. "This has been an enlightening lunch date. Magick and dreams, belly aches and voodoo, when it's supposed to be all hearts and flowers."

"I'm know, and I'm sorry," Anna said, but she couldn't allow them to stray back to benign conversation. "Okay, I have to say it."

"You really don't." Rae held up a hand. "Especially if it requires that ominous tone of voice."

"The way I see it, you've already crossed paths with Arik."

"No."

Anna ignored the denial and forged ahead. "So why not get the full story?"

"No."

"Wow. I know you can be stubborn, but monosyllabic arguments are just annoying."

"Come on, Anna. What did you expect? And I can't believe you're suggesting I should talk to him. You. The one who threatened to give him a lizard penis."

"Ew. I did say that, didn't I?" Anna wrinkled her nose at the imagery. "I was angry for how he treated you. So cold and callous."

"Right. Exactly why I shouldn't open that door again." A sunbeam suddenly highlighted Rae's face, and her sad, sad eyes. "Some should just stay closed."

"I'm sorry he hurt you." Something twinged inside Anna, a reflection of the ache she knew Rae still suffered.

"I keep telling myself it's all in the past, and now here he is again, haunting my every thought. Yesterday I thought of him as a ghost," Rae said softly, "but now I think he's more like my own personal demon. He shows up, and it all goes to Hell."

Rae worked it through for herself, speaking calmly as Anna sat in silence. "I don't owe him anything. I won't feel guilty for brushing him off, or never speaking to him again." She sat up straight and glanced over. "But there was one thing."

"What?"

"Arik mentioned his mother. He seems to think he can help her, and that maybe I can, too."

A sad sigh escaped Anna. "The poor woman. So tragic."

"I know," Rae agreed. "Mrs. Mansur was always good to me. Arik may be losing his mind, and he may have hurt me like no one else ever has," she bit her bottom lip, "but if he's right about any of it . . ."

"You would do whatever you could to help."

"In a heartbeat."

"Then I think you have your answer," Anna said. "And if we're lucky, we might end up with a few of our own."

Rae tilted her head and nailed Anna with a dubious stare. "What do you mean *we*? And I haven't agreed to anything yet."

Anna would also do whatever she could to help, including laying on a thick layer of guilt. "I thought you said this was my time, and I want to do this. In fact, if we don't find out what Arik meant, I doubt I'll be able to relax and enjoy myself."

Rae wasn't fooled in the least. "Boy, that's playing dirty, St. Germaine."

As if Rae hadn't called her out on the ploy, Anna reached for a croissant. "Ian isn't picking me up for a couple of hours, so I say we enjoy this fabulous meal, and then we go get some information."

"I don't know. . ."

"I'll be right beside you the whole time," Anna assured, "and since he approached you, it's the perfect opportunity. And," she added, homing in on the very thing holding her friend back, "you know what they say about vanquishing demons."

Rae went still and hiked a questioning brow.
"First, you have to face them."

10

Rae's belly fluttered with nerves as she and Anna climbed the steps of the grand brick mansion. Though she'd called Arik—who'd been both eager and gracious—she still couldn't tamp down the riot of anxiety shaking her from head to toe.

"One second," she said, holding out her hand to stop Anna from ringing the lion's-head doorbell. "One. More. Second."

Channeling serenity, she relaxed her neck, shoulders, and back, like she would if preparing to meditate. She'd certainly need reduced stress and increased acceptance for any interaction with the man who'd altered her life so profoundly.

Another breath, and she found her center. Then she reached for the doorbell herself and gave one firm push.

She had seen him yesterday and had managed well enough. But she'd had static flooding her mind, numbness from the initial shock.

Today, though, she knew what to expect. A longing for what might've been. Fierce attraction that never died. And anger—deeply rooted anger—fueled by the pain he'd so callously delivered.

These were the reactions she knew to anticipate. The feelings that made her stomach flutter and tense. But she was ready, determined, and bolstered to have Anna by her side.

The door opened to reveal a middle-aged woman, lean and petite, with a friendly face and spiky red hair. She also wore pale blue scrubs identifying her as medical personnel. "Hello, ladies." She beamed at them. "You must be Ms. Scott and Ms. St. Germaine."

Anna returned a bright smile of greeting. "Please, call me Anna, and this is Rae."

"And I'm Dee." The woman stepped back and held open the door. "We've been expecting you."

Rae entered after Anna and stepped into the grand foyer. The medieval tapestry still graced the wall, the tiled floors remained the same, and so did the scent of freshly-cut lilies, sights and smells that transported her back in time. To the first night she'd ever come to this house, when Arik had brought her home to meet his parents.

Nostalgia wrapped loving arms around her as she remembered how much she'd adored them both. Arik's father, the intellectual, who liked to tell bad jokes. And his mother, who'd pulled Rae right in and asked her to chop lettuce for the salad, making her feel instantly at home.

She'd fallen in love with them just as she had their son, spinning visions in her head of the life she would have. The life she and Arik would make together.

She could look back at them, those young-girl dreams, and now they seemed so tender and innocent. And so fragile, so easily shattered by a few harsh words.

Anna's touch on her elbow reminded Rae she was in the here and now. That neither of Arik's parents would be greeting her today, and that Arik's true motives were still unclear.

Hardening her resolve and shielding herself from sentiment, Rae fell into step beside Anna and followed the brisk Dee through a maze of hallways to the back of the home.

The caregiver looked over her shoulder. "Arik is with his mother in the conservatory."

The conservatory. Arik's mother had always loved that room, sitting and reading among the plants. Rae rubbed a hand below her throat, suddenly much more apprehensive.

The last time she'd seen Mrs. Mansur was in the hospital, in a physical state that had darkened the whole world.

They turned the final corner then, entering a tiled corridor with floor-to-ceiling windows along one side. The hall led to an equally bright room, a dome-roofed conservatory made entirely of glass panes and filled with lush foliage.

Rae slowed when she saw Arik. He was on one knee in front of his mother's wheelchair, holding a straw to her lips as she sipped from a glass.

She couldn't make out the words he spoke to his mother, but the tone was soft, love and support propped up by an underlying grief. Grief he probably thought he was hiding.

But Rae could hear the loss echo down the hall, as if he'd shouted.

Sadness crashed over her and, for a moment, she was simply undone, overcome by sympathy for two people she'd once known so well. Who at one time had almost been family.

Almost.

Pieces of broken memories, and those shattered dreams, cut at her with sharp, keen edges until she had to take a few more breaths.

When Anna slowed as well and sent her a look of concern, Rae shook off the last of anguish, squared her shoulders, and continued down the corridor. But she faltered—briefly—when Arik lifted his head, piercing her with eyes so dark, so depthless, Rae could tumble right in.

A smile flitted to his lips, but was gone in an instant. He got to his feet, stoic yet genteel, the gentleman of the house receiving callers.

As he stared at Rae, a wrinkle marred his brow, but then he turned his attention to Anna. And the smile was back. "Thank you for coming," he told her. "It's been a long time. How have you been?"

"Well, thank you."

"Congratulations, by the way. I've heard nothing but good things about Ian."

Anna's expression softened at the mention of her fiancé. "That's kind of you to say."

Rae hadn't been sure what to expect, but the byplay was everything civil and polite. However, she couldn't let Anna carry the burden of this encounter. Arik and his request for a meeting were Rae's responsibility.

Before she could speak, Arik put a hand on his mother's shoulder. "Mom, we have visitors. You remember Anna." He paused. "And Rae."

Following his lead, Rae bent over and spoke gently to the woman in the wheelchair. "Mrs. Mansur." She swallowed against the tears that rose suddenly. "Marit, I'm so happy to see you. I've thought of you often."

The Swedish blonde hair and clear gray eyes were in stark contrast to her frail posture. Propped up by pillows on each side, Marit Mansur appeared unable to move any part of her body.

Except her head, which raised slightly in response to Rae's voice. And unless Rae was imagining things, the bright eyes flared with recognition. They latched on to her face, widened, and blinked erratically.

"She remembers you," Arik said, his tone calm and steady, though his expression portrayed something else. A subtle disturbance only someone who knew him well could see.

After a moment, he addressed Rae. His face, handsome and severe, gave no more clues to whatever stirred within his mind. "Why don't we talk in the library? I know you have questions."

"Miss Marit and I will be just fine," Dee said, taking the drink from Arik. "It's the perfect time of day with the sun dappling in through the trees to pattern the floor."

Not only efficient, Rae thought of the nurse, but kind and comforting. She could see why Arik had hired her to help care for his mother.

Without another word or any indication of his mood, Arik led Rae and Anna back down the hall and through the interior of the house. While many could be easily confused by the rambling mansion, Rae already knew the way, having once considered it a second home.

Ignoring the bittersweet pinch inside, she followed silently until he opened the library doors.

Little had changed here, from what she could recall, as this was a place she'd spent little time.

Arik had often avoided the room, claiming he wouldn't spend his life trapped in books. That he'd rather gain knowledge through experience. Real-world exposure. And real-life adventure.

With a swift jolt and a tug of regret, Rae realized she wasn't alone.

Arik too had given up on a dream.

"Amazing," Anna said, her gaze tracking from the shelves below to the extended archives upstairs. Then she seemed contrite, putting a finger to her lips. "Sorry, but this place still stuns me, and I forgot how big it was."

"My family always made information a priority." Arik slipped his hands into the front pockets of his dark jeans. "Books, history," he sighed, "and legends." He fixed Rae with an unwavering stare. "The last is why I needed to see you."

"All right." Discomfited by his directness, Rae started to cross her arms but forced them to stay by her sides instead. She refused to let him see her disquiet. She would give no indication of the effect he had on her.

Foolish? Petty? Childish?

Perhaps.

But she'd already given him far too much.

"Before we go any further," she said, "I want you to know I only came because of your mother." *Not because of you. Not because of the hole you left inside me.*

"You said something about helping her," she continued in a stern voice. "So that's why I'm here."

"Understood." Arik's jaw clenched before he added, "I'll admit, I was surprised to get your call. But still, I'm grateful."

Rae nodded and went straight to the core of the matter, wanting to get this over with. "Tell me what you meant when you said I triggered something."

"Cutting to the chase, I see." Arik flattened his lips and gave a stiff nod before crossing the room to stand near a large window. "Yesterday morning, I had a visit from Mahalia." He cut his eyes to Rae. "The friend I told you about."

"The voodoo woman," Rae said. She crossed her arms after all.

"Yes. She showed up unexpectedly, agitated like I've rarely seen her and insistent that I listen to what she had to say. She told me about a dream filled with various imagery, but she mentioned a specific time." Arik focused on Rae. "7:44."

When he just stood there looking at her, she shook her head. "And?"

"What time did your plane land yesterday?"

Alarm shivered down her spine. "I don't remember. Sometime before eight."

"Flight 1022?" he asked.

"Yes." Alarm morphed into annoyance. "Get to the point, Arik."

"I verified the details after you arrived, because even after what happened, even after what I saw for myself," he shifted on his feet, "I guess I needed more proof. Your plane's arrival was recorded at 7:44."

"The time Mahalia told you," Anna said, edging forward. "What exactly happened? What did you see?"

Arik indicated a globe set in a wooden stand. "At precisely the time Rae returned to Savannah, this globe lit up from inside." He continued to study the antique. "Since it's at least three centuries old and has no power source, I can offer no rational explanation for this phenomenon."

Rae exchanged a glance with Anna and knew she and her friend were thinking the same thing.

Magick.

As if responding to her panic, to her suspicion, the pit in Rae's stomach deepened and began to ache. Hiding what was going on internally, she frowned and waved a dismissive hand. "Well, if that actually happened—"

"If?" Arik asked, jerking his head toward her. "You're more entrenched with the supernatural than the average person, so why would you question—" He broke off abruptly as insult flashed across his face.

"I see," he said at length. "It's only me you doubt."

Refusing to be baited, Rae went on as if she hadn't heard him. "Fine. It happened as you say. But what does any of this prove? How does it connect to your father or, more specifically, to your mother?"

Arik rolled his shoulders as if to stave off tension. "This globe belonged to my father, and he only kept items here that pertained to our family legacy."

Rae started to reply, but Anna interjected, "Arik, tell us what you know."

"Not as much as I'd like, because my father kept most of it secret. I think he was trying to protect me." Arik strode to a large desk near the fireplace and picked up a brown leather book. "After his death, I came here. I searched every nook, every secret drawer or hidden panel I could locate. Finally, I found my father's journals. The ones he'd wanted to ensure I never read."

Rae eased to a bookshelf and pretended to study the leather spines embossed with gold or silver, but she kept her ears tuned to Arik's story. He told Anna of his family history and the centuries spent compiling research materials.

Rae knew most of this from before, when Arik had told her everything. But then he spoke of things she'd never heard, things better suited to a tale of espionage than to claims of magick.

Cryptic codes. Foreign languages. Secret groups.

Arik finished and grew silent, prompting her to turn around. "So you don't know anything for certain," she said. "In fact, the timing of my arrival could be a coincidence."

Anna pursed her lips and said nothing. But Rae received her message loud and clear.

She heaved a breath. "Like I said, I'm here for your mother, so how do you think I can help?"

"I don't know," Arik said, raking a hand through his golden hair.

A signature move so familiar to Rae that she pressed her joined hands against her sternum, a worthless tourniquet for the bleed in her heart.

"I was hoping if I talked to you and told you all of this . . ." Arik dropped the book to the desk. "I just don't know. I'd hoped you might tell me something new. Something that might make a connection."

Shoulders deflating, he homed in on Rae, his eyes ablaze with frustration, yet shadowed by fear. "This legacy is more dangerous than I ever realized. What happened to my parents is proof of that."

He shrugged, held up his hands, and then dropped them in despair. "But you clearly can't help us. And Mom . . . well, she can't tell me anything. She can't speak at all."

Tugged again by sympathy, Rae took a step forward.

But it was Anna who said, "Maybe she doesn't have to."

11

Cooling relief swept through Arik when he understood what Anna was offering. "You'd be willing to do that?" To use her powers as a seer, a psychic. "You'd be willing to look?"

Anna, Rae's long-time friend and staunch ally, sent him a gentle smile. "Of course. I'm sorry this never occurred to me before, but I didn't know the details of your mother's condition and, truthfully . . ."

She paused, giving Arik the opportunity to say what she was delicately trying to avoid.

"You were angry with me," he said in a matter-of-fact tone. "I can't say that I blame you, and I never thought to reach out to you either."

"I'm a big believer that things happen when they're supposed to, and with what you've told us about Rae's visit coinciding with activity in the globe, well . . ." Anna slid her eyes to Rae, who stood nodding slowly to herself.

"I'm with you," Rae said. "That's a good idea. A great idea." A smile bloomed on her beautiful lips as she looked at Anna. "I'm so glad you came with me today."

A second source of relief hit Arik like a painless arrow to the chest. *Rae had brought Anna.* He curled his fingers tightly to his palms and fleshed out the logic.

This might be the extent of Rae's involvement. The activation of his father's globe may have started the chain reaction that resulted in Anna being here today. And she'd come with a new perspective on how to help his mother.

Could it be that simple? Could that be the link?

The surprise of real hope buoyed his spirit and his steps as he returned to the center of the room to stand between the two women. "I can't thank you enough, Anna. I really can't."

"Of course." In a surprising move, she walked to him and touched his elbow. "Is now a good time?"

"Yes. Yes." Arik glanced at Rae. They shared a moment, her face reflecting his own cautious joy. Then the elation fell away, leaving guarded wariness in its place.

It stung to have her look at him with such distrust, her lack of faith somehow worse than the open disdain he'd come to expect.

She hated him because he'd loved her so much, enough to end a relationship with his other half. Because that's how it had felt. How it still felt.

Like he was missing a part of himself.

He'd never wanted Rae exposed to the poison of his family history. Since her return, his nights had been troubled and sleepless, hours spent worrying over her connection. Over the cruelty of putting her in harm's way, especially after the pain he'd caused her.

After he'd sacrificed everything by giving her up.

Her absence would always be an open wound but, at the very least, the loss they'd suffered shouldn't have to be in vain.

Encouraged by Anna's idea, Arik gestured to the doors.

"What about Dee?" Anna asked, heading in that direction. "How much does she know?"

"Ah," Arik fumbled for a response. "Nothing really, not about the legacy or what really happened to my parents. She knows I do some importing of rare goods and assumes that's why I do so much research."

He opened the door for Anna and Rae. "And I don't dissuade her of that belief."

"I understand, but just for your information," Anna's grin was conspiratorial as she passed, "she can be trusted."

The reminder of her psychic ability galvanized Arik as he led them back through the house. At a slightly quicker pace.

They returned to the conservatory to find Dee reading out loud to his mother, a passage he recognized from *Wuthering Heights*. One of his mother's favorites.

Pausing, Dee raised her head. "Back already?" She closed the book and stood up from the stool she'd positioned beside the wheelchair.

"Dee," Arik began, thinking of Anna's assertion that he could be fully honest with the caregiver. But he reconsidered the explanation he'd been about to give her, not quite ready to make that leap. Instead, he asked, "Would you mind putting together a snack?"

"No problem at all." Tucking the book under one arm, she asked Rae and Anna, "Any requests, ladies?"

"No, thank you," Rae said. "We just had lunch."

With a bob of her head, Dee left them alone. And would be gone long enough, Arik hoped, for Anna to do whatever it was she had planned.

Anna had quite a family history of her own—as he'd learned years ago from Rae—but details had always been vague when it came to the St. Germaine prophecy. And while he'd also known that both women practiced witchcraft, he'd never had need of Anna's particular gift. He'd never seen her in action.

"What can I do?" He rubbed his palms together. "Do you need anything?"

Anna shook her head and pulled the stool in front of his mother, while Rae sent him a quelling look. One he took as his cue to back off and be quiet.

He was happy to oblige.

"Marit," Anna said in a soothing voice, taking his mother's hands in her own. "If you don't mind, I'm just going to sit here with you."

Arik tensed when his mother flashed her gaze to him, but then she slid her eyes slowly back to Anna, she closed them, and released a breath.

"She's comfortable with you," Arik said in a hushed voice, his heart rending—as it did on a daily basis—to see his mother so restrained. So isolated from the world, and in many ways, from him.

Anna also shut her eyes, and Arik saw her body relax. Seconds ticked by with no sound, no movement, except a single glance from Rae. She folded her arms over her stomach, her expression alert.

Arik wondered if optimism and dread warred within her as they did him. For no matter how she felt about him, she'd grieved with him when his father had died and had always shown true affection for his mother.

"Thank you, Marit," Anna whispered at last. She released his mother's hands, rose, and came over to Arik.

Her slumped shoulders and kind smile told him she hadn't gotten the information he needed.

"I'm sorry," she said, the apology serving as confirmation.

"Did you see anything?"

"I did. Images of you when you were young, and of your mother and father together. She has happy memories of your family, foggy at the edges, like looking through frosted glass." Anna tilted her head. "I wish I could help you, but if this isn't the way, then we can at least be grateful that her thoughts are of loved ones, and of happier times."

Disappointment crushed Arik, but at the same time, he appreciated knowing his mother wasn't tormented. That visions of the attack, and the murder of his father, weren't the memories trapped forever in her mind.

"Thank you for trying." He did his best to hide his reaction, though the setback was a blow. He was back to the original problem and still had no idea how Rae was involved.

Fortunately, Dee returned with a tray of refreshments and placed it on the small table kept in the conservatory for such purposes.

A tingle of bells erupted in Anna's pocket, and she pulled out a phone. "Ian's texted me that he's outside." She turned to study Rae briefly, but shifted to Arik again as if changing her mind. "I know exactly how hard it can be to have challenges like this, especially now that you've had experiences with . . .well, with the globe."

"The paranormal," Arik said, nodding. "Yes, it's an adjustment, even though I've known you and Rae for years, and now Mahalia."

He thought he heard Rae suck in a breath, but she turned quickly and went to his mother, speaking to her in low tones. Likely saying her goodbyes.

But Arik didn't want her to go.

"Don't hesitate to call me if you have any questions about today," Anna said, drawing his focus again. "Or if anything else happens." She pressed her lips into a line of worry. "Even if you discover Rae has nothing to do with any of it, you and I were friends once. I'll help in any way I can."

Humbled, Arik could only nod and tell her, once again, "Thank you."

She patted his shoulder and moved around him. "I'll show myself out," she said quietly, giving him a moment with Rae.

But Rae had seen Anna move. She schooled her features into a blank stare and walked right past him. Without a single word, wave, or farewell—not even a *go screw yourself.*

"Rae, wait." He pivoted to track her fast march from the room, gave silent thanks Dee had come back to sit with his mother, and promptly gave chase.

Rae was making a run for it. That much was clear. But Arik feared he'd never get this chance again if she made it out the front door.

He caught up to her in the foyer, just as Anna stepped outside. "Rae, stop. Just give me a minute."

She grabbed the handle, stopping the door mid-swing. "I've got to go," she bit out, not bothering to face him.

"There are things I need to say to you, things you should know. Please stay and talk to me."

Her head whipped around. "You have Mahalia to talk to now."

"Mahalia?" Arik puffed out a breath in shock. Is that what she thought? "No, no. She's much older, more a motherly figure than—"

"Forget it," Rae said abruptly. "It doesn't matter."

"Yes, it does." Arik grabbed her wrist, so she couldn't run. Not this time. He knew he could never have her again, because he'd destroyed that chance. But if he could only explain. If he could make her understand.

"Rae, listen to me." He gentled his grip, trying desperately not to think about how soft her skin felt against his fingertips. "I have to tell you, and I should have long before now. What I did back then wasn't because I didn't love you."

She shook her head vigorously, using her free hand to push against his to free herself. "I can't do this now. Not here. This house . . ."

"I did it because—"

"No!" She jerked loose and backed away. "I won't hear this from you. Nothing you can say will make a difference or change the past. What's done is done, and you made yourself clear a long time ago."

Her eyes shined suspiciously, turning her light brown eyes to gold. But her jaw was set, her expression mutinous. "You cut me off with no explanation, no kindness or compassion. After all we'd been to each other, you told me to go away. To get out of your life."

She took another step in retreat, grabbing the handle again. "So I got out. And that's where I'll stay. So congratulations, Arik. You got exactly what you asked for." She jerked open the door.

Sunlight flashed in his eyes like fire, then it was gone. And so was Rae. Stunned and defeated, he stood staring into space, listening to the echoes.

Of a door slamming on the last of his hope.

12

The metal door opened abruptly, torchlight blinding her unused eyes as she tumbled to the stone floor. Exhausted and defeated, she lay in a heap, unable to move, unable to speak, her throat gone raw from unanswered screams.

Shutting her eyes against the light and her awareness against an unwelcome reality, she tried to close herself up inside her mind. If she tried hard enough, she might make it back to the comfort of unconsciousness. To the blissful dark and gentle silence.

After so long trapped in the iron maiden, her body felt boneless, depleted of energy. Only the raging pain of her stab wounds confirmed she still lived at all.

Or did she? Could she truly be alive yet remain in a place like this? Being tortured by these abominations? These inhuman creatures? Perhaps this was Hell or Purgatory, some heinous punishment for a life she couldn't even remember.

As these thoughts rolled around in her head, a blow to her thigh brought fresh agony and jolted her to a more lucid state. Another hard hit and she slit open her eyes. Bare feet, long-toed and sickly-white, were inches from her face.

The ghouls were back. They had her surrounded.

The next kick struck her stomach, forcing an *oof!* from her gut, followed by a low groan. Recalling her previous punishment, she tightened her throat and swallowed the sound.

Another of the pale monsters kicked her anyway, so she

curled into a tight ball, attempting to protect herself.

I'm so weak. I can barely move. How could she fend off these merciless brutes?

One of the ghouls whined from behind its wire-sewn lips, and the horde responded by grabbing her arms to hoist her up.

She couldn't stand, so the ghouls supported her. Then like before, they wrenched apart her jaws, force-feeding her another of the slimy, viscous globs.

But this time, she swallowed greedily, desperate for any scrap of sustenance. Unaffected by the form and texture, she opened her mouth wide for more of the thick goop. They rewarded her with a second helping.

And fuck all if she wasn't grateful.

Her eyes popped wide as she sucked on the sludge. *Fuck all?* Where had that come from?

The words seemed familiar and strangely comfortable, as if she'd used them often in the past. Ignoring the ghostly beings around her, she squeezed her eyes shut and tried to remember.

Who am I? Or who was *I? What is my name?*

Her internal search for identity was cut short when more hands grabbed hold and jostled her until she looked at them. "All right. I'm still awake, assholes." Her words rode on a tide of fury, but as soon as they echoed in the torture chamber, she clutched her arms and legs together and tucked her head.

The lashing she'd expected never came, and it was only then she risked turning her head to survey the room. No dark ones present. No masters to split her skin.

Still, she had to be more careful. How many wounds could she sustain? Even here, there had to be an end. Some version of death.

But as she worried over this bizarre existence, she glanced down at her naked body. Her flesh was riddled with bloody punctures, holes left by the chamber of spikes. And as she watched, they began to heal, knitting themselves whole as if by magick.

Feeling bold—and likely delusional—she dared to laugh out loud. Her burst of humor caused a rumble amongst the ghouls, several of them grunting at her in what sounded like censure. *Unh-unh-unh-unh.*

"Fine," she whispered, experiencing a surreal sense of camaraderie with these pathetic souls. They shared the same captors, after all, so she put a finger to her lips and nodded assent.

The ease of movement surprised her. She had her strength back. A quick study of her arms found them free from cuts or gashes. Even bruises.

The crud they kept stuffing in her mouth must have healed her. That had to be it. She ran her tongue over her teeth, searching for any remnants.

Before she could consider why the ghouls kept returning her to health, they began pushing and shoving her, ushering her through the dungeon and outside to the curving tunnel.

Turning left, they steered her deeper into the labyrinthine corridor, her bare feet shuffling along the rocky floor. Time and again, the ghouls stepped on her toes, so tightly were they pressed around her.

The tunnel dipped suddenly, descending to a lower level. There, she sensed an aberrant chill. One she'd come to associate with the dark masters.

As if in an underworld basement, she picked up on the smell of dampness, a scent like mildew. Liquid ran down the stone walls, rivulets glistening in firelight from sconces. From the craggy ceiling overhead, droplets fell with a *pok-pok-pok* and splashed her skin, adding another layer of the fierce cold.

The mass of ghouls pushed her farther down the narrow passageway. At the end, blackness encroached, dense shadows consuming all light.

Where the dark ones waited.

Fakrah. One of them spoke, the voice resonating with bass in her brain. Painful, like before, though slightly more tolerable.

That, or she was simply getting used to constant agony.

The ghouls halted in response to the command and parted to create a pathway between their tall sickly forms.

She stood shivering—cautiously silent.

The same master who'd spoken turned to stare at a metal door embedded in the stone. The entrance opened slowly, as if on command, to reveal a huge, gloomy space beyond.

An overpowering scent flooded from within, like stagnant water, sluggish with mold and decay.

"*Vos,*" the master said, his dark gaze now fastened on her.

Through the pain in her head, she had a flash of comprehension, as if she understood the word. Was it only her imagination? She didn't speak their guttural foreign language.

But she would swear he'd just told her to "go."

Her heart pounded beneath the bones of her chest, beating painfully as if fighting for escape. What if she'd misunderstood? What if she did the wrong thing?

Uncertain and fearful—terrified of offending the dark ones—she stayed rooted to her spot, eyes wide, breaths rattling through her lips.

"*Vos,*" the master repeated, this time pointing to the door.

No mistake. He was directing her to enter the room.

Her legs felt thick and heavy, weighed down by dread, but she dragged herself forward. The penalty for disobedience was a lashing. A burning pain she knew well.

While the dark chamber was still unknown.

Arms crossed over her naked torso, she inched forward. With every step, the temperature dropped, and the stench seemed to pervade her pores.

The dark masters obliterated the light as she passed between them, so she felt her way with her feet, taking a step down once she entered the room. Standing on a damp slab of rock, she waited for further instructions, her ears homing in on a new sound—softly rippling water.

She strained to see but couldn't make anything out. Trapped in total darkness, she had no idea what the vast, open space contained. Her only clue was the odd slushing noise, like hundreds of hands undulating in liquid.

Something cool brushed against her back, and she cried out before she could stop herself. Every muscle in her body tensed as she waited for the lash.

But seconds passed without attack.

She released a controlled breath, her eyes darting to the side as a ghoul slid past her, holding a torch. The pale creature looked at her and waved his hand, indicating she should move again. That she should advance farther into the room.

With at least some illumination in the chamber, she squinted and studied the area. The chamber was enormous, a vast cavern with walls and ceiling of stone. Yet other than the wide step where she stood, the entire space held black water.

They expected her to go farther in? To enter the water? Would they leave her here, floating in cold, inky liquid as some form of punishment, a different version of the iron maiden?

The place was freezing. Her teeth began to chatter, so she bit down on her bottom lip. Still, she flinched when the black water sloshed onto the small platform and wet her feet.

Brow furrowed, she watched the lake and pondered the subtle waves. She didn't feel any wind, so why did the surface move?

The ghoul thumped the middle of her spine with the heel of his hand. Farther behind them, the voice of the master ordered, "*Vos.*"

Go.

Steeling herself against the frigid cold, she dipped one foot and bit back a gasp. Liquid should be frozen at this temperature, but the physics of torture-land seemed to have its own laws.

Hoping to satisfy the dark ones, she continued to ease her leg into the depths. As her limb submerged, it disappeared, as if devoured by the obsidian pool.

A long, slick object grazed her ankle. In a lightning-fast move, she jerked her leg up and fell back onto the wide stone ledge. "What was that? What's in there?" Panic flushed her system with adrenaline.

The ghoul grunted forcefully at her and pushed on her shoulders. She slid forward but twisted around to latch on to his leg. "No! I won't go!"

A gash appeared on her thigh. At last, the masters showed displeasure.

She could ignore the pain. She could go back into the pit. Or the spikes. But her mind conjured horrid images of whatever lurked within the black depths.

Another of the ghouls rushed down to help dislodge her grip from the first one's leg. Its long fingers dug into her neck and wrenched her toward the lake.

Hands clenched on the edge, she used all of her new strength to hold herself in place, staring at the choppy surface. She understood the source of the waves. She saw why the water churned.

It was alive with snakes.

"No, no, no!" She dug her heels into the rock and flung her body backward.

She'd let those dark bastards lash every inch of her flesh before she went into that water.

But the stone ledge was slippery and more ghouls had joined the struggle. They slid her closer.

She pushed back harder.

Even as she fought to stay on the step, a red-eyed serpent slithered up onto the slab, flicking its tongue as if sensing prey.

One ghoul gave a muffled shriek and ran for the door, leaving the others to wrestle with her. Those who remained gave her one last shove before they too bolted for safety.

Because more snakes had discovered warm flesh. More long, sleek bodies found their way onto the step.

In a frenzy of fear, she swatted her hands at the snakes and tried to crabwalk to the door. But before she gained any ground, a serpent struck. The creature sank its fangs into her calf and pumped in searing venom.

Her shrill scream echoed in the cavern.

The metal door slammed shut.

As blackness overtook the light, she focused again on the sound of ripples. On the waves created by a thousand swimming reptiles.

Swimming closer to her.

Another snake struck the flesh of her hip. Then two more bites to her back and stomach. As the onslaught continued, she scrambled to press against the door.

But there was no escape. No light. No warmth. And nothing to save her.

Crying and whimpering, she tried to slap and kick the snakes away, but her foot only slipped over the soft bodies as more and more piled on. Before long, she lost track of the bites, consumed by the poison burning through her veins.

Sliding into the dark water, she prayed she would pass out. She prayed for death.

But as the serpents coiled around her arms, neck, and into her hair, she at last understood the terrible truth.

Death would bring no reprieve from this torment.

Because she couldn't die.

13

The grand hall of the St. Germaine house had long been designated as coven central. With its massive fireplace, proximity to the kitchen, and more than adequate seating, Anna and her friends always seemed to congregate there for the most important discussions.

Like whether to play the toilet-paper-dress game or panty piñata.

Snuggled in between Kylie and Lucia on the green velvet couch, Anna tossed back her head and roared with laughter. "Willyn did not bring this. You two are setting her up." She continued to chuckle, and occasionally gasp, as she read through the tags with "words of wisdom" for her wedding night.

"I swear she did." Kylie crossed her heart. "She has a dirty little mind hidden beneath all of that sweetness. Just ask her."

"Or ask Dare," Lucia joked, clinking her glass with Kylie's across Anna's lap.

"Oh, no." Anna rolled her eyes to the rafters high above. "When you two start drinking appletinis . . ."

"Those little green drinks aren't what you should be worried about." Claudia made the announcement as she and Viv exited the kitchen carrying two trays of what Paige had aptly named "frou-frou drinks." Both wore pajamas, as requested, for this low-key, girls' night, stay-at-home bachelorette party.

"This," Claudia said, placing a hurricane glass in front of Anna on the coffee table, "is called a mystic marvel." Red hair bundled on the back of her head, she grinned down at Anna. "We thought it was appropriate."

"Oh, yeah?" Anna picked up the deep pink concoction and sniffed. Then flinched. "Whoa. What did *we* put in this?"

"Tequila and—*umph*." Viv's description halted when Claudia shoulder-bumped her. "Easy, fire crotch," Viv said, drawing a laugh from the three on the couch. The teasing took them all back to the first time they'd heard that awful nickname.

"Good one." Kylie winked at the Asian witch. "You're learning."

Viv gave a mock bow.

"It's good," Claudia insisted, eyeballing the fuchsia-colored drink. "Take a sip."

"Um . . ." Anna sniffed again and was about to risk it when a voice rang out from above.

"Hey, consider yourself lucky." Paige hung her head over the railing of the walkway. "I argued for penis pickle shots."

Anna snorted and was immediately grateful she didn't have any mystic marvel in her mouth to shoot out of her nose. "That is too disgusting! I never liked pickles much. Now it's a sure thing."

Giggles and chatter trailed along the upper hallway and down the stairs as Paige and the remainder of the coven made their way down to the grand hall. When Anna spied Paige, her eyes bulged. "They got you in pajamas. I can't believe it."

"I bought them for her," Hayden said, also wearing pink pajamas with various candies floating on the fabric, her signature color showcasing her natural glow and caramel-hued hair.

"Did you put a spell on Paige to make her wear them?" Anna asked the coven's medium as she waved soldier-Paige closer for inspection. She gaped anew. "Bunnies? Paige is wearing bunny pajamas. This is the best wedding present you guys could have given me."

"Take a closer look," Shauni piped up. She and Willyn flanked Hayden while Paige put on a fashion show, hand on hip in her version of a supermodel strut.

Anna peered at the light blue material. "The bunnies are holding hunting knives." She sat back and bobbed her head. "Paige, they couldn't be more you."

"I know, right? And look." Paige moved in and pointed to another of the sweetly-smiling creatures. "Some of them have M-16s."

"Too bad Mrs. Attinger and Claire aren't here to see this." Kylie sipped her appletini, resplendent in her own sleepwear boasting an oversized cat who had stars for eyes and a creepy, crooked grin.

"Mr. Attinger and Joe took them to The Olde Pink House for dinner tonight," Anna said. "Their own celebration."

"How sweet." Hayden's bottom lip trembled. "Because the little girl they helped raise is getting married tomorrow."

"Here. Plug the works." Paige shoved an electric blue drink toward Hayden. "We cried at the shower, but tonight is party-zone only."

"This time, I agree." Willyn snatched the shot glass from Hayden and tossed it back. "I pumped and stored enough breast milk to earn me at least five cocktails, and I intend to drink them all."

"Then let's get started!" Lucia leaped off the couch and headed for the sound system, having already created a playlist with songs guaranteed to make Anna shake her booty.

Or so the Spanish beauty had claimed.

As the first thumps reverberated through the expansive room, Shauni sidled over to Anna. "I hope the guys have a good time tonight. Michael and Nick carted in every kind of junk food known to man. And they promised the only strippers entering the townhome would be through the television."

"Can they do that?" Viv asked, crinkling her nose. "*Would*

they do that?"

"Nah." Shauni shook her head. "Michael only said that for my benefit, because I teased him about the lineup of action and horror movies they'd chosen."

"Well, I saw the liquor Nick was loading." Viv's lips kicked into a crooked grin. "But I think we still have them beat."

"Here's to drinking the men under the table!" Kylie finished off her appletini and reached for a pretty mixture of yellow and red in a triangular cocktail glass. She sipped, shuddered, and licked her lips. "Man, when did I become a lightweight?"

"You always were." Paige frowned at the trays. "No beer?"

"In the fridge," Claudia said, then turned to Anna. "So why didn't you invite Rae and Emma tonight? You know we would have welcomed them."

"I know, and I did." Anna wiggled her bottom to the beat. *Guess Lucia was right.* "But those two don't get much time to visit, and Rae . . ." She trailed off and lost her rhythm. "Rae wasn't in much of a party mood."

As the women of her coven were no fools, those gathered with her picked up on the change of tone. "Everything okay?" Claudia asked.

Anna moved her head slowly side-to-side. "Hmm, yes and no. She has some unresolved issues regarding an old flame." Understatement of the year, Anna thought, choosing that moment to take a swig of her mystic marvel.

"Holy Hannah!" Her lips puckered automatically. "Who made this?" She cast an evil eye to Claudia and Viv, both of whom pointed at the other before bursting into laughter.

"Okay, we both did," Viv admitted. "And we may have been a little overzealous with the pours." She grabbed Anna's shoulders and shook her playfully. "But it's your bachelorette party, and your sister-witches have created the mother of all hangover spells."

"So toss it back and have no fear." Willyn let out a *wooo!* and grabbed another shot.

"And don't forget, *mis hermanas*," Lucia cranked up the volume, "to shake your booties!"

Surrounded by her sisters and thrilled to be marrying the love of her life, Anna raised her terrible pink drink and did just that.

~~~

One hour and three drinks later, Anna plopped back onto the green couch. With her head woozy and bottom all shook-out, she stretched her legs and melted into the plush, cushy velvet.

Vaguely, somewhere to her left, she heard Claudia say, "Oh, no. Anna's done for."

In response, Anna wiggled one finger in the air. "Just need a sec," she murmured, uncertain anyone heard it but her.

Apparently Kylie wasn't the only lightweight in the group these days, since behind her closed lids, Anna watched a black and gray cyclone spin. And spin. *Maybe I should ask for that spell now. I don't want to get sick.*

But the relaxed state—assisted by inebriation—took her under, and before she could say a word, she slipped into a soothing pool of darkness. There she floated, calm and serene, and so very tired.

As dreams and daydreams often do, the sensation changed, and she found herself out of the water and walking in Forsyth Park. She followed the paver walkway past benches and shrubs, beneath a canopy of huge live oaks.

Nearing the white fountain, she stopped to observe a trio of people. A family.

Anna cocked her head as recognition tried to wiggle in the depths her brain. *How do I know them? Have I seen them before?*

Adrift in the fog of sleep, she struggled to make sense of why she'd come to the park and why she couldn't stop staring at the little tow-headed boy. The father had the child on his lap, smiling and playing, pointing into the splashing fountain.

But the man looked up sharply when pewter clouds rushed in like the tide, blanketing the sky and dimming the light. Thunder rumbled ominously, and the father wrapped his arms around his son.

Only then did Anna notice the emptiness of the park. No one walking a dog or throwing a Frisbee. She and the family were alone.

Alone as the storm closed in.

The mother rotated her head slowly until her terrified gaze locked with Anna's.

And awareness clicked inside Anna's head, like a key turning to throw open a lock. *Marit*. Arik's mother. So the little boy had to be Arik, and his late father.

"Get out of the storm!" Anna yelled, the actions of the dream still controlling her.

While the man and boy huddled together beside the fountain, Marit turned toward Anna and held out her arms. She opened her mouth and began to scream.

The sound of horror wrenched at Anna, but she found herself suddenly paralyzed, unable to run to their aid or even call out.

A soul-splitting cry poured from Marit's lips as tears streamed down her cheeks. The scream intensified, growing shriller as her terror increased.

Lightning slashed and thunder roared, then Arik's mother crumpled into a small black shape on the concrete. She changed into a black bird.

She became a raven.

Still screeching, the bird jumped into the air and tried to fly to Anna. But the acrid scent of brimstone rose in the air, a forewarning of imminent doom.

Fire erupted from the bird's feathers, creating a burning ball that dropped to the ground.

And sent the whole world up in flames.

"Help!" Anna shouted, blinking furiously and shaking her head when she found Hayden staring into her face.

"Anna, wake up. Wake up." Hayden's eyes brimmed with fear as she gave Anna a shake.

"What the hell did you guys put in those drinks?" Paige hiked her brows at Claudia and Viv.

"It wasn't that," Anna muttered, rubbing both hands over her hair. Though sobered by the rush of adrenaline, she rolled and set her feet on the slate floor, taking deep breaths of clean, fresh air. Air that didn't smell of sulfur and ash.

"Well, partly it was the drinks. But more. Damn it, more." Anna rubbed the heel of her palm against her forehead. "I should have known."

Lucia turned off the music and heavy silence encased the room.

Hayden rubbed the middle of Anna's back. Shauni rushed over with a glass of ice water.

And the rest of her coven formed a protective circle around her.

Accepting the water, Anna sipped and let the dregs of the dream—the vision—clear from her troubled mind. Her friends didn't ask questions or nudge her to explain. They waited patiently until she was ready to speak.

"I'm sorry to ruin the party," she said at last, leaning back into the couch.

"Don't be silly." Willyn's firm voice conveyed her concern. "We can see you're upset."

Anna nodded and sought out Claudia. "I told you Rae didn't come tonight, because she'd had trouble with an old boyfriend."

Claudia nodded.

"That's not the whole story." She glanced to Viv as well. "And I should be thanking you for the strong drinks."

"Oh, I'm sorry," Viv said.

"No, I mean it." Anna drank more of the cool water to parch

a throat that felt raw from an imagined scream. "I might not have had the vision or seen the truth if I hadn't passed out the way I did."

Kylie rubbed her hand over her arm as if warding off a chill. "A meditative or relaxed state can make you more open. You've said that before. But what did you see? Should we be worried for you? Or for Rae?"

Anna's kneejerk reaction was to say "no," but that simply wouldn't be true. "Well, *I'm* worried. About Rae, Arik, and his mother."

"Arik is the ex?" Lucia asked, frowning as she crossed her arms.

"Yes." Anna gave them a brief rundown of what had happened the day she and Rae had visited the Mansur mansion. She included Marit's state of paralysis and the images she'd gotten from the woman. Images she'd thought to be benign.

Lastly, she circled back to her original dream of the raven.

"Why didn't you tell us about the first vision?" Paige had her hands on her hips and stood in her I'm-ready-to-kick-it stance.

"I wasn't positive what any of it meant or if there was a credible danger. But when Rae arrived, I knew in my gut that the dream was about her." Anna pressed her lips together. "I'm certain that raven was Rae. But this time, it was Arik's mother, and I'm not sure why."

"But the world burning around you is a pretty clear warning," Willyn said.

"And the warning includes Arik's mother." Anna rubbed her temples, trying to line it all up in her head. "The pictures I got from Marit, the way they were frosted at the borders." She stood up and curled her hands into fists. "I should have known something was off, but considering her condition, I just thought . . ."

"You thought they reflected her mind," Viv stated plainly. "A mind that may have been damaged along with her body."

"Yes. And I've been so consumed with my own life. With the wedding." Guilt started eating at the edges of her conscience. "I should have *known*."

"Anna," Willyn still had the no-nonsense tone, "you did everything you could, and you used your ability to look further. It may have taken a couple of days, but you have been given a sign."

"A sign that Marit and Rae have something in common with the raven." Viv pulled black-framed glasses from her purse and put them on. "Even if you don't know what that is, you know something bad is involved."

Anna considered the logic, went over it all again, and decided she couldn't have done anything different or moved any faster. "You're right. All that matters is what I do next."

"And what is that?" Shauni asked, emerald eyes wide. "You're getting married tomorrow."

"When I was at Rae's and Arik's homes, I did a quick spell of protection, just a one-size-fits-all ward against negativity and harm. It should be fine for the time being." Anna pictured Marit and how she'd screamed in fear. And she thought of Rae, certain her friend was still vulnerable. "But more will need to be done."

"Look, Rae will be here tomorrow, so you can fill her in then." Still beside her on the couch, Hayden took Anna's hand. "And if you think it's necessary, we can split up and take watch at their houses."

"No, I think we have a little time." Anna imagined little Arik at the fountain with his father. "Parts are moving, fragments coming together to make a whole, but my intuition tells me a piece is still missing."

But what piece? How could Anna figure it out when Arik barely understood his own history and the powers-that-be only spoke to her in riddles?

"We have a little more time," she said again. But something

was coming, that much was definite.

Anna squeezed Hayden's hand and offered a smile of gratitude to her friends. "You're all so sweet and supportive."

"You know we've got you covered, Anna." Kylie smirked. "Even though our trials are over, you'll always be our head witch in charge."

"*Sí*." Lucia gave a stiff nod. "We'll make sure your friends are safe and that you get your happily-ever-after. It's only fair after all you've done for the rest of the city."

"And the world." Claudia's expression was sober. "Bastraal was a powerful demon. He and witchy Ronja wouldn't have stopped at Savannah."

"I know, and believe me, I've been enjoying the happy times, and looking forward to a future without the shadow of evil lurking in every corner." Anna mimicked Paige and put her fists on her hips. "But if someone I care about is in trouble, then I have to help. I have to do all I can."

"And so will we," Shauni assured her. "In fact, I'll send out some birds and cats now. They'll let me know if they detect a harmful presence." With her gift for communicating with animals, she could make sure the homes of Anna's friends had round-the-clock surveillance.

"Perfect," Hayden said. "Now, Anna, you can take a breath, try to relax, and get back to pre-wedding joy."

"We've got you covered, babe." Paige winked. "Besides, you know it's not a coven party until someone tempts Fate or summons a demon."

Anna heaved a sigh and worked up a smile. "Ain't that the truth."

Comforted, as always, by the eight women who stood ready to take up defense, Anna did as suggested and took another deep breath. She put aside her fears for Rae and the others with the knowledge that they had some talented, reliable, and very experienced witches guarding their doors.

With her pulse slowing and panic subsiding, she gestured to the pink box sitting on an end table and glanced to Willyn. "I think I'm ready to try panty piñata now."

Then she raised her glass to Claudia and Viv. "But I'm sticking with water."

14

Anna adjusted her headband and, feeling no pain, gave thanks for the magickal headache cure her sisters had created. Sparkling with faux diamonds and sapphires, the band reflected the colors she'd chosen for her special day. A white dress in the abiding Victorian tradition, with blue rosettes around her waist and trailing down the back.

The witches who'd come to be like family had already gone down to take their seats in the garden. And while Anna would have loved to have them all stand with her today, as they'd stood with her in the past, the unanimous decision had been no bridesmaids at all. Since including Rae, there would have been nine, which was simply a bit too much.

Speaking of Rae. Anna sensed her a split-second before a soft rap sounded on the bedroom door.

"Come in," Anna called, a thrill coursing through her to have her oldest friend see her in bridal white.

Rae opened the door, popped inside, and crossed both hands over her heart. "Oh, Anna."

"Rae," Anna whispered, "can you believe it? This is actually happening." What was it about the fairy tale that always seemed just out of reach?

"You're gorgeous. You're perfect." Now Rae steepled her hands as if in prayer. "The most beautiful bride ever."

"People always say that." Anna faced the mirror and pressed a hand to her stomach where butterflies flew.

"That's because," Rae said, moving to gaze into the mirror over her shoulder, "at her special moment, every bride *is* the most beautiful." Carefully, affectionately, Rae stroked a strand of Anna's hair.

Anna recognized the symptoms, as there had been a plethora of watery eyes and sniffling noses today, so she notched up her chin and quelled the surge of emotion. "Don't cry, Rae." Her own eyes began to sting. "I need you to help me out here and be strong."

When a tear spilled over, Rae wiped it quickly away as if it stung. "Who's crying? I don't see anyone crying." Putting on her best imitation of Tom Hanks, she quoted from one of their favorite movies. "There's no crying in baseball."

"Or weddings," Anna said on a laugh. "At least not mine. I rarely wear mascara as it is, so if it runs, I won't know what to do."

Rae lifted her hands. "You're surrounded by women and none of them got you waterproof?"

Anna tilted her head and blinked at herself in the mirror. "Maybe they did. I honestly don't know." Regardless, the threat of tears had been defeated, thanks in no small part to Rae's humor.

"Before you walk down the aisle," Rae's lips curved up in the smart-ass smile Anna knew so well, "I only have one crucial question."

"And that is?" Anna asked, playing along.

"Who decides to get married on a Wednesday?"

Anna's laughter rang out like the clearest of bells. "I guess someone who found herself intrigued by old wedding customs and the poems that went with them." She turned around and recited, "Marry in April whenever you can, joy for maiden and for man."

"You're no maiden."

"Ahem." Anna pretended she hadn't heard the jibe. "As I was

saying. I discovered another that read, 'Monday for wealth, Tuesday for health, Wednesday best of all.'" There she paused and looked at Rae.

Her friend froze in the act of reaching for the wedding bouquet on a nearby table. "That's it? What about the rest of the days?"

"I don't know." Anna held out her hand for the mix of white and blue hydrangeas. "I got to Wednesday and stopped."

"Of course you did." Rae sighed deeply and got a weepy expression on her face again. "I would hug you, but there's no way I'll risk messing up hair, makeup, or dress. Not with," she glanced at the bedside clock, "ten minutes until show time."

"Okay, air hug." Anna held out both arms and mimed a double-cheek kiss.

A *tock-tock-tock* sounded on the door just before it swung open to reveal Claire. She stepped inside, Mrs. Attinger bustling in after her.

"All ready?" Claire looked to the ceiling and blinked fast, her lovely brown skin sporting blush and her eyes set off by mascara. "No tears. No tears."

Anna chuckled. "Why is it we wear makeup on the occasions we're most likely to cry?"

"One of life's little mysteries," Mrs. Attinger delivered drolly. "Now let's go, honey. Don't keep that young man waiting a single second longer than necessary."

"I don't intend to." Anna performed a restrained happy dance, protecting her dress and bouquet. As Rae waved and scooted down the hallway, Anna walked with the two older women to the little silver elevator.

She stepped inside alone, as it would only fit her and the dress, and cast a bright smile to her honorary mothers. Mrs. Attinger sent her a loving look and took Claire's hand. Then they set off in the direction of the stairs.

Shortly after, the bell chimed on the bottom floor. Anna

exited and was met by the tall, handsome man who would walk her down the aisle and give her away. "Quinn." She placed a kiss on her brother's cheek, and the look they shared required no more words.

Glancing through the back windows, she and Quinn waited until Claire and Mrs. Attinger slipped into chairs beside their husbands. Then Canon in D began to play.

She stepped out into lovely midday light, just perfect for a wedding day. For meditation and magick, she often preferred the soft, silent moon. But today, she thought, lifting her face to the healing rays—today was for the sun.

A soft purr drew her attention. She looked to find nine cats lined up like sentries, her own gray girl, little Ivy, sitting in front. When the girls had asked if they should bring their pets, Anna had wondered if the animals would understand about such human practices, or if they would even care.

But the small, adorable faces seemed to be smiling—from Hayden's sweet Daisy to Viv's grumpy Kiko—and Anna knew she shouldn't have doubted. After all, these cats had served as soldiers for the coven, and she was doubly glad Claire had insisted on making a special wedding-day treat. One prepared for a feline palate.

Anna couldn't stop her soft chuckle as she hooked her arm in Quinn's and began her march past a bevy of watchful cats. If anything, this wedding was eclectic, from the music to the guests, to the combination-ceremony itself. A service she and Ian had created to reflect them both.

"Ready?" Quinn asked after a few steps, his little-brother grin full of pride and affection.

Anna winked. "More than you know."

With a nod, Quinn faced forward again. He escorted her over sandstone pavers, through glorious spring gardens and smiling faces, until they stood before the gazebo and a very open-minded minister.

Azaleas bloomed blushing pink and pristine white, while birds swooped in the powder-blue sky. But the most wonderful sight for Anna was the tall blonde man in a tuxedo, beaming with anticipation, waiting for her hand.

Quinn pressed a gentle kiss to her cheek, and stepped back as she went to Ian.

But before placing her hands in his, Anna paused to acknowledge each of her sisters, whose undying loyalty and love had seen her through to this happy ending. After she and her coven had shared a brief, meaningful moment, she turned and reached for Ian.

Lost in his adoring gaze, Anna listened to the minister's inspiring words, and before she knew it, Quinn reappeared with a cord, wrapping it around both her and Ian's right hands. Bound in the way of the handfasting ritual, she and her groom took turns speaking their vows.

She heard the holy man ask her a question, and her heart all but burst from her chest when she said, "I will." Then it was Ian's turn, the slight hitch in his voice bringing Anna's tears rushing back.

But then the kiss—at last the kiss—and sheer joy lifted her up. Up onto her toes, up into his arms.

Cheers and applause broke out from the guests, along with a few whistles from the coven men. Together then, as man and wife, Anna and Ian went back up the aisle, nodding to friends and family along the way.

Once clear of the seating, Anna took the opportunity to pull Ian back into the house for a private moment before the reception was in full swing. Even as the door closed behind her, she heard Quinn directing people to the tent where tables, refreshments, and a dance floor had been set up.

She'd brought Ian inside for a rather serious discussion, but first she had to say one thing. Wrapping her arms round his neck, she tugged him close and whispered against his lips,

"Hello, husband."

Ian answered by taking her mouth in a slow and deliciously sweet kiss. Several seconds passed before he was able to say in return, "Hello, wife." He dropped his forehead to hers, and for a moment they stood there, basking in the momentous change in their relationship.

"I wanted to get you alone before the party started," she told him.

"Did you now?" He raised a single brow, lustful intentions clear.

Desire swirled in her belly, a long liquid pull that almost distracted her from her purpose. Almost.

"I'm afraid you'll have to wait a little longer," she teased, nipping at his bottom lip. "Because I only get to wear this dress once in my lifetime, and I intend to keep it looking nice."

"I'll help you take it off. Carefully."

"And," she said, fighting the temptation the imagery inspired, "I need to talk to you about something." Her chest tingled with apprehension. "Something important."

Caressing her cheek with his thumb, he gave her his full attention. "I'm listening."

"I had another dream—well, more of a vision, really. Last night when I was with the girls."

His eyes, like granite flecked with blue, clouded with concern. "And you're worried, which means I'm worried. Are you in danger?"

"No." Anna's gaze flitted outside and back to his. "Not me."

"Rae," he said with certainty. "Another vision of the raven?"

"Yes, only this time I saw Arik's mother instead." She'd filled him in on the visit with the Mansurs when he'd picked her up from their home. "She was the raven this time, but Rae was represented by the bird before. I'm positive. And I'm so sorry about the timing of all of this, but—"

"Shh." He touched a fingertip softly to her lips. "You're

worried about your friend. There's no need to apologize for that. Ever. And . . ." He angled his head, "I think I know where you're going with this."

Her heart kicked one time. "You do?"

"I do. So I'll call the resort and see if they'll work with us." He shrugged and smiled. "And if they don't, then we'll send Joseph and Sylvie on the honeymoon they never got to take."

"That's a nice idea." Anna's tone was low and laced with guilt when she added, "I feel like I'm ruining this for you, after all of your planning."

"Hey, listen to me." With one knuckle, he notched up her chin and stared deeply into her eyes. "I can change the plans or put them on hold. Whatever needs to happen. I understand the importance of this kind of threat, when it has to do with magick—"

"And evil."

"Then there is no second-guessing. I'm not just a coven man now," he wrapped her in his arms and pulled her close, "I'm a coven husband. And we do what's got to be done. All of us, right?"

Humbled by his generous heart, Anna whispered, "We do."

"You stood by each of your sisters when they faced their trials. You stood by me—hell, you saved my life. So how could I expect anything different now?"

"Ian," she began, but he spoke over her.

"Through sunlight and shadow, Anna. That was my vow." He lowered his mouth to hers for another brief kiss. "And I'll never break it."

When the tears came this time, Anna let them fall. "I love you, Ian. So very much."

"And I love you." He gave her a squeeze. "Now I think you'd better go have a talk with Rae. But as soon as you're done," his smile was rich with promise, "I want to dance with my wife."

~~~

As the other guests made their way to the tables and chairs, Rae lingered in the garden. She could remember Anna's mother fussing over her young roses, the same bushes now several feet tall and bursting with blooms in yellow, white, and crimson.

Leaning in, inhaling the floral scent, she let her mind float back to those innocent days. Happy days.

Pre-heartbreak days.

By this point she'd accepted Arik's presence in her thoughts, his image looming like the dark imprint after a bright flash. Of course she'd think of him today, while attending a wedding. Romance and love were thick in the air, brightening eyes and quickening grins.

Just one more reason she'd decided to take a stroll, not quite ready to face the celebratory crowd or toasts to the future.

Not when her own past had reared to take a bite.

She was thrilled for Anna, her oldest and best friend, and would never do anything to detract from her day. But still . . .

Her lip trembled as she touched her left hand, as she remembered the ring—and the love—

that had once shimmered so brilliantly for her.

She'd had so much confidence in their relationship and, after all these years, she still couldn't comprehend Arik's behavior. After the trust she'd placed in him, how could he just cut her out of his life? Swiftly, cleanly, and without a single tear.

Rae turned her face up to the warm sun, wondering if she'd never known him at all. Perhaps she'd been blind in love, swayed by her perfect man and idealistic fantasies. Because the blow had been devastating. And she'd never seen it coming.

Deep inside where logic ruled, she knew his coldness, his change in personality, had only been a result of his parents' tragedy. Who wouldn't be affected by such senseless brutality? His father had been taken, his mother altered terribly, and

Arik left alone to put the pieces back together.

"But I would have been there for you," Rae whispered, feeling a pinch of that loss even now. She would have helped Arik through, as well as his mother. If he'd given her a chance.

Stamping her foot on the stone path, Rae shook her head in frustration. The same old questions, with no new answers. Just more pain and doubt, more of the misery that plagued her whenever she came back home.

And the gnawing in her gut told her it was past time for her to go, to put the hurt and memories far behind. The nuptials were complete and the cake soon to be cut, so Anna would be leaving town herself.

Though Emma had wanted her to give it a few more days, Rae's bags were loaded in the trunk of her sister's car. And inside Rae's purse the boarding pass she'd printed flashed like a beacon, signaling a message loud and clear.

Go. Go. Go.

Yes, she would go. She would run again. But she spared one more thought for Arik, recalling the tenderness he'd shown his mother, the dismay when Anna had discovered no information.

And the burning intensity in his eyes when he'd asked her to stay. To talk to him.

Rae moved from her hand up to her wrist, where the skin still felt sensitive from his touch. What could he possibly say that would matter now? An apology might be nice, if long overdue, but it wouldn't heal her or stop the ache.

She didn't need his guilt or regrets. What she needed, what she'd only ever needed was his—

"No!" Her denial flew away on the breeze. "I don't need anything from him." As she crushed a fist to her chest, her heart pounded and her stomach clutched.

"I've got to get out of here." She released a shaky breath. "I can't take this anymore."

Turning on her heels, she marched around the rose bed,

following the garden path through a miniature labyrinth of manicured hedges. When she exited the other side, she almost rammed straight into Anna and Ian.

The tall blonde man—Anna's Viking, as Emma loved to call him—held up his hands. "Whoa," he said, before sending a crooked grin to his bride. "You do know her well."

"I told you she'd be here," Anna replied, though her attempt to return his smile fell flat.

Rae picked up on the undercurrent right away. "What's wrong?" She flashed her eyes from one to the other. "Why aren't you two at the reception? You know, the one in *your honor?*"

"I needed to talk to you," Anna said. "Before you left town."

Rae made a sound that was half sigh, half grunt. "Give me some credit. I wouldn't have left without saying goodbye."

"But I know you're leaving today. Or at least," Anna sent a sidelong glance to Ian, "that's the plan."

Now Rae's intuition was on high alert. "Okay, St. Germaine, spill it. Whoops." Rae caught herself. "Can I still call you that? Technically, it's no longer your name."

Anna's expression softened and her eyes misted. "You can always call me that. Promise you will."

"I promise. Now talk," Rae added quickly, "because you're scaring me." She waved her hand at Ian. "You even brought your husband for backup."

"I insisted on being here," Ian said, "because I want the assurances to come straight from me."

Rae opened her mouth but Anna spoke first. "Rae, last night I saw something, images involving the raven again." Her pause was exceptionally heavy. "And I also saw Marit."

Jolted, Rae let the words sink in before she grabbed Anna's hand. "What did you see? Is something going to happen to her?"

"I'm not sure, but," Anna squeezed her fingers, "Arik was right. Whatever's going on, you're connected." Another huge, pregnant pause. "That's why Ian and I are delaying our honeymoon."

"What? No. You can't." Rae shook her head vehemently. "I won't let you."

"Sorry, Rae. It's already done." Ian's look was sympathetic. "Whether you decide to stay or go, our decision has been made. I tell you that, so you won't feel guilty."

"Well, thanks, but I do anyway."

Anna studied her solemnly. "I don't think you should leave. Not until we know what's happening and discover what's posing a threat. A threat serious enough that I keep having visions."

She clasped her hands together across the front of her gorgeous white dress. "I'm worried for you, Rae. For all of you."

"I know you are. Oh." Rae pulled Anna into a hug. Then she dragged in Ian as well. "But your honeymoon."

"Will be there when the time is right," Ian said, leaning back to give a firm nod.

"Thank you." Rae inclined her head and held his stare. "I already knew you were a good man, but . . ."

"We're here for you, Rae. Whatever you need." The blue of Anna's eyes darkened with concern. "The raven is symbolic and connects you to the Mansurs. And while I haven't puzzled it all out, I am certain of one thing. Arik and his mother are in trouble."

Numbness flooded Rae's body from head to toe. "If they're in trouble, then so am I."

15

Rae curled her fingers into tight balls, digging her nails into her palms. "Can we talk?"

Emotions flashed over Arik's face like a slideshow—surprise, relief, confusion. "Of course. Come in." He waved her inside his home. "Mom is napping and Dee isn't here today," he said, a subtle way of telling her they could speak openly. And privately.

She'd decided to come over early and by herself. While she was in town, while all of this craziness was throwing her and Arik into the same space, she might as well tell him how she felt.

She hadn't come to the decision lightly. But when she'd risen with the dawn, clarity accompanied the brand new day. If she ever hoped to heal and move on with her life, she needed to vent some of the roiling fury she'd carried for so long. Some of the bitterness that still festered in her heart and spirit.

Arik had poisoned her, and now, at last, she would release the toxicity. Though that wasn't the only reason she was here. Beneath the anger and resentment, after all he'd done, the truth was she still cared for Arik. And his mother.

"I thought of calling first," she said, "but I . . . I just didn't. I knew the odds were you'd be home, so I rolled the dice."

"And you were right." His smile was tense and tight, uncertainty tugging at the corners of his mouth. He slid open huge pocket doors that led into the parlor. "Can I get you anything to drink?"

The civility in his tone cut like a shiny new razor. "Will you just stop with the polite routine? Stop acting like I'm someone you've just met."

He turned to her, lips pressed together and a storm brewing behind his dark eyes. "No, we haven't just met. Far from it. Which is why I'm trying to tread lightly."

"You don't have to." Rae glanced at an elegant, gold-colored chair. But decided to stay on her feet. "Because I won't."

She held up her hand to stop him from talking. "I have things to say, things that are long overdue."

Arms hanging loosely at his sides, he inclined his head. "I imagine you do."

"I'm angry with you, Arik. No. I'm furious. And I have been for nine years." Just saying the words loosened the knots of anxiety twisted up inside of her.

So she was able to soften the delivery when she continued. "I know now, just as I probably knew then, that what happened to your parents not only hurt you, but maybe did enough damage to change you on some level."

His lips parted like he might reply, so she rushed on. "Your world was destroyed, and you suddenly doubted the very things you'd always been sure of. You lost your faith in everything. Including me."

"Rae—"

"Wait." She spread her fingers as if to ward him off. "Please, just let me get this out."

He stayed quiet, but didn't look happy about it.

"It was the worst time of your life. I *know* that." She'd seen the evidence firsthand, in his harrowed face and despondent moods. "But I was the one person you should have trusted. I could have helped you, but you never even gave me a chance."

"I couldn't," he whispered.

"Yes, you could have. You could've talked to me, leaned on me, even yelled at me about how cruel and unfair the world had been to you. Because it was."

"Yes." Arik ran a palm down the leg of his black pants. "Then I turned around and treated you just as unfairly."

Rae could feel the moisture pooling in her eyes. "Yes, you were also cruel. And so very cold."

Arik tensed as if she'd delivered a blow.

"You just threw me away, Arik." She pressed a fist beneath her heart. "You threw *us* away."

Misery racked his features. "I never wanted to hurt you."

"How could ending what we had not hurt me, Arik? When you lost your father and your mother was injured, I ached for you. I grieved *with you*." Then he'd cast her aside, and she'd mourned for him as well.

"You don't understand, Rae. I had no choice." Staring past her, he closed his eyes and took a deep breath. When he looked at her again, he seemed suddenly calm, as if he'd accepted a hard reality. "I didn't push you away to hurt you or because I didn't trust you. I did it to protect you."

"What?" She'd anticipated an apology. *At least*. But what he said made no sense. "What are you talking about?"

"I'm sorry my family history is affecting you, Rae. I never wanted that. I never wanted it to *touch* you. And what's happening now is exactly why I ended the relationship."

Comprehension dropped on her like a load of bricks. "Are you saying you knew?"

"That you'd be a part of it? No. *No*." Arik stepped toward her. "But I was trying to prevent that very thing. Just look at my mother." He flung out an arm. "Her only crime was being married to my father. His legacy—*my* legacy—cost her *everything*."

His wide shoulders tensed. His jaw clenched. "And I vowed not to let that happen to you."

"I don't understand," she said, hands shaking, knees watery. Maybe she needed that chair after all. "The years we were together, in all that time, you never said a word about danger."

"Because I truly didn't know. After my father died and I found his journals, I learned more about what he'd been keeping from me. Then Mahalia entered my life and filled in a few more blanks.

Stunned into silence, Rae could only listen.

"I strung enough of the information together to realize my father was dead and my mother was in a coma because of this damned family curse. And that's what it is," Arik said, vehemence dripping from every word. "Not a legacy. A *curse*. One that destroys anyone close to it."

The ramifications of this new admission tumbled over Rae, as if those bricks had broken loose and were striking her one at a time. Her mind struggled to replace the well-cemented outrage she'd harbored for nine years. *Almost a decade.*

Blind to the revelation going on inside her, Arik continued. "So I told you to go. I made sure you hated me." He moved closer to her. "And losing you, knowing I had your hate," he drew a halting breath, "it almost killed me."

The very real agony in his tone reached deep into Rae and squeezed her already-bruised heart. *He* had almost died from the pain?

Then that sensitive and aching heart began to *thump-thump-thump,* faster and faster, her blood roaring with startling discovery. Arik had loved her, even as he'd torn her apart.

All that time wasted. All the nights she'd cried herself to sleep. All the perilous feats she'd performed in search of the most elusive photos.

And each time wondering if a fall to her death would finally deliver freedom.

"But you wanted me safe." She didn't realize she'd spoken the thought out loud until Arik caught her gaze and drew near.

"Yes. Damn it, Rae. Yes." He raked a hand through his tawny hair. "I came close to giving in a couple of times. Of tracking you down and telling you the truth." He spoke with clear regret. "But you'd left Savannah by then, and I assumed you'd moved, that you had a happy life. So how could I drag you back, especially with the legacy still a threat?"

A happy life? Rae almost choked on the irony. "You were so callous. Arik, you were *brutal*."

"Can't you see that I had to be? I had to make sure you stayed away. But despite the suffering we've both endured, you're still at risk." He scowled and shook his head. "I'd send you away again if it would make any difference."

She stiffened. "But I'm not leaving this time. Not unless I choose to go." And that was another revelation. When had her desire to run begun to shift?

Because now she felt *compelled* to stay.

If she could withstand the pain in her stomach. The deep, sharp pull worsened every day.

"You're right," Arik said, relenting at last. "Maybe I should have trusted you. Maybe I should have given you a choice before. But I was an emotional wreck, and I let my feelings control my behavior."

He lifted his hand but stopped suddenly and dropped it to his side again. "Apparently, I still have that problem. I grabbed you when you were here before, because I desperately wanted to talk, to tell you what I'm telling you now. I was out of line, and I'm sorry."

The rich brown of his eyes burned into her. "I lost the right to touch you a long time ago."

"Yes. You did," she whispered. So why did the mention of his hands on her send pleasant chills down her neck?

"No matter what happens now, I want you to know I didn't hurt you because I stopped loving you." His deep voice soothed. It seduced. "I hurt you . . . because I loved you. I loved you *so much*."

The chills turned to warmth and spread to her belly.

It should have been a warning.

After all this time, she'd expected rage to carry her through this moment. She'd thought disdain would keep him at a safe distance when they finally had the conversation she'd imagined in her head hundreds of times.

But the heat in her blood wasn't rage. And what she felt for Arik wasn't disdain.

By the stars, it wasn't.

Instead, a long-abated hunger roared back to life, the kind of raw need she'd only ever had for one man. *This man*. And beneath the physical craving, she sensed something else. A small flare and ripple.

The remnant of a dream struggling to revive.

Yearning overtook her, made her rock on her feet.

Arik put his hands on her arms to steady her.

Her head swirled. "Arik, I need to . . . I can't . . ." Was that *her* sounding so breathless?

"I'm sorry, Rae. Sorry for everything." He eased in closer, his tender gaze giving strength to the sensation growing inside her.

"If only I wasn't bound by this legacy." He touched her cheek, softened his voice. "If only I could—"

Chimes rung in the air, as loud to Rae's ears as the bells of Notre Dame.

She and Arik both turned their heads.

16

"Who could that be?" Arik cursed under his breath, fingers squeezing Rae's arms softly. Her natural scent—female and slightly sweet—slipped around him, drawing him in like silken ropes.

He didn't want to let her go.

"Someone's here," he said gruffly. "I'll see who it is."

Rae blinked slowly, as if waking from a dream. "Arik, wait. I was going to tell you." She laid a hand over his. "There's another reason I'm here."

Her hesitant manner and furrowed brow told him something was wrong. Concern overrode all else, and he removed his hands from her arms. "Who's at the door, Rae?"

"Anna and another woman from her coven. I thought we'd have more time, but—" She licked her lips, eyes darting toward the foyer. "Anna had a dream, or a vision. They pretty much amount to the same thing. But she saw your mother."

"Mom?" Arik started to ask but paused, deciding he'd rather hear the details from the original source. He was out of the parlor in three strides, opening the door in another two. "Anna, come in," he said, with no attempt to hide his worry.

She entered along with a tall woman whose flaming-red hair had been pulled into a long, straight tail. He met her eyes as Anna introduced her as Claudia.

"Hello," Arik said, barely controlling the urge to demand an explanation. Anna had had a vision about his mother, a vision that had sent her straight to his home. One day after her own wedding.

He didn't think he was going to like what she had to say.

"Thank you both for coming," Rae said, stepping up to stand next to Arik.

He'd forgotten how good it felt to have her at his side.

"I haven't had a chance to tell him about your dream," Rae told Anna. She balled her hands together. She was jumpy. Nervous.

Crossing his arms, Arik braced himself. "I hate to be rude, but I need you to tell me what's happened."

"All right," Anna said. "It seems my visit with your mother was productive after all." In a direct, no-nonsense way that he appreciated, she told him what she'd dreamed.

She explained how she'd seen him as a child with his parents at Forsyth Park. Then, in a calm and steady voice, she told him how his mother had reached out for help. How she'd screamed in terror.

She finished by speaking of a raven and a world on fire, and as she did, she focused on Rae.

"Anna also dreamed of me." Rae lifted a shoulder. "And I was also the raven."

"But you're not sure what any of it means." Arik glanced up the stairs in the direction of the bedrooms. Where his mother slept soundly.

But did she sleep peacefully?

"I'm sure a darkness is lurking," Anna said. "And I'm afraid it wants something from you. Or Rae, or your mother." Anna's shoulder rose and fell. "Honestly, I'm at an impasse."

"Which is why she asked me to come." Claudia addressed him, her expression kind but her manner as forthright as Anna's had been. "All of the witches in our coven possess unique gifts. Mine is psychometry, the ability to touch an object and receive details about its history."

"She can see things that actually occurred," Rae jumped in to explain. "I thought if you showed her your father's globe . . ."

"Yes. Absolutely." Arik released a breath he wasn't aware he'd been holding. "I welcome any help I can get. I'm out of my depth when it comes to magick or the supernatural."

"It's this way." Rae tilted her head to indicate the hallway that led to the library. As seemingly as comfortable in the house as she'd ever been, she led Anna and Claudia back.

Arik followed, his anxiety rising again. The fear he'd suppressed since the morning Rae returned and the globe illuminated. As he trailed behind the trio of women, he looked at Rae. He thought of his mother.

And his instinct to protect reared up like a beast unchained.

His hands balled into fists. *I won't allow them to be harmed.*

For the first time in his life, he truly grasped the value of his father's training. Though he'd never explained the reasons to his son, he'd demanded Arik practice daily. That he *fight* daily.

And now the weapons he'd mastered might finally be put to use.

"Arik?"

He jerked his head up in response to his name. Rae, Anna, and Claudia were all staring at him. They'd entered the library, and he hadn't even noticed.

"The globe," he said as if reminding himself. "Beside the fireplace." He pointed to the wooden stand.

Claudia handed her purse to Anna and made her way across the room. She looked to Arik, and at his nod, placed one palm on the globe.

The room seemed to hold its collective breath as he, Anna, and Rae looked on in silence.

But after only a few seconds, Claudia frowned. Concentrating on the antique, she curved both hands around the globe and leaned her body closer. With a shake of her head, she sighed and pulled away.

"I'm not getting anything. If I didn't know any better . . ." She trailed off and put a finger to her mouth. "I feel as if the globe is protected. Honestly," she faced them, her expression one of bafflement, "it feels like an enchantment."

"A spell?" Rae asked, jerking a glance to Arik. "Did your father's journals say anything about witches or magick practitioners of any kind?"

"No. Well, not as far as I can discern." Frustration put an edge to his voice. "The only thing that's clear are references to a group known as the Huktai. I've worked for almost a decade to break my father's code. All that damn gibberish."

Catching himself, he lifted a hand in silent apology.

"It's okay." Rae came to him, but she didn't touch.

Her nearness bolstered him, but not enough to stop the dam from breaking. "If he knew people could get hurt, then why didn't he teach me more? All the katas in the world do me *no good* if I don't know who the enemy is. Or *what* it is."

Energy ramping, Arik began to pace. "What am I supposed to do with an old globe and journals that amount to nothing but riddles?" He held out his hands. "Riddles I just can't solve."

His angry words bounced off the books. The hundreds of books that told him nothing.

"Maybe we can try something else." Claudia spoke into the strained hush. "I know what happened to your parents, and I'm sorry to bring it up."

Alert again, Arik homed in on the witch. "Go on."

"If you have something that either of them were wearing that night, maybe an object they were carrying?" She let the question hang in the air.

"My mother's necklace." Even as he spoke, Arik was moving to the huge desk. He opened a drawer and retrieved a blue-velvet box. "They took it off at the hospital. They said it was better if she didn't wear it." He opened the box with a dull *snap*. "Considering her condition."

"I know this is difficult," Claudia said, walking back to stand on the other side of the desk.

Arik lifted out the small locket. As it dangled on the chain, he pictured the photos inside. A wedding photo of his parents on one side. A shot of baby Arik on the other. "Please. Do whatever you can."

He held it out to Claudia.

She cupped her palm beneath, and Arik let it drop.

Claudia gasped as soon as the gold touched her skin. Her neck tensed, cording on each side as if strained. She stumbled back. Her eyes rolled up.

"Claudia!" Arik skirted the desk, getting to her just in time to catch her mid-fall. He lowered her to the floor, and Anna and Rae were beside them in an instant, both kneeling with alarmed expressions.

Arik cradled Claudia, trying to protect her head when her back arched violently. Bent taut as a bow with her hand vised around the locket, she began to spit out phrases in short bursts. "Drawing symbols. Woman. Scarf."

Scarf. Arik immediately flashed to Mahalia and dread chilled his blood.

No. Not her, he realized. *Mahalia's mother.*

"Blood. A chicken foot." Claudia moaned, sweat popping out on her forehead. "Rusty nails."

Coffin nails? Arik hissed out a breath. "Sounds like voodoo."

Her entire body quaking, Claudia forced out more through gritted teeth. "They don't want her to tell. They don't want her to tell!"

She threw her head back again, so forcefully Arik feared she'd snap her own neck.

"It's enough," Anna said, her own neck tense with worry. "Arik, get the locket."

"I'm trying." He'd been working his fingers under Claudia's, but they were clamped down. Rae began helping him, prying

Claudia's fingers open as gently as possible while Anna touched Claudia's face and chanted quietly.

"Almost," Rae said. "I think she's loosening—"

Before she could finish, Claudia's fingers splayed and the locket dropped to the tiles with a tinny *clink*.

Gasping again and again, Claudia thrust her hands wide, one latching onto Arik and the other on Anna. Then she bolted upright, her eyes round as silver dollars. "What. Was. That?"

"Are you all right?" Anna cupped her friend's face with her hands.

Claudia bobbed her head, wisps of her fiery hair falling in her face. "You were right about the darkness. It's close. No. No. Not just close." She looked to the ceiling. "It's *here*."

"My God." Arik tracked her gaze. "My mother. I have to go to her."

"The darkness," Claudia said again. "It has a . . . smudge."

Arik paused to listen, torn between hearing more and getting to his mother. In his mind, a menacing shadow was looming over her at this very moment.

Claudia locked her hand around Anna's wrist. "We've felt it before, or something similar." Her breaths were calming and she sounded more coherent. But no less horrified. "When we opened the box from Nick's basement."

"No. It can't be." Anna slumped. "Not again."

"What are you talking about?" Arik got to his knees and let Rae slide in to take his place to support Claudia. Flames erupted within him, a wildfire of terror. He had to get upstairs. "You said they didn't want her to tell. You meant my mother."

Claudia nodded.

"Anna, please." His voice was stretched to the breaking point. "What do you know?"

"Your mother may have been cursed."

"Yes, I know the woman Claudia was talking about."

"But voodoo didn't cause your mother's condition." Anna

shared a glance with Rae then stared at Arik. "Voodoo alone isn't powerful enough."

Arik's gut twisted as fear spread through like a sickness. "Then what is it?"

Anna stood to face him. She drew a breath. "Demons."

17

The clouds parted to let pale streaks of sun break through, and Arik could finally see the peaks of a grand house rising above a lush, thick forest of moss-draped trees. The boat he'd ridden to St. Germaine Island coasted up beside a pier, engine throttled back to a low, muffled rumble.

Anna had suggested they return to her home right away, insisting that until they knew exactly what they were dealing with, the warded and magickally defended house was the safest place for his mother. Not to mention the experience of the people who congregated there. The nine tried and tested witches and the men who'd stood with them during the prophesied trials.

In fact, Anna had driven the boat herself after finding the yellow house on the mainland empty. She'd mentioned a couple named Joe and Claire before slipping into the house to grab a set of boat keys.

Without question, Arik had climbed aboard the large vessel, carefully transporting his mother. Now, wrapped in a sheltering blanket, she was held firmly against his side. A chill had ridden in from the ocean, carried on the winds of a quickly growing tempest.

They'd hoped to make it to the house before the weather hit, but even as Claudia and Rae tied up the boat, cold drops began to pelt Arik's skin. "Hold on, Mom. I'll get you out of this rain."

Her wide eyes rolled to him as her body trembled. Pity and guilt almost caved in his chest. She was so frightened. His poor, sweet mother. *What did they do to you?*

He wondered how much she understood of what was happening. Did she comprehend what they were doing or why they'd left the comfort of home? The warm, familiar rooms where she felt secure?

He'd hated dragging her out on the water and the rough, bumpy sea, but he wouldn't rest until she was safe. Until she was protected by the strongest of magicks.

And that meant the Savannah Coven.

Thank God for Rae and Anna. He was deeply grateful for the help they'd given, as he was far beyond his comfort zone.

All along, he'd felt ready to find the answers he sought, determined to know all his father had withheld. But the more he learned, the more confused he became.

An enchanted globe was bad enough. But demons? He gripped his mother tighter.

Demons?

Just what had his parents been up to that night? Had they willingly gone to meet Mahalia's mother? And if so, what had gone wrong?

And what did beasts from the darkest depths of Hell have to do with his family legacy?

Fearful like he'd never been before, he pulled the blanket up to cover his mother's head. Once the boat was secure, he stood with her in his arms.

A dark-skinned man was on the dock, knees bent and hands outstretched. "Let me take her. She'll be fine. I promise."

With a terse nod, Arik transferred his mother to the man's strong arms and climbed out. With Arik right behind him, the man walked at a fast clip up the pier to a truck where Anna's brother Quinn stood waiting to open the door.

The first man slid Arik's mother inside and made sure she was stable, then he notched his head to the side and told Arik, "Go ahead and climb in. We'll follow in the carts."

"Thank you, uh . . ."

"Joseph," he supplied, and then he patted Arik on the shoulder. "She's in good hands. The very best." With that he turned and called Anna's name before pointing to a golf cart parked beneath a shelter.

Arik got in beside his mother, murmuring soft encouragement. He expected Quinn to drive the truck, but it was Rae who climbed in and threw the vehicle into gear. She looked in the rearview mirror as Quinn loaded the wheelchair into the back and covered it with a tarp.

Then Quinn tapped twice on the tailgate, and Rae slowly turned around on the gravel lane. She tossed a glance to Arik's mother. Then to him. Her honey-brown eyes held a mixture of compassion and unwavering determination.

And Arik knew he'd been a damned fool. She was right. He *could* lean on her. "Rae," he said, his voice barely audible beneath the pattering rain. "Thank you."

Her expression softened further, and her lips parted. But whatever she'd been about to say, she decided to keep to herself. Facing forward, she followed the road until they pulled up at a residence of wood and stone. The architecture made Arik think of a castle.

Rae stopped the vehicle, hopped out, and ran up the steps to bang on the double doors. One large wooden panel opened instantly and two more men came outside.

Arik recognized the fair-haired man as Ian, Anna's new husband. He learned the other's name when Rae called to him, "Dare, do you mind grabbing the wheelchair from the back?"

Rae and Ian came to the passenger side as Arik carefully picked up his mother. "Can I help?" Ian asked.

"I've got her, thanks." Arik shook his head and skirted around Ian. The truck door shut behind him. Rae stayed right with him as they carefully navigated the wet steps and went inside, both dripping all over a stylish slate floor.

She helped Dare unfold the portable wheelchair while a new woman rushed up with a dry quilt. "Here," she said, "let me put this down and you can set her in."

"Thanks, Willyn," Rae told her.

Arik wouldn't attempt to keep the names and faces straight. Anna had said all of the coven and many of the men would be waiting for their arrival, but his mind felt muddled and cloudy. Too full of fear to worry about pleasantries.

By the time his mother was wrapped in the quilt and in the chair, Anna and Claudia had piled into the foyer with Quinn and Joseph right on their heels. "Ethan?" Anna asked directly of the blonde named Willyn.

"He's gathered supplies and is in the great room setting up with Sylvie." Willyn turned to Arik to add, "Ethan is a demonologist, and Sylvie practices hoodoo. A kissing cousin to—"

"Voodoo," Arik finished with a nod. *Oh, yes. We've definitely come to the right place.*

Another woman chose that moment to hurry up. "I think you're on the right track." Her golden eyes encompassed him, Anna, and Claudia. "I was speaking to a spirit in the kitchen, and as soon as you arrived," she winced slightly at Arik, "he vanished right away."

Arik could only blink. "Did you say a spirit?"

"Yes. A ghost." She crossed her hands lightly over her chest. "I'm Hayden, and I communicate with the non-living. I mention this only because he left so quickly. Because he was afraid. You see," she explained, her voice quiet and sympathetic, "those who are lost are more susceptible to . . . demonic influence."

"More confirmation then," Arik said, glancing down at his mother. She'd closed her eyes and seemed to be dozing.

Though she likely wouldn't be for long. He looked at Anna. "Okay. What do we do?"

"Everyone who's here is in the great room," Hayden told

them both. Then to Anna, "We couldn't reach Trevor and Cole. They're interrogating a suspect. And Michael is in emergency surgery at the vet clinic."

"That's fine," Anna said.

Rae gripped the handles of the wheelchair. "To the great room, then?"

At Anna's nod, Rae met Arik's gaze and began rolling the chair across the smooth floor. As they moved, he vaguely registered a vast gathering area, a glittering chandelier high above, and trappings that spoke of wealth and elegance. All cloaked in a light scent of citrus he recognized as wood oil.

They walked through the sitting area and down a hall, stopping at an arched doorway. Quinn edged around them to open the door, allowing Rae and his mother entry. Behind them, Arik stepped into the great room.

And felt as if he'd stepped through time.

The construction of this portion of the house dated much farther back than the rest. The walls were of ancient rock and mortar and supported a high, pointed roof. Wooden beams intersected overhead to create a pattern.

Head tilted back, Arik studied the design. The beams formed a star. No, he realized.

They created a pentagram.

"This place is sacred," Rae said with reverence. "And the safest place for us to be." She looked pointedly at his mother, so he understood what she really meant.

The safest place for *her*.

"Right over here." A man waved to draw their notice. He had black hair, black jeans, and a black T-shirt. Even his eyes were dark and fathomless. But his smile seemed genuine and meant to comfort.

"Who is that?" Arik asked, nudging Rae aside to take control of the chair. He felt suddenly uncertain as he eyed the various tools and implements spread across a white marble table. Not a table. An altar.

Just what did they have planned?

"That's Ethan. Don't worry." Rae placed her palm on Arik's back as if sensing his sudden trepidation. "You can trust everyone here. I promise."

When Arik stood unmoving, simply staring, she gently took his chin and forced his eyes to hers. "I promise," she whispered. "Please, trust me. Trust Anna."

Swallowing down the bitter taste of fear, he sighed heavily. "I do." He rolled his mother toward the altar. *I do trust you.*

"Right here is fine," Ethan said, indicating a spot in front of the marble stand.

Arik faced his mother toward the door they'd entered, her back to the altar, and locked the wheels of the chair. He took a moment to study the rest of the room.

More people streamed inside, in addition to the few who were already lighting candles. He did a double-take. "Black candles?"

"They actually repel negative energy," Rae said. "Everything that's being done is for our protection." She didn't have to ask him again for his trust. Her eyes did that for her.

"All right." Arik put his hand on his mother's shoulder and watched as the others—many of them complete strangers—gathered around to form a circle. From their open body language and shared glances, he sensed strong bonds between them all.

Friendship, love, camaraderie, loyalty. Concepts practically foreign to him.

He'd been alone so very long.

Again Rae touched him, an unassuming caress on his arm. And the weight of the universe came crashing down. The weight of the risk he'd chosen to take.

Because he finally had some of those long-awaited answers, and damned if he wanted them now. Both his mother and the woman he'd loved—the woman he'd tried to save—were caught up in an evil he didn't recognize. An evil he couldn't begin to comprehend.

To hell with this legacy. He didn't *want* to be alone anymore. He wanted his mother back to normal, and he wanted Rae back in his life. Books and research and quests couldn't fill the void of his solitary existence.

But they were both being threatened by this unknown force, and if any of them were to be freed from that danger, then there was nowhere to go but forward. No way to predict what would happen next.

Arik didn't know enough to question. He didn't know enough to confront. He could only sit back as Ethan—the demonologist—employed the methods he thought best. Like Mahalia said, the fates had cast the die. So he had no other choice.

This had to happen.

As he faced an uncompromising reality, Arik's heart pounded viciously, each beat a painful kick inside his chest. His mother and Rae needed help, even if it put their lives in peril.

"We should start," Ethan said, his voice startling Arik from his morbid thoughts.

"It's time?" Arik saw that the others were looking at him, waiting for his consent. The candles had all been lit, flames flickering around the perimeter of the round room.

Ethan held a small bottle along with a rosary.

"Exorcism?" Arik asked, blood rushing to his head fast enough to make his vision go dark. He'd seen clips of those rituals before, where the salvation of a soul resembled torture.

"I don't think it will come to that." Ethan held up the objects for Arik's inspection. "These are both tradition and precaution."

A woman appeared beside Ethan then, hair and eyes a rich brown. "You can stay close," she said in a Spanish accent, "but it's probably better to let us do our work."

"This is Lucia, one of the coven." Rae introduced the new

female, and then another with creamy-brown skin. "And Sylvie, Joseph's wife."

"Hoodoo," Arik said, his throat growing tighter by the second.

"That's right." Sylvie smiled kindly. "Between Ethan and me and Anna's girls, nothing's going to get past us to hurt your mother."

She nodded firmly and winked. And it was as if she'd reached right inside of Arik and turned a valve, releasing a little of the tension he'd been holding in.

Everyone here had shown concern and sympathy, and this final assurance—offered with a smile—was the final stone. The one that took him past the tipping point, easing him from the side of anxious skepticism to cautious acceptance.

"We'll be right here." Rae guided him several feet away. Together they stood apart from the four beside the altar, yet within the circle formed by Anna and the others.

Arik watched Ethan put his finger to the bottle and mark the sign of the cross on his mother's forehead. *Holy water. Not so terrible.*

But he reconsidered when his mother jerked as if burned. And her eyes opened to horrified discs.

"Mom, I'm here. It's going to be all right. Better than all right." He squeezed Rae's hand, still soft in his, and remembered what she'd said. "I promise," he told his mother, willing to bet on faith and the abilities of those surrounding him.

He cast a searching gaze from face to face. Anna stood with Ian, both steady and calm, while Claudia was beside the woman named Hayden, their expressions holding only the mildest concern.

And that was an affirmation that he was doing the right thing.

Then came Anna's brother and a younger woman he hadn't met. Beside them were two females with raven-black tresses. One wore her hair in a braid, and the other was Asian, her arm looped with a man's.

The opposite side of the circle completed the group, a tall woman with a ready stance and white-blonde hair lined up next to a man with a military look. Finally Joseph, then Dare and Willyn.

That left the three in the middle of the great room. Ethan, Lucia, and Sylvie, all focused on Arik's mute, quadriplegic mother.

Please, let this work. Please, let her . . . He shut his eyes and pleaded for his most fervent wish. *Please, let my mother still be in there. Let her come back to me.*

Rae sidled closer, still clutching his hand.

When he looked again, Lucia was behind the wheelchair, her lips moving as if in prayer.

Meanwhile Ethan laid the rosary over Arik's mother, touching several of the beads and mumbling things too low to be heard. After a moment, he fell silent and backed away.

That's when Sylvie stepped up holding a bowl. She dipped her fingers into a dark substance, some sort of granules. Black salt? She sprinkled the small particles all over his mother, singing a quiet refrain in another language.

Ethan returned then, with a large grayish stone.

"That's skeletal quartz," Rae whispered in his ear. "It embodies the four elements—earth, wind, fire, and water—with powers to purify the spiritual self." She stroked his arm encouragingly. "It's the best gem for healing."

Arik tossed her a grateful look, but he couldn't keep his eyes off of his mother for long. Several strained minutes passed, the trio around her working, chanting, moving.

All the while, his mother sat motionless and still.

Arik's muscles bunched. His head ached.

Ethan finally set down the crystal and picked up a smaller item from the altar. A small burlap bag. He pressed it to Arik's mother's nose, holding it there as if expecting a response.

Then he got one.

His mother inhaled loudly, before releasing a blood-chilling shriek.

Arik jolted to hear her make the sound. *Any* sound.

That's when Sylvie moved in fast. She placed a mirror close to his mother's face.

A consecrated mirror. Arik nodded, remembering how Mahalia had once explained the process.

After proper preparation, it was said a mirror would bounce a curse, sending it to the one who'd cast it. But if Mahalia's dead mother had created the hex, where would it go? Would it find her in the afterlife?

Arik brushed aside the pity that welled up for Mahalia. Right now, he had one priority. All the rest would have to wait.

His mother drew another long breath, dropped back her head, and fell utterly still.

"No!" Arik yelled, lurching forward.

But Rae held him back. "Wait. Just wait."

Arik waited. He watched. Unblinking, he stared at his mother, searching for any sign of life.

Suddenly, as if she'd just completed an arduous task, she tried to raise her arms but instantly went limp again and settled against the back of the wheelchair. Though her head lolled to one side, ragged breaths gave proof that she still lived.

But the moan issuing from her parted lips struck a chord of terror deep inside Arik. "Is she okay?"

"I'll check on her," Willyn said, hurrying to join the growing group near the altar.

Half of Arik wanted to go as well. The other half was petrified of what he might find.

What if his mother remained in her vegetative state? What if breaking the curse made no difference?

But she'd moved, he reminded himself. She'd vocalized sounds.

Willyn murmured to Ethan, and he nodded. With a weak grin, he turned to Arik, "The curse is gone." He picked up a different stone from the altar, touching the green crystal to Arik's mother's face and chest. Then exchanged a triumphant glance with Sylvie. "Yes."

"A lot of strength in this place," Sylvie said, holding out her palms as if feeling the air. "And concentrated goodwill." She locked stares with Arik. "Love is the most powerful magick."

All the anxiety broke free and flooded from Arik's body. His shoulders relaxed.

"Her neck," Lucia said then, leaning over to study his mother. "Something's on her neck."

"What?" Arik asked, tensing up again.

"Some sort of mark on her skin."

As if flying backwards through a tunnel, Arik flashed to memories from his youth. His mother pushing his small hand away from her golden hair. His mother sweating while gardening and Arik saying, "It's hot. Why don't you put up your hair?"

She'd always brushed off such suggestions, claiming she had an unsightly scar. One she didn't want even her son to see.

"But she doesn't have a scar," he muttered to himself. Still, his statement drew curious or surprised looks from those near him.

"What do you mean?" Rae asked.

"My mother always tried to hide her neck. She claimed to have a terrible scar. But I've never found a single blemish. I just assumed she'd been overly vain or that the mark had faded over time without her knowing." He leaned forward but didn't advance. "What do you see?"

Lucia hovered two fingers over the right side of his mother's neck. "Here, just behind and under the ear. A symbol I don't recognize."

"Mind if I look?" Quinn asked. He waited for Arik's nod and

walked forward and scrutinized the spot Lucia had pointed out. "I don't know. I've never seen anything quite like this." He bent closer.

Arik's mother sat straight up in the chair, and everyone jumped. Including Arik.

Blinking and heaving breaths in and out, his mother turned her head. She lifted her arms as if imploring.

"Mom." Arik took a few steps, but then halted abruptly. His mother's eyes looked past him. They were fastened on another.

Her extended arms reached for someone else.

"Arik?" Rae asked in an unsure voice. "I think she's . . ."

"Yes. She wants you." Joy over his mother's improvement warred with alarm over why she was so intently focused on Rae.

With a confidence Arik wished he felt himself, Rae hurried over. "Marit," she said happily, taking his mother's hands in her own.

The instant she made contact, Rae's body went rigid. She shook and trembled as if being electrocuted.

Still holding on to Rae and with her eyes shining bright, Arik's mother raised her head, widened her eyes, and in a hoarse, raspy voice—spoke her first word in nine years. "*Akasha.*"

Rae gave a sharp cry, and then, as if released from a spell, she dropped to her knees and sagged forward.

Arik's mother let go, breaking their connection to collapse in the chair once again.

He was at their sides in a split-second, jerking his head back and forth, trying to assess them both.

"She's okay," Willyn said. "Your mother passed out. That's all."

He released a shaky breath and turned to Rae. She was awake and staring at him, but she appeared disconcerted, almost groggy.

"Rae." Arik touched her cheek. "What *was* that? Are you

hurt?"

Before she could reply, Quinn spoke in an awestruck tone. "It's gone. The mark on your mother's neck is gone."

Rae whimpered, grimacing as she slid a hand under her hair, up to her own neck. "Not gone." With her shocked gaze locked with Arik's, her lips quivered as she said, "I think it's on me."

18

Rae ran into the solarium, desperate to lose herself in the tropical surroundings and peaceful quiet. Following the sand-colored bricks, she circled her way through the vegetation, passing huge-leaved palms and blossoming plants.

Outside the sky had darkened, quicksilver clouds roiling with the growing storm. But the constant drone of rain soothed her. The dimness and shadows gave her a place to hide, the lush green isolating her from the rest of the world.

She put a hand to her neck, where the skin still tingled. She might have found a type of sanctuary, but the mark—the symbol—had followed her into the dark.

Footsteps gave away Arik's presence as he raced around the path. He rounded a corner and caught sight of her. "Rae," he expelled on a breath.

The relief on his face gave her the slightest twinge of guilt. He'd been through an ordeal tonight, distraught and worried. He didn't need to be burdened any further.

"You should be with your mother," she said.

"I know. I will." He eased closer, moving lightly, like a man trying not to startle a wild animal. "Willyn is with her. She's a nurse, and she thinks Mom is only sleeping."

How sad, Rae thought. After all those years of being unable to move, Marit seemed to be physically exhausted.

At least the change had been a positive one, and with any luck she'd continue to improve.

Yet while Marit appeared to be healthy and on her way to recovery, the ritual couldn't be called a complete success.

Rae whirled to face him. "What is this thing on my neck, Arik?" She heard the hitch of fear in her voice. "Do you know?"

"I haven't seen it." A few more steps and he closed in. He angled his head but didn't move her hair to examine it. Instead, the first thing he did was pull her into his arms.

Rae had thought she wanted to be alone, that she could figure out the new problem by herself. It's what she'd done for a long, long time.

But the heat and strength of his embrace drew a soft sound from her throat, and she simply melted into him. She slid her arms around to his back, gently flexing her fingers into his corded muscle.

"I'm sorry," she whispered against his dark gray shirt. "I just need to get to my bearings."

"Take all the time you need." Voice gruff with emotion, he stroked a small circle between her shoulder blades.

Rae closed her eyes. She sunk in. And releasing the last shreds of her tattered pride, she just let him hold her.

He smelled the same as he used to, clean and masculine, with an undertone of the crisp aftershave he'd always favored.

More at home in his arms than she had any right to be, she said, "For someone who's traveled the world, I seem to have lost my way." She'd meant it as a joke, just lighthearted banter, but the dire truth in her words created internal bedlam. Emotional chaos to rival the storm outside.

She shifted back to look up into his eyes. "I don't understand what's happening. Why me?"

He didn't offer false consolation or placating half-truths. Instead he asked, "Can I look?"

With a slight nod, she moved to lift her hair. But Arik beat her to it, the brush of his fingers like fire on her flesh. She trembled in response.

"I'm sorry." He went still. "Does it hurt?"

"Not anymore. At first, it was as if I'd been branded, a burning so deep, like nothing I've ever felt before. It shot through my system. Incredible pain." She held her head to the side to give him a better view.

"I don't recognize the symbol, but the writing style reminds me of some I've seen in Dad's journals." He trailed the pad of one finger across her neck. "I would have kept you from this," he said hoarsely. "I would have given my life."

The warmth of his lips on her skin shocked her system in another way, and the surge of pleasure almost did her in. Legs weakened, she clung to his broad shoulders.

"I shouldn't have done that." Arik stiffened, frowning down at her. But he didn't release his hold on her waist.

"It's fine," she said. "It doesn't hurt at all." Though she suspected that's not why he'd apologized.

"In fact, I feel pretty good," she said. "Aside from the obvious concern of what this all means, I actually feel fine. Energized, alert, and I—"

Her entire body went rigid. "It's gone." She slapped a hand to her stomach. "Arik, it's gone."

"What?" Alarm animated his features. "The mark?"

"No, no. The pain in my stomach. It's completely gone." His baffled expression reminded her that he had no idea what she was talking about. "I guess I can tell you now, considering everything else."

Rae's heart skipped as she stared into the depths of his gaze. She would basically be admitting the hurt, and the affection, she'd carried for him all these years. "I stayed away from Savannah for two reasons. The first and more obvious being," she gulped, "you. I didn't want to be reminded of you."

He closed his eyes and exhaled. Then he slowly shook his head. "I've kept you from your home, from your family. My selfishness and fear hurt you, deprived you of the life you'd known."

He looked at her again, and now regret swam in those depths. "I feel like I can't say I'm sorry enough."

"You don't have to anymore. What's done is done, and after tonight," absentmindedly, she rubbed the writing that magick had burned into her flesh, "I understand better than ever why you wanted me gone. Why you would have kept this from me."

She shrugged. "If our roles were reversed, I might have done the same thing." Her lips kicked up in a cocky grin. "Only I would have been much nicer when I broke your heart."

"I did that, didn't I?" Lightning flashed to light up the solarium at the exact moment he cupped her face. "Does it make any difference that it broke mine, too?"

Heat from his touch streamed down her spine, while his sweet admission stole her breath. "Arik." One moment his name was on her lips, and the next his mouth lowered to capture her sigh.

She'd never known another who could stoke fire in her heart, and in her soul.

With one. Soft. Kiss.

Her blood stirred with anticipatory thrill.

But then he lifted away, leaving her feeling slightly bereft and empty inside.

His fingers tightened on her hips. "I'm not going to apologize for that."

Rae's pulse thrummed and her skin felt sensitive, like she'd been dusted in starlight. She leaned back to gather her wits, pressing a palm to her belly where hot, liquid desire pooled.

The motion drew Arik's notice and his features tensed. "You never told me the second reason."

"Hmm?" Rae blinked to clear the crimson-edged lust from her mind. "Oh, my stomach."

She shook herself, recalling the more serious issues at hand.

"You see," she said, "whenever I came back here, I experienced some discomfort." She quirked her lips and decided to be brutally honest. "Actually, it felt like a chasm opened in my gut, a crater that got wider and deeper the longer I stayed in town. I just related the symptoms to you and to my . . ."

She glanced down then back up to him. "My unresolved feelings. But I know now—I'm *certain* now—that wasn't the case." She huffed and glanced aside. "I'll be damned. Anna was right."

"Right about what?" he asked.

"Magick. It's the only explanation. The pain left as soon as your mother and I touched. As soon as the mark transferred to me."

Arik's hand flicked out and fluttered the leaves of a Hawaiian ginger plant, sending the wonderful scent washing over them. "I don't remember you having this discomfort."

"That's because it didn't start until after you broke it off with me." She furrowed her brow and stared into the shadows, searching her memories of that time period. "No, wait. I remember waking up in the middle of the night with a stabbing pain."

She gripped his arms. "The next morning, you called me to tell me to come to the hospital. I remember how badly my stomach ached as I got dressed. I was afraid I'd be sick at the time when you needed me most."

Realization lit up his face. "You were affected by what happened to my parents."

"Specifically, to your mother." Rae bobbed her head as it all began to make sense. "The curse, *her* curse, also had something to do with me." Jittery now, she released her hold on him and hugged herself.

Lightning cracked the sky as if to slice it apart. The resounding thunder shook the glass panes around them.

"What if I was wrong?" Arik put a hand to his forehead. "What if I shouldn't have pushed you away? Maybe you were meant to be here all along."

"Or maybe I was meant to go. And meant to come back now. Anna's dream, the globe—these things occurring so near my return." She raked her hair away from her face. "That's no coincidence."

She moved to a bench and sat. "All this time I've been running, wrapped up in my own self-pity and feelings of betrayal."

"Rae—"

"No." She bounded to her feet again. "It's okay, Arik. Please, don't feel bad for me. Because you've suffered, too. For nine years, you've worked tirelessly to find a meaning behind your family history, a reason for your parents' attack. You've taken such good care of your mother."

She went to him and slipped her hands to the back of his neck. "You never left her side. You never gave up."

Her body deflated. "Like I did. I always thought you were the one with the choices. I had no idea what you were going through."

"Don't do that." His arms twined around her waist again. "We could spend forever second-guessing what we should have done."

"You're right." She firmed her lips, determined not to spend any more time feeling sorry or sad. "Now we have to take stock of where we are and what we want."

Looking up at Arik, she began to see what mattered most to her. And it wasn't the excitement of seeing a new place or capturing sights most never saw except through photos. It wasn't climbing to the highest height or disappearing into a deadly cave.

What mattered to her were the people she cared about. The people she loved. Like her family and Anna.

Her heart tumbled in her chest. *Arik*.

"Maybe," she whispered, fingers threading in his cool, silky hair, "we are *exactly* where we're supposed to be. Exactly where we were always destined to end up."

"I'd like to think so," he said, then his lips skimmed her hers again. "I don't know what lies ahead for us, Rae, but if you're willing to trust me again, I think we can help each other."

Her laugh was short and light. "That's the craziest thing. I trust you more than ever." She leaned into him. "I saw how hard it was for you in there. The concern and horror that racked your face." And hollowed his eyes.

He shuddered and pulled her close. "I couldn't bear the thought of losing her." He lowered his head to lightly rest against hers. "Or you. When you screamed . . ."

"*Shh.*" She turned to press a gentle kiss on his cheek. "I'm fine. I really am. And tonight, you need to stay here, to be with your mother."

"I am. They're getting a room ready upstairs." He nuzzled into her hair and spoke softly. "Will you stay? I need you close, at least under the same roof where I know you're safe."

"Of course." She wouldn't leave him. Not tonight.

Her pain was gone and the possibility of her dream had returned. She had no reason to run again. Not from her home. Not from Arik.

And not from whatever fate magick had decreed for them both.

At length, he lifted his head. "I'll sit with Mom tonight. Hopefully by tomorrow we'll know more about how she's doing. And then," he held her gaze, "I'd like for you to come with me."

"Where?"

"To Mahalia's." His shoulders rose and fell. "I think it's time for the two of you to meet."

"Yes," she said calmly, still locked in his arms. "I think it's time."

~~~

Anna was in the park again.

As if a movie had been rewound, she stood in the exact moment when Arik's mother looked over at her. And began to scream.

Like before, the storm rolled in, lightning shattering the sky and thunder deafening her ears.

And also like before, Marit Mansur morphed into the raven.

But this time the bird flew to Anna, making it all the way from the fountain to soar up and over her head at the last second. She would have turned to watch it, but as the raven brushed by, a *whump!* brought Anna's gaze to the ground.

A dark blue book lay on the cement. The raven had dropped it at her feet.

Pages frayed and a deep scratch across its cover, the book looked worn and well-used. A bright red ribbon hung from the bottom, beckoning to Anna, promising knowledge.

She stretched out her arm. She tried to reach the book.

But the universe erupted again, and like before, flames burned all around. This time, however, Anna didn't escape. This time she felt her own skin heat and bubble. She smelled her hair as the strands ignited.

And as she was consumed by fire, a strange cackling filled the air. Harsh laughter rippled on the flames.

A woman's laughter. Taunting laughter.

As she whipped her head in search of the source, red and gold flames morphed into a shape. They formed a visage. Though the woman's face remained unidentifiable, Anna's heart swelled with dread.

Dread and bone-deep horror.

Fear drove her from sleep, and she woke up in her bed, sitting up, her hands on her knees and perspiration dampening her hairline.

"What is it?" Ian asked, rising quickly to wrap a supportive arm around her back.

Anna's lungs heaved and her mind revolted. "Something's wrong. I don't know." But there was no denying the threat she'd perceived.

"Only a nightmare. That's all it was. By the goddess." She wiped at her hair. "It was only a nightmare."

Ian tugged her over, pushed her head to his shoulder. "Do you want to tell me?"

"I think it was a warning." She clenched her eyes shut and willed the images away. "I know in my heart something is coming, but I don't know what." She snuggled closer and let his warmth soothe her.

"A woman was laughing at me. Taunting me."

"Who?" Ian stroked her hair. "Baby, who?"

"I just don't know." Fighting off chills, Anna pulled up the blanket. In the dead-still and dark of night, she whispered, "But she was laughing."

19

She didn't know how many hours had passed—or how long she lay on the verge of insanity—before the door finally creaked open again. The tiniest crack seemed to flood the black room, illuminating what had become a chamber of death.

The vast cavern reeked with the stench of decay and oozed with bile and blood.

Blood from thousands of dead snakes.

Exhausted, and in enough pain to wish for her own end, she lay sprawled across the stone ledge, one leg dangling in the obsidian water. She no longer feared a serpent's bite, for her body was covered in punctures, and her own blood now ran thick with venom.

She'd long ago grown immune to the pain, stamping out agony with a rise of pure, unadulterated rage.

All around her, sinewy corpses floated in the lake, some with their long spines twisted or snapped, and others with their heads bitten clean off.

Bitten off by *her*.

Turnabout, you legless bastards. She could barely see out of one eye, so swollen was her flesh from countless strikes. But she rolled that eye toward the open door. And gave her watchers her most baleful glare.

"*Voren*." A master spoke from outside in the tunnel, and she had no trouble deciphering the language. He'd told her to "come."

"Fuck you," she whispered, her puffy lips making it sound more like *fahg ooh*.

A lash appeared on her breast, punishment for disobedience.

Reaching deep for the last of her strength, the last of her willpower, she rolled onto her side and pushed up with one arm. Swallowing, she moistened her throat, licked her lips, and inhaled deeply. "I said. Fuck. You."

With a rebellious snarl, she waited to be whipped again. But to her astonishment, a second strike never fell on her already destroyed skin.

Instead, the master rumbled an order, and three ghouls scrambled inside to surround her. One pried open her mouth to push in a ball of the nutritional and restorative sludge.

She spit the slime back into its face.

"*Unh-unh*," the ghoul protested, its wire-sewn lips flattening with displeasure. Digging fingers into both sides of her jaw, it forced open her mouth so another pale servant could shove more slop inside.

They held her mouth shut, one rubbing her throat until she swallowed involuntarily. Instantly, the burn in her veins began to fade, and the holes in her body began to close.

After a brief coughing spell, she drew a ragged breath and shouted, "Fuck you all!"

Her angry shout echoed in the cavern of death, but the only response was from the three white-skinned monsters who hauled her to her feet and dragged her out to the corridor.

Deciding she was done contributing to her own abuse, she fell slack and closed her eyes. They wanted her moved? Then they could damn well carry her.

After another directive from the dark master, the horde of ghouls waiting in the tunnel lifted her like a rocker in a mosh pit. Then they bore her inert form through the shadowy halls.

Up an incline and out of the tunnel they marched, until at last curiosity got the best of her, and she slit her eyes open.

They'd returned to the original room, with pillars all around and the endless black void overhead. The mob carried her to the center and gently—so gently it was almost comical after what she'd endured—rested her on the ground.

Precisely where the slime pit had once served as her grave.

"*Vos.*" A deep voice resonated, but the order to "go" wasn't for her. The meek, pale servants spread out and formed a perimeter, ghouls lining up to create three sides. And the dark ones standing guard along the fourth.

"So you've got me surrounded." She sat up and rested her arms on her bent knees. "What next, huh? Fire? Spiders? Pulling out my guts? How about that prickly-pear, or whatever they call that nasty ass-stretcher?"

With her body restored and her attitude riled, she slowly turned her head to the dark masters and leveled them with a stare. "Just bring it on, so we can be done with it."

Begging didn't stop the torture. Obedience didn't bring relief. So what did she have to gain by continuing with either?

The snakes had been her worst nightmare. The slippery shits had carried out the most gruesome, cringe-worthy, and relentless assault. But she had fought. And she had survived.

Fuck all that. She had *conquered.*

Impatient, pissed off, and sick of being so disgustingly dirty, she thrust her head out in challenge. "You hear me?" she growled. "What's next?"

As if in answer, one of the masters raised an arm, the black haze that obscured their bodies rising along with the extended limb.

No order had been spoken, but a ghoul responded as if it knew what was expected.

Scraping its long white feet over the ground, the ghoul grunted and crept forward. Then it began to run.

It ran straight for her.

A muted howl sounded in its throat just before it launched

itself through the air, one hand curled in a massive swinging fist.

She had been healed. She felt strong. So she rolled clear of the attack and quickly gained her feet. The strange creature skidded in the dirt, spun around, and charged her again.

She widened her stance, held up her arms, and clothes-lined the asshole, catching it with an arm across the throat.

The ghoul gave off a dull *umph* as its feet kept moving, but its upper body jerked to a halt. The pale form hovered parallel to the ground, before dropping with a *thud*.

Soundlessly, she fell on the creature. And wasted no time snapping its weak neck, a handy trick she'd picked up in the serpents' lair.

A collective groan issued from the remaining ghouls.

Dusting her hands, she faced the masters and cocked a hip. With a sneer on her face, she lifted her eyebrows, mocking them with an is-that-all-you-got? expression.

One of the masters laughed then, if the gravelly rumble could be considered laughter.

The inhuman sound sent prickles down her back, like the legs of a tin centipede.

Why was he laughing? She glanced around, but none of the ghouls made a move.

She didn't have to wait long before a large mass streaked overhead, the *whoosh* of wings ruffling her matted hair. Then a screech ricocheted in the dark, stabbing her heart with sharp, cold fear.

Terror was acrid in her mouth, but instinctually, she readied for another fight.

And based on the size of the monster, this might be her last battle.

The beast took her by surprise by dropping from above, instantly enshrouding her with its claw-tipped wings. Rough like leather and dark as soot, the creature's skin scraped over hers.

A stinging pain shot through her shoulder, and she realized the thing had clamped down on her with its elongated jaws. With its head so close, she reached up and over, scratching her fingers across its face until she felt the soft give of its eyes.

She dug in, and gave a screech of her own, refusing to let go until the monster did.

As if recognizing the stalemate, the flying fiend released her and took two jumps back.

Knowing she had no choice, certain she must fight for her life, she lunged at the menacing beast and latched on to its neck.

With a thrust, she kicked off of its stomach and flung herself onto its back. Again, she gouged its eyes, and when it reared in defense, she took its pointed jaws in one hand, and grasped the back of its head with the other.

She tensed her muscles and—

"Stop," the masters called as one, the unity of their order conveying its importance. And confirming its finality.

Both she and the winged monster paused in their struggle.

Had the language translated in her mind? How was she understanding more and more of what they said?

One of the dark ones stepped forward. He waved his hand, and the beast shook her loose before lifting off into the void.

Breathing hard, she pushed back her hair. She held her ground.

The master advanced, and as she watched, the shadowy mist cleared, revealing the hidden face behind the haze.

She would swear her heart stuttered to a painful stop, and she wished the master had remained obscured.

For there were some things you could never un-see.

The chilling laughter rattled forth again as the dark one extended his hand. He said in his wicked voice, "Come, my child."

His hideous face split into a smile. "You are ready."

20

Arik sat in Rae's kitchen, sipping a mug of coffee and jiggling his leg beneath the table.

And feeling like a complete coward.

He silently urged Rae to hurry up with her shower and change of clothes. The two of them had swiftly fallen into old, familiar routines, and Rae truly seemed to have forgiven the past.

But despite their mended fences, he wasn't quite ready to cross paths with her sister Emma.

He and Rae had been awake early this morning, having taken turns sitting up with his mother throughout the night. Just past dawn, Willyn had come to the room, offering to relieve them and promising she would let Arik know if anything changed with his mother's condition.

With the house still quiet and his mother sleeping soundly, he'd taken her up on her offer. But instead of getting any rest for themselves, Arik and Rae had decided to return to the mainland.

They still needed to see Mahalia.

The sound of Rae tromping down the steps broke Arik from his musings. And gave him no small amount of relief. In a shot, he was up and at the sink, cleaning his cup and putting it in the drying rack.

"Well, aren't you tidy?" Leaning against the door jamb, her hair still wet and wearing a simple dress of yellow linen, Rae studied him with a wry grin on her luscious lips.

The sight of her was enough to make Arik feel like he was burning alive from the inside out. And he welcomed the heat.

"I'm not going to lie." He raked his gaze down over her long, toned legs. "I could stand a few minutes alone with you."

"Oh?" She glided—no, she *sauntered* over to him, stopping just shy of touching him and with her hands held behind her back. "Whatever for?"

"I'd tell you, but we haven't even had our first date," he teased, unable to resist pulling her into his arms and pressing a chaste kiss to her lips. "But as much as I'd like to move things along in that department," he ran his palms down her curves and was rewarded with the hitch in her breath, "I'm afraid Emma will be back at any second."

When she feigned disappointment, he hiked a brow. "Demons and curses? I'm actually getting accustomed to the idea, but . . ."

"But you're not ready to face my sweet sister." Laughing, Rae brushed her fingers through his hair. "Is it wrong that hearing you say that gives me some sort of perverse pleasure?"

"Not at all. I expect our rekindled relationship to have starts and stutters, all things considered." He stepped toward the hallway, pulling her with him. "But Emma on the other hand, she's going to be full bore in one direction. And I don't expect smooth sailing."

"You are so right." Grinning, Rae snatched her purse from the antique sideboard of golden wood. "I should have showered more slowly, because that's a reunion I'd pay good money to see."

"Just not today," Arik said. But he hadn't made it halfway to the back door before it opened to admit three talkative women, all sporting various versions of athletic wear.

Karma. You really are a sneaky little—

"Holeeee shit." The startled—and wholly appropriate—

exclamation burst from the woman wearing an aqua-blue running outfit that complimented her figure as well as her golden-brown complexion.

"Bell!" Rae cried, rushing forward to greet her high-school friend and give her a hug.

"Ah-ah, girl. I'm sweaty." Bell fended her off but happily kissed Rae's cheek before gracing her with a beautiful smile. "I'm so glad you stuck around long enough for me to see you this time." She playfully slapped Rae's shoulder.

Then her mischievous gaze shifted to Arik. "And I think I see why you did. Seems you ran into more than one acquaintance on this trip home."

"It does seem." The words were offered in a cool, brittle tone as Emma stared Arik down the way a predator did its prey.

And like the true nature of prey, he felt the hairs stand up on the back of his neck.

For good cause. Emma had plenty of reason to despise him. Not only had he hurt her sister, but the pain he'd caused Rae had also driven her away from Savannah. Away from her home and family.

Emma and Rae had always been tight, and Arik had the unfortunate distinction of being the first thing to truly separate the two.

"Arik?" a third woman whispered, her stare narrowing as she looked over Bell's shoulder.

"Yes, my darling girl. That's him." Bell crossed her arms and grinned.

The petite brunette glowered. "Arik the Disgraceful. What are you doing here?"

So he'd been relegated to a dog name. Arik blew out through his lips. And not even a good dog name.

"Oh, Bryn." Rae's laughter was high-pitched and false. "We don't have to say that anymore." She turned and told Arik in hushed voice, "It was just a joke. A girl thing."

Arik's gaze streaked back to the young woman with a lovely tilt to her brown eyes. And he couldn't help smiling. *Bryn*. He should have recognized her right away. This grown woman, as outspoken as her Aunt Rae, was the teenage girl he'd once taught to play chess.

But before he could say anything to her, Emma marched forward and slammed a water bottle down on the sideboard. "It wasn't a complete joke. His behavior *was* disgraceful." She plunked her hands on her hips. "So now all of a sudden you two are . . . what? Friends?"

She gave Arik a onceover before glaring daggers at Rae. "All's forgiven?"

Emma Scott was undoubtedly one of the kindest, gentlest souls Arik had ever come to know. But when it came to her loved ones, especially family, she was fiercely loyal and protective.

"Rae, wait," he said, to stop her from responding. Then he addressed her sister. "Emma, I don't blame you for whatever you're feeling right now. I know this is unexpected."

She only pursed her lips but didn't reply.

But Bryn did. "Unexpected? More like a shock. As in electrotherapy kind of shock." She all but shoved her way past Bell. "You made promises to my Aunt Rae. You gave her an engagement ring."

"Bryn, hold on," Rae started, but her niece ignored her.

"Then you just jerked everything out from under her. And you," Bryn added, pointing at Rae, "you were a mess. I was young, but I remember. And I also know he's why you've stayed away. So what? We're not supposed to say anything when you spring him on us like this?"

With her piece said, Bryn crossed her arms at the exact time that Emma did the same.

Bell, however, simply stood there grinning like a fool. When Arik caught her eye, she winked. "You're up, loverboy. Watcha' got to say for yourself?"

In fear of more retribution from the Scott women, Arik wisely suppressed a grin. Bell used to get a kick out of calling him "loverboy" or Rae and him "lovebirds."

At least one person appeared ready to let bygones be good and gone.

But he did owe Emma and Bryn some consideration. So he steeled his spine and spoke directly to the two who'd once been his extended family. "I would say Emma and Bryn are both entitled to their anger. And rightly so," he added meaningfully. "Because they don't know the full story."

"And it's a story we are not going to get into right now." Rae stepped between him and the trio of women, her hands up as if calling for a cease-fire. She huffed loudly and sent him a look that clearly said *don't argue*.

At his nod of agreement, she turned to Emma and Bryn. She put one gentle hand on each of them. "Truth be told, I love you both so much at this moment that I don't know whether to laugh or cry."

She kissed each of them on the cheek. "I know you only want what's best for me. So thank you."

Emma shrugged. "Just tell us what's going on," she said, her tone so defeated, yet so concerned, it took all Arik had not to spill the whole story and beg her forgiveness. His decisions, his actions, had caused a farther-reaching effect than he'd let himself realize.

"All I can say right now is that Arik had a good reason—a *very* good reason—to do what he did to me." Rae tossed a quick glance over her shoulder at him before facing them again. "But things are complicated right now, and I'm going to have to ask you for a little patience. He and I are both working together to solve a problem, and—"

"What problem?" Bryn demanded.

"I really can't go into it. I need you to trust me on this." Rae touched her niece's cheek when Bryn started to pull away.

"*Please*, just wait for a little bit. I need to work this out." When Rae spoke again, her voice was shaky. "Because this time, I want to stay home."

Emma sniffed as if she was about to cry. She shook her head at Rae, the exasperation clear in her pinched lips. "Fine. We can wait one more day. You get *one day* to have your secrets. And that's it."

"But—" Bryn tried to interject but fell quiet when Emma touched her shoulder.

"One day." Emma looked to Arik as if making sure he heard her as well. "We've missed out on having Rae in our lives for the past nine years. That's on both of you. So all either of you get is one. More. Day."

That said, Emma grabbed the water bottle. She brushed past Rae, stomped past Arik, and disappeared up the spiral staircase.

Bryn still stood glaring at him.

He might as well start trying to make amends. "Bryn," he said, tilting his head and trying on a small smile. "You're so grown up I didn't know you at first."

"Yeah. A decade will do that." Her eyes, her voice, were hard as stone.

Arik shared a glance with Rae as he considered how to best approach the once-young girl who'd become an adult in his absence.

But then Bryn's hard expression fell apart. Her stiff tone broke. "She wasn't the only one who loved you, you know. She wasn't the only one you just walked out on." She clenched her fists at her side and punched them downward, as if to beat off her traitorous emotions.

Then, without another word, she shook her head and left in the direction Emma had.

"Bryn, wait," he tried as she hurried past him. But she ignored his efforts and ran up the stairs.

Now even Bell lost her grin. "I don't know what you two have going on, but even I deserve to have my say." She sighed. "And what I'll say is this. First, Emma and Bryn will be okay. They just need a little time."

She held Rae's gaze for a moment, and then Arik's. "Second. Whatever this is, just please be careful. Be *certain*. Because none of us want to go through another Rae and Arik Cold War. If you get my meaning."

She gave a decisive nod and reached back for the door that was still standing open. "Now I've got to go." Her merry smile was back as if she hadn't just given them a gentle scolding. "Got to tend my garden and go for my mani-pedi. Then it's Friday afternoon tea at the Gryphon with my daddy. Standing date."

Bell started to slide out, but she paused and turned back. "You know we all love you both. Don't forget that." And then she was gone, the latch clicking into place behind her.

"Well," Rae said, slumping as if she'd just survived the aforementioned war.

Feeling just as hollowed out as Rae looked and, deciding he couldn't have said it any better, Arik ran a hand through his hair. And simply nodded.

21

"I love this place." Ten minutes later, Rae shielded her eyes against the sun to take a better look at the ancient live oak and the charming treehouse built high in its sturdy limbs. "Is that stained glass? How pretty." Colorful glass panels of various sizes had been framed and hung from beneath the wooden platform.

Rae's initial reaction to Arik's "voodoo woman" had been doubt and defensiveness. But one look at the adorable yellow cottage, picket fence, flowering shrubs—and of course, the treehouse—and she decided she already liked this Mahalia she'd heard so much about.

Arik tossed a crooked grin up to the adult version of a child's hideaway. "That's pure Mahalia, all right. You never quite know what to expect."

Movement farther down the road drew Rae's notice. "I see what you mean." Humor laced her voice as she spotted the woman heading their way. She wore a white peasant blouse and broom skirt of the same color, the fabric swinging just above the pavement with each dauntless step.

A scarf wrapped around her head, white as well but with a colorful floral pattern. She held a walking stick in one hand, an old physician's bag in the other, and on her face, she sported round sunglasses. The look was both bold and whimsical, her fashion sense reflecting the fun spirit of the treehouse.

As she drew near, her lips bloomed into a lovely smile. "Well,

well. This must be Rae Scott you've brought to meet me." Mahalia opened the fence gate and joined them in the yard. "And I didn't need to toss the bones to know that." She chortled at her own joke.

With a distance still between them, Rae held up a hand in greeting. "Hello, Mahalia. It's nice to meet you."

"And you." Mahalia jabbed a thumb over her shoulder. "I've just been down the road visiting some friends at Bonaventure."

Bonaventure Cemetery. Rae nodded understanding. Cemeteries and graveyards were a big deal in Savannah, made all the more attractive and enchanting as if to encourage the living to remember the dead.

"I've got some sun tea making out back." Mahalia strolled toward the porch steps. "Should be about ready now. Why don't you two come on in? Have you had breakfast?"

Oh, yes, Rae thought, grinning like a school girl who'd been offered fresh-baked cookies. She definitely liked this lady.

But before she could accept the hospitality, Arik spoke up. "Actually, Mahalia, a lot has happened in the last twenty-four hours."

She tipped down her sunglasses to look at Rae. "So I see."

"We came with news." Frowning, Arik glanced to the house. "And I'm afraid it's an outside conversation."

"Is that right?" Mahalia asked, the cheer draining from her face like melted wax. She nodded solemnly. "So you want to talk about my mother."

Rae didn't grasp the meaning of "outside conversation," but given the sensitive topic and Mahalia's reaction, she wouldn't ask until she was alone with Arik.

"I appreciate you remembering that, boy." Setting down the walking stick and doctor's bag, Mahalia eased over to a gigantic azalea bush and ran her thumb across a pale-purple blossom. "You talk," she jerked her head at Arik. "I'll listen."

"We've learned more about what happened that night." He

didn't have to elaborate on which night he meant. "As you and I thought, your mother was there with my parents. And," he hedged, shifting on his feet, "it turns out that my mother was the victim of a voodoo curse."

Mahalia nodded again, still focused on the flower.

"Voodoo," Arik continued, "reinforced by demonic power."

The last got Mahalia's full attention. Staring at Arik, she pulled the glasses free from her face, backed up, and plopped down on the steps. "Demons."

Chest heaving, she glued her gaze to the stretch of lawn as if transfixed. At length, she turned to him and asked, "You sure?"

"Yes. Rae's friend and her coven have been helping us. Anna got involved because—"

"Anna St. Germaine?" Mahalia broke in.

"Yes," Rae answered this time. "She's a childhood friend."

"Well then." Mahalia sighed in acceptance. Then she balled her hands up in her lap, rocking back and forth. "Oh, Mama, what did you do? What did you do?"

And why? Rae wondered, though again, she would let Arik take the lead in this discussion.

"She told me she had to do *one thing* to keep us safe," Mahalia said as if reading Rae's mind. "If I'd only known what she was involved in. If only I'd stopped her. Now her soul's got to fight for redemption." She rubbed her forehead and whispered to herself, "Oh, Mama."

"We can't know what the demons did to her." Arik moved to kneel before his friend. "Or what they might have threatened her with. Maybe," he said, letting his pause give weight to what he was about to say. "Maybe they threatened her only child. Or her grandchildren."

Mahalia looked up at him, and Rae could see the wet shimmer beneath her eyes.

"I don't know much about demonology myself," Arik went on, "but from what I've seen so far, and according to Ethan, an expert in the field, demons don't exactly abide by any rules. They use, they hurt, they manipulate to get whatever it is they want."

"My mother was a gifted woman," Mahalia said.

"Yes, she was. And they must have needed her. They needed her enough to force her to make a terrible choice."

Surprise rolled over Mahalia's features, followed by confusion. "You don't hate her for what she did to your mother?"

"No. I tried to but can't seem to make it stick." He took Mahalia's wrinkled brown hands in his. "You need to know that the curse is gone, and my mother seems to be healing. We're hopeful she'll make a full recovery, but it's too soon to tell."

Mahalia let out a breath and tilted her head back. "Praise be."

"So the curse is gone," Arik repeated. "It's over."

As far as we know. Rae couldn't help putting her fingers to her neck, tracing the symbol they still didn't understand.

Despite the mark, she still felt healthy and vibrant, with no apparent curse or ill effects.

Not yet, anyway.

Arik still crouched in front of Mahalia. "I know what it's like to carry guilt on your shoulders. Guilt that doesn't rightfully belong to you."

Mahalia shrugged.

"Whatever our parents did, whatever they got caught up in, we are not responsible." He shook her hands. "Do you hear me?"

Pursing her lips, the older woman tugged her hands free from Arik and used them to pat both sides of his face. "I hear you, boy." A weak grin lifted one side of her mouth. "When did you get to be such a know-it-all?"

She wiped at her eyes, and gazed lovingly at Arik. Then she threw up her hands and stood as he helped her up. "What am I saying?" She winked at Rae. "He's been a wiseacre since the moment we met."

Rae's laughter was soft and tinged with relief. The information Arik had brought Mahalia couldn't have been easy to hear, yet she was already back on her feet. Smiling and cracking jokes.

Now Rae was certain. She *adored* this woman.

And was suddenly very grateful she'd been a part of Arik's life all this time. That he hadn't been completely alone.

"Now can we have that tea?" Mahalia asked Arik.

"Well, there's more," he said and smiled. "But I think we can talk about it over a cold glass."

"What more?" Mahalia put a hand on her ample hip. "Tell me now."

At this point—since it concerned her—Rae stepped in. "Once the curse was lifted, a sign appeared on Marit's . . . on Arik's mother's neck. One none of us has yet identified."

"Hmm." Mahalia rubbed her chin. "Did you bring a picture? Or a drawing?"

Rae and Arik looked at each other before he said, "We brought the real thing. Only it's no longer on my mother's skin."

"It's on mine," Rae finished. She leaned in to give Mahalia a better look and pulled aside her hair.

Mahalia squinted. She peered closer. Then she leapt back and slapped a hand to her heart.

Rae's arms rippled with goosebumps. "What's the matter? Do you know what it means?"

"No, but I've seen that sign before. I've seen—" With a shake of her head, Mahalia waggled a finger at Arik. "I'm sorry, boy, but we're going to have to skip tea and breakfast altogether. I've got work to do."

"What's wrong, Mahalia?" A wrinkle of worry formed between his brows.

"It's what she tried to tell me," Mahalia told Arik. "I know that sign."

But it was Rae's eyes she met when she whispered, "It's the symbol my mother kept trying to draw."

22

Arik veered onto Drayton Street beside Forsyth Park when his cell phone rang through the speakers. The screen on his dashboard lit up with Anna's name, so he pressed a button on the steering wheel to answer through the car's system. "Anna," he said, "is everything okay? Mom?"

"She's fine. In fact, she's doing even better." Anna's voice was in surround sound. "She's roused a couple of times and managed to sip some broth."

Rae reached over to squeeze his arm and smiled from the passenger's seat.

"But she kept her eyes closed pretty much the whole time," Anna continued. "Willyn says she's doing well and her vitals are stable. She thinks your mother is just worn out."

"I can imagine," Arik said, once again overcome by sadness over what his mother had endured. If there was any fairness in the world, she wouldn't remember her days of paralysis or have any long-term effects. Physical *or* psychological.

"But I'm calling for another reason." Anna hesitated. "As much as I hate to even say the words . . . I had a dream last night."

In response to the silence from Rae and Arik, she quickly added, "But it wasn't all bad."

"Not *all* bad?" Rae asked.

"Arik," Anna said, ignoring the indirect question, "do you remember your father having a blue journal? One with a deep gouge across the front?"

"Blue?" Arik turned it over in his head. "Not that I recall. He had over a hundred books he'd scribbled notes in, but he seemed to favor black and brown."

"Anna," Rae interjected, "we're on our way to Arik's house, so he can grab a change of clothes and some essentials. We're almost there now and can take a look through the journals. Then we'll call you back."

"No need for that." Anna's voice disappeared.

Rae leaned forward to stare at the screen. "Did she just hang up on us?"

"She did," Arik said, pointing. Down the road, Anna stood waving from the sidewalk in front of his house. He pulled into his drive just as Ian exited a silver Lincoln parked at the curb.

Arik and Rae slid out of the car and met Ian and Anna on the lawn. Anna seemed eager, but Arik lacked her enthusiasm. He wasn't optimistic that the journal was in his home. And even if it was, he doubted they'd be able to find it.

After he greeted Ian and the two men shook hands, Arik turned to Anna. "I'm fairly certain I've never seen the book you described." He gestured to his expansive brick home. "And I've covered every inch of the house over the years. Every nook and cranny, every secret hiding spot or *potential* hiding spot."

When she continued to appear unaffected, he pressed his lips together. "Trust me, there are too many places to be searched. If it's here, and if we hope to find it, we probably need your whole coven for the hunt."

"Actually, I already know the journal is here. And I didn't bring all the witches." She notched her chin toward the front steps. "Because we only need one."

Arik turned as the Spanish witch who'd helped with the ritual walked out from the shadows and waved. "Lucia," he said, lifting a hand in return as they walked up to join her on the porch.

He moved past her to unlock the door, speaking over his shoulder. "Not that I have any doubt you can do it," the door swung open and he let the ladies enter first, "but how exactly are you going to find the book? And how can you be sure it's here?"

"Ah, sí. This is where my special little talent comes into play." Lucia chuckled and patted the front of his shoulder. Then she pulled out a piece of paper from a pocket in her olive-hued pants.

She unfolded it and showed Arik a picture. "Anna is a talented artist, no?"

"Very," Arik agreed, studying the depiction of the blue book more closely.

"I saw this in my dream and knew it was important." Anna folded her hands across her stomach. "So I sketched it and gave it to Lucia."

"Now that I have the true image," Lucia said, picking up the explanation, "I can locate this journal anywhere in the world." She spread her hands as if to encompass the planet.

Duly impressed but no longer surprised by the talents of the coven, Arik breathed a sigh of relief. "I'm just glad we don't have to go around the world to find it."

"No, it's here," Lucia said. "And I hope you don't mind that I took a peek in your door. I wanted to see how your foyer was tiled and maybe get some ideas. Since our houses are of a similar age." She grinned like a hoyden. "And in the same neighborhood."

"What?" Anna and Ian said together.

Lucia gave a little shimmy. "The white house across the street with the sold sign? That's mine."

Anna dashed back to the window with Rae in tow. Both women looked out and squealed. "It's huge and so lovely," Anna said.

"You bought the old Chadwick place?" Rae's face shone with

delight and intrigue when she went to take Lucia's hands. "I can't believe it. You and Arik will be right across the street from each other."

Rae's obvious pleasure gave Arik's stomach a hard twist. Not because he wasn't also excited to hear Lucia's news.

But because he'd rather Lucia be his *and Rae's* new neighbor. He still imagined sharing his life with her, just as they'd once planned.

First, he thought with a stiffening of his back, they had some daunting issues to tackle. Not only of the paranormal variety, but personal as well.

He ran a hand through his hair. How was he supposed to find time to talk to her? To tell her how he felt—how he'd *always* felt—between breaking hexes, deciphering symbols, and searching for hidden journals?

The selfish part of him wanted this entire business to be over and done.

But the part of him that still grieved for his father and demanded payback for his mother—well, that part refused to let him quit.

His thoughts wandered from his father's secrets, to the mysterious blue book, and back to the phone call that had prompted this little search party. "Anna," he said, breaking in on the women's chatter, "aside from the journal, what did you dream about?"

"That's right." Rae quickly diverted from house-warmings to the question she'd never had answered. "You never told us the bad part."

"That's because it's just more of the same." Anna sent Ian a sidelong glance before she explained, "I went back to Forsyth Park. I saw Arik and his parents again. Only this time, the raven dropped this book at my feet and when the world burned . . . a woman appeared in the fire, laughing at me."

"Who was it?" Arik asked.

"I don't know. But I can tell you she bears nothing but malice. Whether for you or me, I can't yet say."

Arik nodded. "So my mother became the raven who gave you the book?"

"In a nutshell." Anna bobbed her head.

"Then what are we waiting for?" Arik turned to Lucia. "Let's find this journal."

Lucia clapped her hands together. "That means I'm up." She proceeded to roll her shoulders, blow out through her nose, and stand perfectly still for about three seconds. Then her gaze jerked to the ceiling. "Upstairs, second floor, back corner." She pointed to confirm the direction.

"Sounds like my mother's room," Arik said. Which at one time had been his father's bedroom as well. The five of them trouped up the staircase that began on one side of the large foyer and curved up and around to the second-floor landing.

Once on the upper level, Arik gestured toward the rear. "This way." He led them to his mother's bedchamber, a genteel space decorated in ivory and light aqua-blue tones. He stood back, allowing Lucia to follow the trail only she could detect.

She went straight to his mother's dresser, the same one she'd had for as long as Arik could remember. His initial reaction was to tell Lucia he'd already been through every piece of furniture in the room. But he didn't speak, reminding himself of the extraordinary things he'd seen over the last week.

As he and the others watched, Lucia pulled out a drawer from the bottom and set it on the area rug. "I don't want to be invasive," she said to Arik, pointing her hands to the contents. "There are personal items here."

"It's fine," he said, but then he kneeled down beside her. "I'll help." He lifted out a few folded scarves, a sachet that smelled as if it had once held fresh lavender, and a large green-velvet box he knew contained his mother's costume jewelry and various trinkets.

"The segments in this box are jewelry sized." He placed his palm against the lid. "I don't think there's room for a book."

"Not there," Lucia agreed, before sliding the tips of two fingernails along the lower edge of the drawer. And with a slight pull, she easily lifted out the false bottom.

Nestled between two old hand towels, lay a blue tome with a scratch marring its cover. "It even has the red ribbon hanging out." Awed yet again, Arik held up the journal for Anna to inspect.

"That's what I saw," she confirmed.

Before he'd even gained his feet, Arik was flipping through the pages. "More of the cryptic codes," he said, frustration rolling up his back and neck in waves of tension. The strain at the base of his skull turned instantly to a pounding ache.

"Here, let me." Rae set her hand over his, a plea for patience in her light brown eyes. The simple touch calmed him instantly, making him aware of his heightened stress.

"Good idea," he said, handing her the book with one hand and using the other to trail down the silky sheen of her hair. He felt the need to soak in her soothing energy. He yearned to hold her close. To just hold her.

Knowing when he needed to relax, he sat on the edge of his mother's bed while Rae perused the pages. A few minutes passed quietly, with only one aggrieved sigh coming from Rae.

Arik doubted she realized she'd released the sound, an indication she was finding nothing useful.

Another long minute dragged by, and then she cried, "Yes!" startling everyone else into action. Arik leaped up and went to look over her shoulder as Anna, Ian, and Lucia crowded in from the front.

"The last entry is in English," Rae said, her fingers splaying the pages, marking her place as she held the journal out to Arik. "I think it's for you to read. By yourself if you'd prefer."

He glared at the writing as if afraid the legible words would somehow convert to the indecipherable scribbles he was used to seeing. "Okay," he said, though he made no move to accept the book, his hands remaining down by his sides.

Rae sidled closer, the warmth of her side pressing against his. A silent show of support.

Needing no further urging, he took the journal. "I think everyone should hear," he said to the others before refocusing on the beige paper. "It's my father's handwriting."

Had he known there was a chance he'd never return that night? Had some sense caused him to leave his son one small clue?

Arik cleared his throat and read aloud.

Tonight is the night! After all the years of research and the decades of lost knowledge, we will finally, finally, learn the full story. We know the location of the missing piece, the one item that can unlock our past, and give us the truth of our ancestry.

Tonight we go to retrieve the medallion, hidden these last few centuries in a place so near, a place I have visited often.

But only recently have I discovered the document to tie it all together. At night! That was the missing element. The light of the moon must be shining down.

And only my Marit can see the way.

My beautiful Akasha.

And only her chosen one can accompany her there.

My whole life, I knew the medallion had to be in Savannah. How fitting that all this time, the future has been lying with the past.

Marit is getting dressed, so I write this entry as I wait for her. My beloved, my savior. Tonight we have our reward.

Tonight we go to Bonaventure.

"Bonaventure," Rae said, rubbing her arms. "A cemetery, of all places."

"And that word again." Arik snapped the book shut. "Akasha," he breathed, feeling the odd sound on his tongue. "I meant to ask Mahalia if she'd ever heard it, but I forgot after she saw your neck." He angled toward Rae.

"I forgot, too." She raised a shoulder. "She was so upset by the symbol and its connection to her mother."

"Rae," Ian said, "from my perspective last night, it seemed as if Marit called *you* Akasha. Did it feel that way to you?"

Rae rubbed under her ear, as Arik had seen her do so often throughout the day. "I can't be sure," she said. "I don't remember much during those few seconds she and I were connected. The electricity hit, and I went blank."

"The word Akasha, and the symbol on your neck." Ian crossed his arms and looked every bit the lawyer. "Two things associated with Arik's mother. And now you."

"Or so we think," Anna said. "We can't be certain Marit was calling Rae that word."

"But I think she was," Lucia chimed in. "That's the impression I got."

Arik took Rae's hand before he sighed and said, "So did I."

Rae held his gaze for a long moment. "So if I am this Akasha, just as your mother was, if she somehow passed this sign and a name on to me . . ."

Arik finished what she couldn't quite bring herself to say. "If you're the Akasha like my mother was, then you might be able to see whatever it was my parents went to find." He swallowed against a throat gone dry. "What they went in search of the night they were attacked."

"He mentioned a medallion." Rae's eyes were still lasered to his. "And only the Akasha can see the way."

As if they were alone in the room, Arik and Rae continued to stare at each other.

At last, Anna asked in a quiet voice, "Are you two planning what I think you are?"

Arik waited for Rae to answer first.

"We have to go to Bonaventure," Rae said, her hand tightening on his. "We have to go to the cemetery."

Arik glanced down at the journal he still held. As he remembered his father's mention of moonlight, his heart clenched as if trapped in a vise. "And we have to go at night."

23

When Rae walked into the library, Arik was still poring over the book. They'd decided to postpone the trip to Bonaventure, since heavy cloud cover blocked the moon and threatened more rain.

That, and he'd wanted to inspect the journal more closely, to scour the pages for anything he could translate, any speck of information that might tell them more about the cemetery, the medallion, or what to expect.

She cleared her throat to gently draw his notice.

He glanced up, and looked so darn cute, with his golden hair mussed and a blank expression on his face. Until he noticed her and gave a heart-stopping grin.

"Anna just called. She said we shouldn't try to get to the island tonight." Rae gestured to the high windows. "The storm just landed on the island, and it's too dangerous to be out in a boat."

"Storm? Tonight?" He glanced out the window to the falling dusk and then to a brass clock on the wall. "How long have I been at this?" He ran both hands over his head and propped his elbows on the desk. "I feel like I just came up from a thousand leagues under the sea."

"You've been drowning, all right. It's almost seven."

He glanced out the window again. Clouds the color of pewter loomed in the sky, blanketing the last of the dying light. "I can't stay away from Mom this long."

"Anna also said," Rae told him, strolling closer, "that you are not to worry about your mother. They all know the pressure you're under right now, and the trouble you're facing. That *we're* facing. And she insisted that there are plenty of them to take shifts sitting with Marit."

Skirting the desk, she leaned against it beside his chair. "Believe me, Arik, they don't mind helping. It wasn't that long ago that the coven faced something similar, and they are well-acquainted with strength in numbers."

"I know." Arik pushed the blue journal aside. "I just hate taking advantage of her hospitality and leaving Mom alone." He rubbed a hand over his thigh in agitation. "What if she wakes up and I'm not there?"

Rae pulled her cell phone from her back pocket and wiggled it. "I have Anna and Willyn in my contacts for video chat. You'll see your mother the minute she wakes long enough to realize where she is."

"You've got it covered, don't you?" He hooked a hand around her hip and shifted her to face him. "You've got *me* covered."

"I do try," she said and laughed.

When he leaned in to put his head on her chest, the keenest yearning tugged inside. She released a sigh. How had she ever expected to get over these feelings? To stop loving the one person who seemed to have been created just for her?

After nine years, he was still the only man who could turn her inside out. The only one who could wrap up her heart in golden ribbons, simply by offering a slow, sweet smile.

Rae laced her fingers in his hair. She'd always loved feeling it, like gilded silk. For a moment, they sat contentedly that way, only soft caresses and comforting strokes.

Outside, rain broke free to pummel the earth, and Arik lifted his head. Then he rose to press a brief kiss on her mouth.

"Another thunderstorm," he said, moving to stand between her legs. Now he looked down on her, his palms on her collarbones, thumbs lightly teasing her neck. "Déjà vu."

"I don't mind this repeat performance." She closed her eyes beneath his tender ministrations, remembering their brief but meaningful interlude in Anna's solarium the night before.

"There's something about the sound of rain." He pushed her hair back over her shoulders. Then gazed at her as if longing to devour. "And the wildness of a storm."

"Mm-hm." She recognized the heat in his stare—compelling, intense, looking at her as if she were the only woman in the world.

His palms skimmed down her arms, making her tremble. "Will you promise to give me a kiss in the sunshine?"

"Yes," she said, turning her hands over to catch hold of his. Still clasping his fingers, she stood to meet him.

"And a kiss on Sunday?" Arik looped both of their arms behind her back and trapped her against him.

"I promise." Her voice purred with sensuality.

He took her mouth, delving deep before retreating with a slight pull on her bottom lip. "And a kiss at Christmas?"

Nine months away. She knew what he was asking. "I hope so," she said, readying herself for a leap, a jump into full honesty with an undercurrent of vulnerability. But she'd found her words from the night before to be true. She *did* trust him.

"I want that, Arik. More than anything." She fought the ghost of old fears when she admitted, "You're still my favorite dream."

"I can't tell you what it means to hear you say that." His features seemed pained as he released her hand to stroke her cheek. "What's inside me, what I feel for you—then, now, and all the days in between—I want to make you mine again, to promise you forever . . ."

He hesitated, and she quaked within.

"But I'm afraid I've lost what we once were. That if I offer my heart, you'll call me a liar and a hypocrite." His arms cradled her, not with lust but with a tenderness that bound them together with silvered threads. "I'm afraid you'll throw my love back in my face."

"Arik," she whispered, in complete surrender, "why would I throw away the one thing I've longed for all these years? Not just love. Not the love of a man." Her eyes blurred as tears rose. "But *your* love, Arik. Only you."

His breath left him in a rush, and he crushed her in his embrace. "How is it I've missed you for so long, yet it feels like you never left?"

"I know," she said on a laugh. "It's the same for me. I've been so angry with you, but those lost years seem like a fading mirage."

Here, Rae thought as he lifted her in a sumptuous kiss, here was where she truly belonged. In Arik's arms, in his life. In Savannah. As he pushed her back on the desk, she gave herself over to him.

And knew she was finally home.

Yearning grew and fires burned, their bodies tight and hands searching. Arik moaned against her lips and slid his hand under her dress, stroking her thigh with a feathered touch.

Her breath caught when he eased her panties to the side.

"Is it too soon?" His mouth brushed hers as he spoke.

"Hell, no." Undone by need, Rae tightened her grip. "It's been too long."

~~~

Tracing her soft flesh, Arik marveled over the things that still fascinated him. The things that always had him wanting more. Her satiny skin, her sweet, female scent, and the long lashes feathering above her cheekbones when she closed her eyes.

Like now, when he plunged his fingers into her. "Rae. God,

Rae." He reveled in the feel of her. Wondrously hot, enticingly wet.

His fingers moved, working inside and out, stroking the spots he knew she loved.

As her warmth tightened around him, her head fell back, her gaze met his. "Arik," she whimpered. Then her eyes glazed over as she came.

Heavy-lidded with contentment, she went limp, barely able to cling to his arms.

It was all he could take.

In one move he picked her up from the desk, carrying her up the library stairs to the mezzanine, ducking into a secret panel that exited into a corridor of the south wing. Right beside his bedroom.

He kicked open the door, entering a very male domain with heavy wood furniture. The bed, large in Victorian style, was all too inviting as he laid her on the velvet cover.

His fingers dug into her hips as he gazed at her long, lovely form. He leaned over to nibble at her mouth, and she ripped his shirt up over his head.

Returning the favor, he eased off her dress and tossed it to the floor to pile with his shirt.

In a blur of stolen kisses and searching hands, they managed to divest themselves of their remaining clothes.

And that was fine by him. The only thing he wanted touching his skin was Rae. Her hands, her mouth, her eager lips. He covered her then, pressing the length of his torso against her flat stomach and pert breasts.

Her nipples hardened at the contact, and he heard someone groan. Then he realized it was him.

She took his finger in her mouth and suckled, the erotic move driving him right up to the edge. "Damn, woman, I've missed you so badly. I've missed talking to you late at night and first thing in the morning." His body ached, his blood fired with desire. "I've missed seeing you, touching you, tasting you."

He pressed himself between her thighs but held back, just to tease. "And making love to you."

"Now, Arik." She writhed beneath him. "I need you now." She ran her fingers down his neck, his chest, and over his abs taut with restraint.

When she reached around to rake her nails down his back, animal instinct took over for them both. He fisted his hands in the rich, dark of her hair and positioned himself.

Still, he waited. "I never stopped wanting you, Rae."

And as he always used to do, he caged her face with his palms. "I never stopped loving you."

~~~

While Arik hovered above her, Rae paused, taking a second to study the man she loved.

She remembered this ritual from before. Remembered her heart slamming into her ribs and the sweet anticipation as his fingertips trailed sweetly over her cheeks, and then down between the valley of her breasts. Along the sides of her belly and finally, slower, he gently teased her thighs apart.

He'd always enjoyed heightening the expectancy, drawing out that last perfect moment.

This perfect moment, as his mouth found hers again, his tongue stoking the sounds of her pleasure. Before he slid inside her, and slowly withdrew. Only to plunge again.

Arik rocked within her, and she locked her legs around him, slipping into ecstasy while he took her with long, leisured thrusts.

Both familiar and thrilling, his lovemaking filled her with a wondrous mix of desire and affection. And when he said her name, like a prayer, shivering pleasure washed through her body.

Melded together like molten gold, they moved in sync. The rhythm quickened, pushing her further, until a glorious ache began to throb inside her. Tightening, pulling, promising bliss.

Her system raged under his gifted hands. Her heart trembled and threatened to burst.

When his mouth captured hers again, her heart did open. It took him inside. And as sweet madness consumed them both, she held on to him. She held on for her life.

Arik flooded her senses. He consumed her soul.

And when pleasure pushed her over that edge, the two of them fell together.

24

As specified in the journal, silvery moonlight fell across the stone entrance and locked gate of Bonaventure Cemetery. Rae took in the giant oaks, their drapery of Spanish moss swaying in the breeze. And a few quicksilver clouds churning overhead.

A graveyard big enough to get lost in. At night. With the potential for demon activity.

The nape of Rae's neck crawled with chills.

Other than the wind in the trees, the only sounds she heard were the cries of night birds and the barely audible slam of a car door—the last of the coven witches and their men arriving, having parked some distance away and in spots deemed inconspicuous.

Officially, the cemetery was closed, but the business they had here tonight required stealth and secrecy. Fortunately, the office was dark and quiet, and the low fence wasn't much of a hurdle.

"That will be the last of them," Anna said from where she stood at the fence, studying the vast expanse of graveyard. "I'll go wait with the others."

Though it was up to Rae and Arik to find the mysterious medallion, the coven's magick was a weapon against demons. As were the charmed weapons they'd created for their own war against the underworld.

The men had battled monsters before as well, armed with various weaponry imbued with magick and forged with demon-sensitive metals. So having all eighteen of them here tonight was a no-brainer.

Especially since this was the last known destination of Arik's parents. The place they'd intended to go the night of the violent assault.

When her pocket vibrated, Rae pulled out her phone and heaved a sigh.

"Emma again?" Arik asked.

"Yes. I told her I'd call her tonight, after we were finished."

"She's already given us more than one day." He reached over and rubbed her back encouragingly. "She's bound to be getting frustrated."

"I know, and I feel guilty dodging her calls." Rae shoved the cell phone back in her pocket. "But what am I supposed to say? 'Well, I recently helped Arik lift a curse from his mother, and now I've been marked by magick. Oh, and by the way, there may be a few demons coming after me now.' Yeah," she scoffed. "I can see that going over *real* well."

"Your sister is familiar with magick. She can handle it."

"Yet you didn't stop by Mahalia's to tell her either." Rae slid her gaze to him.

"I'd rather wait until we know more. After yesterday . . ."

"I know." Rae took his hand. "She was distraught."

"And I'm not ready to put her through that again. Not until we have some answers." Arik squeezed her fingers and tossed a glance back to the large group who were deep in discussion.

Rae followed his gaze, noting the moving hands of Paige and her husband Chris. The two ex-Army soldiers were probably devising a strategy for the mission.

Studying the intent expressions of concentration they all wore, Rae again felt thankful to have everyone's help. From the front gate to the back edge near the river, Bonaventure Cemetery stretched half a mile in that direction alone. If she were truly the Akasha now, searching the massive area would fall to her.

But with dense trees and a virtual forest of monuments—plenty of hiding spots—she could focus better knowing her back was covered.

Arik hefted the wicked-looking sword he held in his other hand. "You know, my dad always called this the go-to weapon. If ever in doubt, this was the blade to carry." With a glint of metal under moonlight, he put the sword in the scabbard he wore.

"I always wondered if he wasn't a little bit mad." His grin flashed in the dark, but held a touch of grief. "Why would anyone need a defense like this?"

Rae shivered to imagine what kind of beasts had inspired such weaponry. Monsters Arik might soon be hacking at if things went wrong.

"Hey." Noticing her distress, he took her chin gently in his hand. "Maybe this will all be over tonight. If we find the medallion, we might get the information my parents wanted so badly."

"I hope you're right." She released a breath, comforted by his warm touch. "Then you and I can finally get on with the life we've denied ourselves."

Doing her best to be optimistic, to imagine the best outcome, she lowered her voice. "Including a few kisses in the sun."

The look he gave her held a hint of mischief. "After last night, I think I'm becoming partial to rain."

Rae laughed and pressed her lips to his. "Well, here's one in the moonlight. We can check it off our list."

"The first of many," he whispered, rubbing his thumb over her bottom lip before pulling away.

"We've been talking." Anna's voice drifted to them as she walked up. "The grid search Arik suggested makes sense, and we can all spread out to keep you both surrounded, sort of a fluid net cast out on all sides. The girls and I should see any uninvited guests approaching, and we'll be paired up in couples."

"Sounds like a plan," Arik said.

Anna waved to the others, and then she, Arik, and Rae hopped the fence. The others swiftly followed, and once everyone was over, they headed behind the brick office building. Choosing the area near the right side of the perimeter road, they began the search.

With the other women and men fanned out in all directions, Rae and Arik began methodically checking every square foot. The blue journal had stated that only Arik's mother could see the way, and that she was the Akasha. But in reality, none of them knew what seeing "the way" actually meant.

Rae kept her eyes peeled for the elusive medallion, also mentioned in the book, but they were all still operating on the assumption she could detect anything at all.

With painfully slow attention to detail, they walked up and down each row of a particular section. Along with a variety of headstones, statues, crypts, and other monuments, a dense mixture of shrubs and trees littered the surroundings.

Standing as sentinels, the massive oaks reached long, twisted limbs out over a mixture of ferns, azaleas, and sago palms. Just more obstacles they had to investigate.

Simple gravel and dirt roads cordoned off sectors, but the process still demanded patience. Especially since they couldn't be certain what they were looking for.

After over an hour had passed, mostly in silence, Rae and Arik moved on to a rear segment along the river.

Rae skidded to a sudden stop. She blinked to clear her vision, but the strange phenomenon remained.

"Do you see that?" she asked, pointing to a white marble crypt. The massive burial place was about ten feet tall and almost as wide, with a pale blue glow emanating from the cracks of the doors.

"See what?" Arik asked, speaking low as if he might disturb the residents.

Stunned, Rae froze in place. "You don't see the light coming from that crypt?"

"No," he said. "Let me get closer."

As they crept toward the building, Rae gave a soft whistle. Her signal to Anna.

Anna and Ian hurried over as Arik stood staring at the crypt. "This one?" he asked, shaking his head. "I still don't see it."

Rae walked up behind him and put a hand on his arm.

Arik jerked. "I see it now."

Rae removed her hand to advance.

"Wait," Arik said. "I lost it." He stepped forward to stand beside her. "Rae, touch me again."

She cupped her palm over his shoulder and he nodded. "That's it. I have to be in contact with you to see it."

"Let me try." Anna came up to flank Rae and took her hand. After a few seconds, she shook her head. "Nope. Nothing."

"I love you, girl," Rae said with a smirk, "but I guess that means you're not my chosen one."

Anna chuckled and nudged her with an elbow.

A rustling on the ground, and Rae looked back to see the others crowding around.

"You found something?" Shauni asked, lifting her hand to let a small bird alight on her finger.

"The crypt is glowing," Arik told them before turning back to Rae. "Guess this is where we split off."

He touched the hilt of the sword hanging at his waist and spoke to Anna. "If what my father wrote is true, no one else will be able to go with us. But," he added, his features falling into serious lines, "if you hear anything . . ."

"We'll do all we can to get inside." She inclined her head, holding his gaze in silent affirmation.

Heaving a sigh, Arik asked Rae, "Are you ready?"

In answer, she took his hand. Together they moved to the crypt, each reaching out with their free hand to open the double-doors.

With the barrier gone, the pale light washed over them, and once inside Rae discovered the source. The back wall rippled with blue waves, like the reflection of pool water at night. "Do you see that?" she asked.

"Yes." Arik released her hand. "And now it's gone."

"It looks like a portal or gate. I assume we need to enter together." To get a closer look, she edged around the sarcophagus in the center of the room, a large rectangle of limestone with ivy and trailing flowers etched on the exterior.

When she reached the back corner, a cold sensation pierced her body, like a cool wind blowing straight through her core. She stutter-stepped to a halt and pressed her hand to her stomach. "What was that?" she murmured.

Arik was at her side before she could blink. "Are you hurt? We should leave."

"No. No. I'm fine, but . . ." She put his hand on her midsection. "Right here, I felt something strange. Definitely a source of energy or," she stumbled over the word, "*magick*."

Arik hugged her tight, clearly worried for her safety.

She accepted the bolstering embrace. "You're still trying to protect me."

"I'll never stop," he said, turning to speak softly into her ear.

"And I love you for it." She eased from his arms and faced the wavy illumination.

It was then she caught the glisten of light. Just a small glimmer. She stared into the corner, where leaves and other debris had gathered.

She stepped toward the glint, and the cool breeze wafted over her cheek. Along with the unnatural sensation, a rush of certainty washed through her. "Oh, Arik."

She faced him with sympathy clutching her chest. "I'm

sorry. I don't know how or why . . . I can't explain it, but I feel something."

Brow furrowed, he tilted his head. "What do you mean?"

Baffled, she lifted her shoulders. "I think I sense your father here. This place, the crypt, it might be where . . ." She couldn't finish.

Arik straightened as understanding dawned on his face. "Where he died."

"Yes," she whispered, hating the pain she saw shadowed in his eyes. She wanted nothing more than to take it from him, but there was no running from the truth anymore.

Rae went to the corner and kneeled. She brushed away leaves and lifted out the object, the glinting item that had pulled at her in some inexplicable way.

When she recognized what she held, she forced down her own sorrow. She channeled strength and fortitude. Because Arik would need that from her.

Rising, she turned to him and held out her hand. "I'm so sorry."

25

Arik took the mangled object from Rae. Even in the small beam of his pocket flashlight, he recognized what it was.

"These are my father's glasses." The brown and silver frame was twisted, one lens cracked with a small splatter of brown on its inner surface.

Blood.

As he held the evidence of what his father had suffered, as he imagined how horrific those last moments had been, Arik's vision began to cloud.

His sight darkened with pure black wrath, and inside his body anger boiled, a volcano rising from the depths.

He wanted to rage. To shout. To destroy. He wanted to tear this damned crypt apart. Block by marble block.

Fists clenched and back stiff, he sucked in a breath and imagined the damage he could do.

Then he looked at Rae, standing quietly in the corner.

Air trickled slowly from his compressed lungs—the release of blind temper and the return of logic. Venting his fury wouldn't bring his father back. And it wouldn't erase the mark on her neck.

Whether he liked it or not, she was knee-deep in the mire, right beside him. Just as he'd realized with his mother's ritual, there was no other option but to push on. No choice but to continue forward.

Which meant walking through that gate to face whatever

waited on the other side.

Him. And Rae.

Together.

"Arik?" she asked, a number of different questions in the one small word.

"I'm all right," he lied. "Or at least, I'm dealing."

"I can't imagine what this feels like for you. We can stop now and try another—"

"No," he barked. And felt instantly contrite. "No." He softened his voice. "All that matters at this moment is taking the next step."

He slid the broken glasses into his pocket. Stored them away for another time.

"We're here now." He made a sound of derision. "And we're obviously in the right place." The same spot his mother and father had discovered. "And most importantly, we're still standing. Still alive."

He shifted his gaze to the blank wall, no longer rippling with light. Not for him, anyway, in the absence of Rae's touch. "If I could go in there without you, I would. I'd have Anna and the others drag you away." Frowning, he looked back at her. "But I can't."

"No," she said, drawing herself up and crossing her arms. "You certainly can't."

"I don't know why you've been chosen to be a part of this, but I'm damned sure not making the same mistake twice." One stride and his hands were in her hair, holding her in place as he plundered her lips, kissing her long and deep.

He would never let her go again. If danger was coming, he wanted to be right by her side.

"Okay," she gasped when they pulled apart. "I forgive you for saying you'd send me away." She grinned but put a finger to his mouth to stall his next comment. "But only because I would do the same."

The teasing look in her eyes turned to one of fear. "Because I'm scared for you, too, Arik. But we have to find out. We have to know."

She touched the symbol on her neck. "I don't think this will just go away."

"No," he admitted, despising the truth. "There's a reason my father spent his life—*gave* his life—for this pursuit. And we're as close as he ever came. As much as we might wish it otherwise, this is our fate."

He kissed her lightly again. "But that doesn't mean history has to repeat itself."

Taking a step toward the back wall, he took her hand. And the pale blue light erupted.

"My father would want me to go on," he said, his resolve increasing with every heartbeat. "He'd want us to pick up where they left off." His mother and his father.

Now Rae and him.

"Then let's go in." Rae beat him into the light by inches, her hand still in his. She pulled him through.

Instantly, the world changed. One second they were enclosed by a tomb, the next they stood in a limitless cavern. At least, that's how it appeared, with rock the color of soot for as far as the eye could see.

Arik turned on the little flashlight again, though the small beam didn't do much good. Not in such an enormous chamber.

He and Rae were on a high ledge, overlooking a subterranean gorge. The ravine stretched out in both directions and was too deep to even see the bottom.

Examining the ground beneath their feet, he found that the ledge descended in a zig-zag pattern, like switchback roads on a high mountain. The precarious walkway led down to the gorge and a curved bridge cut from the same dark stone.

"What is this place?" Rae whispered in awe. "How can it be below the cemetery?"

"I'm not sure that's where we still are." Arik held tightly to her, unwilling to let her move too far away.

Somewhere in the shadows, something skittered, and the sound of falling pebbles echoed in the gloom. "Let's move," he said, illuminating the pathway down.

As soon as he repositioned the light, both he and Rae stopped short. "Oh, no," she said, throwing her arm in front of him as if defending him from what he might discover.

A skeleton lay several feet below, the dry bones resting in a pile. Not a random heap, he realized, but the fetal position. As one might curl up if in great pain.

Or if they were dying.

"I'm fine," he assured her, aware she'd thought they'd found his father's remains.

Because he feared the same thing.

Silently, he reminded himself of the goal at hand. *Do what you came for. Then get Rae out of here.*

He drew near the yellowed bones, trailed the light over the skull and pelvis. And heaved a sigh of relief. "It's female. Not my father."

Rae clapped a hand to her chest and also sighed. "How can you tell?"

"The pelvis is . . ." He squeezed her fingers. "I'll tell you later."

"Okay," she tried for a laugh. Then she leaned in and, gripping his hand, moved the cone of light farther out. "What about that one?"

Another skeleton, arms and legs splayed, as if the second person had fallen onto their back and never gotten back up again.

Gritting his teeth, Arik performed the same quick assessment. Relieved all over again to find it was another woman. "Female," he said shortly, his attention drawn to the second skeleton's closed hand.

"She's holding something," he said, excitement coursing

through him. The object trapped in the white cage of her hand appeared to be circular and metallic. Greenish in color like—"Brass," he finished aloud. With the verdigris patina that formed after many years.

He leaned down and pried open the fingers, a few of the tiny bones breaking free and toppling to the dark ground. He ran a thumb across the disc, tested its weight. And glanced back up to Rae. "I think we found the medallion."

"Oh, good. Good." She shifted on her feet, clearly as uncomfortable in the ominous environment as he was.

He stood again, still holding on to Rae, and began climbing back up. "We have what we came for," he said. "Now let's take it back and see what it tells us."

"Your father wrote that it would unlock the past." As Rae drew near the doorway, it lit up again, an invitation.

"I've been thinking about that." Arik tightened his grip on the medallion. "I think he meant it was a type of key." Hands clasped, they looked at each other.

Arik sent Rae a crooked grin. "And I think I know what it unlocks."

~~~

Thirty minutes after exiting the crypt, Arik pulled the car into his driveway. Rae sat in the passenger seat, with Willyn and Dare in back.

Willyn had assured him that his mother was in the capable hands of Sylvie and Joseph, with Claire, Joe, and the Attingers as reliable backup. And at the moment, Arik was more grateful than ever that his mother was safe and sound, and far away.

The more he rolled the idea around in his head, the more certain he was that he knew what to do with the medallion. No magick or special training required, he simply recognized the disc for what it was.

Brass. Likely centuries old if the craftsmanship were to be believed. And in a style he was well-acquainted with.

"How long are you going to make us wait?" Rae demanded, unhitching her seatbelt to scramble out her door.

"Just one more minute." He grabbed her as she rounded the front of the car and gave her a quick smack on the lips. "Bear with me, all right?"

"Ugh." She made an unladylike sound and rolled her eyes. "Fine. Then let's go." She turned to wave at the others as vehicles parked in the drive or at the curb, coven witches and their men piling out.

The unknown still loomed, and the results of what Arik was about to try were still completely unpredictable. So erring on the side of caution—and at this point, good old-fashioned curiosity—the whole crew had come back to Arik's for the big reveal.

Or so he hoped.

Bounding up the stairs with Rae on his heels, Arik turned the key in the lock and let himself inside. By now everyone else was filing onto the sidewalk or tromping up the stairs after him and Rae, so he simply continued the parade through the corridors leading them to one side of the mansion.

To the area in which the library was housed.

"Arik," Rae said in a raspy voice of wonder.

When she didn't say anything else, he glanced over. But she only shook her head at him, with eyes round and her bottom lip tucked between her teeth. As if she were stopping herself from saying anything more.

"You've figured it out, haven't you?" He winked at her, his brilliant Rae.

His *beautiful Akasha*.

But this time, the idea of following his father's path didn't bring melancholy, nor did it cause him frustration. Instead, a sense of peace stole over Arik, because despite the loss and pain they'd endured, he was, at last, about to end his father's quest.

Buoyed by the notion, he helped Rae push open both doors to the library, leaving them spread wide for the large group behind them to enter. And as they did—Anna and Ian, Claudia and Cole, Ethan and Lucia, and all of the others who'd been so fearless and supportive—the huge room filled with a low buzz.

The animated sounds of people on the verge of discovery.

"Take a seat or get comfortable wherever you'd like," Rae directed, taking up the position of lady of the house. A role Arik could hardly wait for her to play for real, and for good.

Because once this was settled and they could take a breather . . . there was the little matter of the ring upstairs. The one tucked away in a drawer in his room, snug in its little black box, just waiting to return to its true owner.

Arik's chest began to feel funny, so he swallowed the jangle of nerves and joy at the thought of proposing to Rae.

Again.

Instead he focused on the item he'd rushed home to examine. The object in the library, a few centuries old, constructed from hardy wood. Wood and brass.

With everyone settled into chairs and sofas, on steps or their own two feet, Arik edged over to the wall, because he wanted to stand behind the antique. To give his guests a clear view of the globe.

Lifting the medallion he had in his hand, Arik caught Rae's eye and gave her a grin. Then he looked to Anna and Claudia, and gave them a nod. With his free hand he felt the bottom of the globe, searching for the strange indentation he'd once felt before.

"It fits," he said under his breath. "I know it fits." Carefully, he slid the medallion into place, using his fingertips to line it up with the hollow on the bottom of the sphere.

He pushed up and slowly rotated. Until he heard a little

click.

Two things happened in quick succession. First, the globe split into five pieces, opening like a flower spreading its petals for the sun.

And second, Rae released a great gasp, her arms spreading, as if she were mimicking the expanding globe.

Golden rays shot from the orb.

Just as a pale purple glow flared in Rae's eyes.

Stunned, Arik stood immobile, terrified he'd just opened a version of Pandora's Box, while Anna and several others gasped or murmured words of concern.

But Rae recovered quickly. She cast him an expression of shock but quickly said, "I'm ok. I'm ok. But . . ."

"What?" Arik made a move to go to her.

She held out a palm. "No. I'm okay. Just energized. All fizzy and light inside." She smiled at him and shrugged. "I have no idea what just happened, but I'm tired of guessing."

She shook a finger at the globe. "So will you please just tell us what's inside that thing?"

Torn between worry for her and the driving need to know for himself, Arik peered into the globe. The five sections had writing on the interior, dark squiggles in what looked like very old penmanship, or calligraphy, or—

"Damn it!" He couldn't stop himself from bursting out. Before anyone could ask, he jerked his head up and said, "It's in the same coded script. The same cryptic language I still can't decipher."

Disappointment ripped at him. He could feel every hope he'd harbored or promise he'd made being torn from inside. The questions weren't answered. The quest wasn't over.

Crushed, beaten, Arik shook his head and said again, "I just can't read it."

A thump and squeak by the open doors had them all turning back to look. A mix of concern and elation thrummed through

Arik, when from her wheelchair being pushed by Joseph, his mother spoke out, clear as a bell. "But I can."

26

Just down the road from the Bonaventure Cemetery, Mahalia kneeled before her altar. She'd spent a full day and half the night searching her house, looking for any scrap of paper with her mother's scribbles.

But as she'd feared, she'd thrown them all away. After her mother's death, Mahalia had cleaned the entire house, clearing away all reminders of those horrific final weeks.

Including all of her mother's attempts to draw the symbol. The mark and other unreadable lines, whatever else she'd been trying to tell Mahalia.

When her exploration of the house turned up nothing, Mahalia realized she would need help. That she would have to ask for divine assistance.

Though none of the sketches remained, Mahalia was certain as the rising sun that the mark on Rae Scott's neck was the same symbol her mother had tried to recreate.

Even without her hands and tongue, her mother had struggled to communicate. Again and again she'd tried.

But Mahalia had never understood the importance.

"I'm sorry, Mama." Mahalia crossed her hands over her heart. "But I'll do right by you now. I'll do whatever it takes."

She reached for a long matchstick and began lighting candles.

Last night, she'd known she would need the help of the *loa*, the voodoo deities, but she'd waited for a day to pass. Now it was a Saturday—Yemaya's chosen day—and the most likely time she would answer a cry for help.

Mahalia blew out the match and set it aside. Candles flickered atop her altar now, the wooden structure draped in white fabric to honor Yemaya. And in red as well, for the patriarch of the loa, Papa Legba.

She would invoke Papa Legba first, as he served as gatekeeper to the Seven African Powers, intermediary to the other loa. She had to call on him if she hoped to reach Yemaya.

Preparing her offerings, she poured a tumbler of rum and set it on the altar. Next to it she set down a bowl of candy. "Papa Legba," she intoned, "open the door for me." She began with the traditional words, and continued with the recitation.

Once she felt Legba had been appeased, she asked for communion with Yemaya. For this, she arranged two more offerings upon the altar—cornmeal and molasses.

When she felt the presence of the second loa, she spoke again. "Welcome, Yemaya, *La Sirene Balianne.*"

As the loa of home, women's affairs, and motherhood, Yemaya was the most able to give Mahalia what she desired.

"Sacred Yemaya, hear my plea. Place my mother's words in my sight. Bring her missive to my mind." Mahalia bowed her head, eyes shut tight. She waited for a response and tried to conjure the images.

She pictured the paper, and her mother's scratches. "I beg of you, Yemaya. Make it clear."

A fluid sensation rolled over Mahalia, and when the drawings crystalized in her mind, she opened her eyes, grabbing the notepad and pen she had nearby.

Without thinking, without interpreting, she let the loa guide her hand. She slowly traced ink on paper, until her fingers went numb, and then fell lax.

Task complete, she set aside the paper, giving proper thanks to Yemaya and Papa Legba. Out of respect, she took her time and closed the ritual.

But once done, she snatched up the paper. The inscriptions were clean and clear, fully legible, and as she'd thought, the symbol was the same as the one on Rae's skin.

But the word beneath.

"Blessed saints," she whispered, her voice shaking.

That word jumped from the paper and speared dread deep into her soul.

"Oh, Mama. I'll finish this for you." She scrambled to her feet and hurried to find her purse. She'd wasted too much time, too many years, and now the past had risen up with a vengeance.

If she weren't in such a rush, she'd call her daughter to give her a ride. She didn't like driving at night.

But she couldn't wait for that. She couldn't spare another minute.

Mahalia huffed in her breaths as she raced outside, frantic to get to Arik and Rae.

To tell them the name of the monster they faced.

27

Water dribbled down her newly healed body. Clean, clear, floral-scented water.

After her battle with the great flying beast, two ghouls—now subservient to *her*—had taken her to a room with water flooding from cracks in the stone ceiling. Once she'd rinsed away the filth, they'd escorted her to an adjoining chamber with a large bathing vessel, filled with the lovely warm liquid she was now exiting.

Lifting her arms, she allowed the two pale creatures to drape her in a soft white material. Then she reached for a nearby platter and picked up a sweetly flavored ball of the nutritional sludge. She popped it in her mouth.

Mmm. The rush of strength and vitality was such a high. She might become addicted to the gooey mush.

Now that she'd been allowed the tasty version.

But, of course, her luxurious reprieve came too swiftly to an end. When the two ghouls dropped their arms, faced the arched opening in the wall, and bowed their heads, she knew a master had arrived.

Her wary gaze rose to the doorway.

"It is time," the dark one said. And nothing more.

It was on the tip of her tongue to ask "Time for what?" But the change in her status felt too new and too fragile to risk backsliding.

Besides, her gut told her the punishments were over. In

hindsight, she was sure they had actually been tests. Yet the reason for those tests remained unclear.

But she definitely didn't want to go backward. Back to pain and filth, back to bites and cuts. Back to the pit.

So she lowered her eyes—but not her head—and followed the master out of the bathing rooms, and then up a set of wide winding stairs that had been carved out of the cavernous stone architecture.

Would she ever see the sky again? Would she forever be trapped in this dark place filled with monsters?

She went meekly with the master because she wanted those answers. She *needed* them. So she let herself be led to a round room illuminated by torches on the wall.

And the only other object in the chamber was a granite table situated in the center. The master indicated she should climb onto the hard surface.

She hesitated, only for the space of a heartbeat, and then she acquiesced.

Once atop the table—which suddenly felt more like a sacrificial altar—she obeyed her instinct and lay down on her back, legs stretched out and arms at her side.

After all, obedience had been one of her first lessons.

As soon as she did, the other masters filed into the room, encircling the table and obliterating her view of anything but their giant, mist-enshrouded forms.

"Do you accept your masters?"

She couldn't tell who had spoken. They hovered so closely, and they all looked so similar.

Still, she nodded and managed a shaky, "Yes."

In a synchronized move, they reached in to grasp the material covering her body. In unison, they ripped the fabric away.

She flinched but didn't cry out.

For silence had been a lesson as well.

"Do you seek the truth?" Two voices rang out together.

"Yes," she said quickly, trembling to be naked and exposed once again.

"We offer our gift." This time several of the dark ones intoned with heavy resonance.

"But you must pay a price." So many voices now, as if all of the masters spoke in a deep timbre that shuddered the air.

"I'll pay," she said, without being prodded, her voice a rough rasp. She longed for the missing parts of her memory and her mind. She was desperate just to know her name.

Instead of answering, the dark ones put their palms on her bare skin, their large hands covering her head, face, breasts, legs.

She closed her eyes and tried not to think about the strange and revolting way their flesh connected with hers. How their touch felt like a thousand seeking tongues.

Then they began to chant, the dialect too ancient and delivered too quickly for her to keep track of. But as they continued the incantation, the tongue-like sensation began to dig into her body, like steel worms pushing deeper and deeper into her tissues.

She had become accustomed to pain and torment, but none of the other miseries she'd suffered had abused her so . . . *internally*. The chanting of the dark ones, their living skin, seemed to be ripping her apart layer by layer.

When the pain at last became too great to bear, she parted her lips to release a scream.

As soon as she did, the shadowy haze covering the masters coiled into one huge line of black that speared into her open mouth. Their heinous energy filled her throat, permeated her bowels, and invaded her brain.

Then at once, the memories came. Hers. Theirs. Knowledge dating back to the birth of stars and light.

The dark enlightenment was beautifully wicked, and beneath the agony she felt the sudden urge to laugh. The desire to cry.

To eat. To hurt. To fuck.

And rising above the others was a deep-rooted need to bring vengeance. To deliver pain.

The delicious torture ravaged her being, and as her body convulsed, she smiled. She climaxed.

She comprehended all she'd endured.

And knew it had been worth it.

28

"Mom." Arik heard the emotion choking his voice. He felt the tears stinging his eyes. But despite the enormous gathering of people, he couldn't be bothered by machismo or saving face as he raced to fall into his mother's open arms.

Her body rocked as if she were sobbing. Or maybe that was him. All he knew, all he cared about, was that his mother was here—alert, speaking, moving and, by all accounts, appearing pretty damned cheerful.

He leaned back and cupped her face. "How do feel? Are you hurting? Do you need to be in bed?"

"*Pfft.*" She waved a dismissive hand. "I've been in bed, and it did the trick." She sent a warm look back up to Joseph and Sylvie, then to Willyn. "Thanks to all of these fine people." Her smile tracked the room to encompass everyone in the library.

"But you," she said, pinching Arik's chin. "You are a sight for these tired eyes. I've been hearing you and seeing you for a long time, but it's been like a dream. Only partial recognition, the world cloaked in a fog."

"I'm so sorry I didn't figure it out before now. I'm sorry I couldn't help you." Guilt was a knife in his chest, twisting with every detail he recalled of the last nine years.

"How could you?" She tilted her head, regret dampening just a bit of her joy. "Your father and I made a decision together. We thought we'd be the ones to learn the truth. To find the medallion and open the globe." She stroked his cheek. "We were the ones who let *you* down, I'm afraid."

She looked past him then, over his shoulder and directly at Rae. "My dear girl." She held out a hand and Rae rushed to take it, caressing his mother's pale skin. "How does it feel?" His mother asked.

Rae squatted to meet her gaze. "The mark, you mean?" She patted her neck. "It's fine. I don't even feel it."

"No, honey," his mother said, her blonde brows clashing together. "I mean the power. The magick of the Akasha."

Mouth falling open, Rae gaped. Then she turned her honey gold eyes to Arik. The eyes that had flashed with another color.

"Magick?" Rae's voice was small and strained. "I have magick? Serious magick?"

Behind her, Anna St. Germaine snapped her fingers and said, "I *knew* it."

~~~

Why am I so surprised? Rae couldn't stop tracing the spot below her ear, the area where she'd first felt the burn. The place where magick had left its mark. *I've known true power existed all of my life.*

Yet knowing others who possessed a gift—like Anna and the women of the coven—was a very different thing than finding out she had one, too. Especially after a tumultuous week like the one she'd just experienced.

"I can't have that kind of magick." Denial simply wouldn't let go. "I've never done anything other than spells. And even now, I can't do anything . . . anything . . ." When words failed, Rae wiggled her fingers. She wiggled her nose. "See? I don't *feel* anything."

"That's not true," Arik said, zeroing her focus back on him. "You said you felt energized after Mom transferred the symbol to you. And just now, you said the same thing."

"You just opened the globe, correct?" Marit gestured to the orb still parted into five leaves.

"Just before you came in," Arik said.

"I'm sure your powers will take effect. You just have to learn how to use them." Marit spoke earnestly to Rae. "Don't be afraid. We're in this together. I'm just sorry I can't teach you myself, but the gift has been stored in the globe. No Akasha in the world has had her magick since the globe was created and placed under a spell."

"Can you tell us about this spell?" Claudia piped up from her seat on a luxurious, crimson sofa. "I've never felt anything quite like it before. I sensed it was an enchantment, but the energy felt . . ."

"Ancient," Marit supplied. "Yes. The magick is old." She leaned toward Arik. "The very oldest."

A stillness fell over the room, as the impact of her statement hit.

"Roll me over there, son. I've told most of what I know." Marit nodded toward the globe. "Your father and I hoped to learn enough to fulfill our duties, possibly break the cycle." She pressed her lips into a tight line. "But, we didn't."

"Why don't we bring the globe to the center of the room?" Arik asked, glancing to Hayden's boyfriend, Trevor. He looked capable of hefting almost anything.

"Sure thing," Trevor said, knocking Cole's elbow. "Help me out. It looks pretty old."

"And if it breaks, you don't want to be the only one blamed." Cole shook his head and winked at Rae before popping a red candy in his mouth. "Some things never change." He turned to follow Trevor.

The two men were homicide detectives, partners Rae had learned. Their solid relationship shone through, and their good-natured ribbing lifted a little of the tension still zinging around the room.

"Thank you, boys," Marit called, drawing smiles from a few of the women. As Arik steered her over beside a table and lamp, she glanced up at him. "Your father and I didn't save you from this as we'd always hoped, but I can't tell you how happy I am that Rae is your Akasha."

Her sparkling eyes fell on Rae. "I always suspected. And always approved."

Rae returned the affectionate look, but her instincts tingled. She'd homed in on something Marit had said.

And so had Arik. "What do you mean *my* Akasha?" He locked the wheels and kneeled beside his mother again.

Marit grimaced. "I can't keep track of what we did and didn't tell you. I'm not sure of the whole story, as much of it was lost over time. Too much secrecy can turn against you in the end." She lifted her brows. "But I do know every Akasha is mated with a Huktai. For her protection."

Now Arik was the one who looked surprised. "Are you saying I'm a Huktai? A member of the group in Dad's journals?"

"Yes, and so was your father. *That* is the family legacy. Why do you think he always had you exercise and spar? He said knowledge could be given in a day, but not the fighting skills. The Huktai possess both, dating back to the beginning, before . . . well, before most recorded history. The chronicles are passed down through the Huktai, warrior scribes responsible for keeping the legacy alive."

Warrior scribe. Rae smiled inside. Pretty accurate description of how she'd always thought of Arik.

"Yes, the inheritance must continue," Marit went on, "at least, until the evil is finally vanquished."

"The evil?" Rae's mood took a hard turn, and she dropped into a vacant leather chair near Marit. Her pulse seemed to be whooshing in her ears. Probably because her heart had begun thumping erratically.

"We never knew specifics," Marit said. "Just that it was

very old and arcane. The facts have been obscured over the centuries."

"How is an Akasha chosen?" Anna came to stand behind Rae, putting a supportive hand on her shoulder.

"No one knows. But the mark, along with its obligation, passes when an Akasha dies. Or," Marit shrugged with a tiny grin, "she gets too old. Fighting dark powers is a young person's game."

"Your mark was suppressed by the curse." Ethan's coal-dark eyes focused on Marit before shifting to Rae. "That's why the symbol didn't appear on you until we performed the ritual."

Marit nodded, but her gaze turned inward. "That makes sense." She put a hand to the base of her throat and shuddered. "That night. After they separated your father and me."

Arik gripped her arm. He held tight.

"I'd been struck from behind and knocked out cold, but I woke to a woman's voice. Her voice, and others. I couldn't understand them, but the sounds they made . . ." Marit clasped her hands together and pressed them into her lap. "This has gone on so long—the secrets, the murders, the rivalries."

"Rivalries?" Arik asked.

"I'm not sure. Neither was your father." She turned to the globe. "I'm getting tired now, so I need to read this." She shot a glance to Rae. "Especially now that it's been opened and the power released. Who knows what other forces have felt the shift? We can't take any chances."

She stared down into the globe for a moment, and then waggled her fingers. "Can someone bring me the magnifying glass? This script is so old, and the lead dialect is French."

"I've got it." This came from the handsome blonde vet married to Shauni as he reached up to the high mantle and retrieved the magnifying glass. The large, round lens sat atop three wooden prongs curving outward like elephant tusks.

After scanning the inside of the globe, Marit blew out through her nose and shook her head. "There's so much here. I'll start from this leaf, which seems to be the beginning. But I'm afraid I'll have to paraphrase."

"Of course," Rae said, recognizing the signs of weariness creeping over Marit. She'd claimed not to want a bed, but the continuing drama was clearly taking its toll.

Marit ran her finger down the first section, her lips moving as if speaking to herself. At last, she sat back and spoke. "The woman who helped create this globe was a French witch who lived in 1573. Her name was Marie Rousseau, and she cast the spell on the globe to preserve the legacy." Sadness played over her expression. "Because she knew she was soon to die."

"Tell us," Rae said. "Tell us her story."

"She writes of terrible times, the witch trials spawned by that vicious book. *Malleus Maleficarum*."

"The Hammer of Witches," Quinn said, crossing his arms.

Marit nodded. "Marie was also an Akasha, and she claims the author had a mistress born of a malicious clan. This group, this clan, also had power. A dark power the mistress supposedly used to influence and convince Heinrich Kramer to write the book. A tool created for one purpose, and that was the extermination of witches."

Indicating the open globe, Marit continued. "Throughout the ages, there has been a battle between the light and the dark, with both sides rising and falling, winning and losing during different periods. But the story of the Huktai and Akashas goes back to the days when malevolent forces ruled the earth."

Another sigh and Marit said, "I can't make out the exact time period, but at one point this great evil was driven out, cast into another realm." She turned to Arik. "This is where the Huktai came into play. "The warriors and scribes who first joined together did so to create the artifacts. Enchanted relics that barred the evil from returning."

"How?" Lucia sat forward in her chair, chin propped on her

knuckles like a little girl hearing a campfire story.

"The scribes created a language. A language that combined their native tongues with that of the dark evil. A potent language inscribed onto five tablets. These were called the aethyrical texts."

"The aethyrs," Anna said. "Other realms, other dimensions. I've heard of this."

"Yes. Like the dimension to where the dark forces had been banished. The aethyrical texts were created to seal the doors between their world and ours." Marit sat up straighter. "But the Huktai needed magickal help to craft the texts. They needed witches, five witches."

"Five texts. Five witches." Rae gestured to the globe. "Five sections."

"Like the pentacle." This from Ian, standing beside Anna.

"Exactly like the pentacle." Marit drew a breath. "The witches who were summoned from their temple of worship embodied the energies of the earth. The five elements represented by the five points of the pentacle."

"Earth, air, fire, water. Even I know those," Nick said from where he sat on the bottom of the stairs with Viv. "But I'm not familiar with a fifth."

Now Marit smiled widely, her eyes brightened by the secret she was about to share. "The fifth element is spirit." Slowly, she turned to look at Rae. "Also known as Akasha."

Rae threaded her fingers together, rubbing her thumbs on the backs of her hands. "I don't understand."

"The five original witches held the power of the elements. And the heart of the elements—the energy that binds them all together—is spirit. Now you, Rae, have been given the full extent of that power." Marit reached out to put her hand on her arm. "It has fallen to you to activate the others."

Rae spoke with hushed reverence, and a little bit of fear. "What others?"

"The other witches. Earth, air, fire, and water. You will need all the Maidens if you are to defeat the enemy."

"Maidens?" Arik asked, lifting his shoulders in confusion.

"The five witches passed down their powers, their duties, and their names to those who continue the fight." Marit steepled her hands at her chest. She inhaled before whispering, "They were called the Watchtower Maidens."

The doorbell chimed suddenly and everyone jolted.

With prickling along her skin, Rae felt like *she'd* been listening to a campfire story. A ghost story, if the bumps on her arms and leap of her pulse were any indication.

She leaned back and put her hand over her heart, worried the thing was going to beat out of her chest.

The doorbell rang again, followed by insistent thumps.

"Sounds like Mahalia." Arik ran a hand through his hair. "I'll be right back."

"I'll get it, man. Don't get up." Chris hustled out the door and disappeared.

Marit closed her eyes as if she needed to recharge, and everyone else took a pause as well. This night had been full of revelations.

Rubbing the bridge of her nose, Rae tried to come to grips with this latest development. How was she supposed to activate the other witches? And how would she even know who they were?

It was all too much, and she was wearing down. A nice long nap appealed to her, too.

When Chris returned, it wasn't with Mahalia. The angry and persistent visitors were none other than Emma and Bryn.

Rae jumped up. "Emma? What are you doing here?"

Emma surveyed the library and its many occupants. "Me? What are you doing? I think that's the better question." She jabbed a finger at Arik. "Your day is up, by the way."

"Emma, I was going to explain everything, but I didn't know

where to begin. And I didn't understand it all myself." Rae swept her arm around the room. "We're just learning now."

"Learning what?" Bryn demanded, hands on hips and legs apart as if she were ready to go a round in the ring. "Something you can tell everybody except us? Your family?"

"It's complicated," Rae started, but then she gave up and dropped her arms to her sides. "You know what? I'm sorry. I was trying to protect you until I had a handle on things. But that is apparently *not* happening tonight."

"I'm sorry. Really sorry." Exhausted and unable to argue, she went to Emma. "I . . . it's just so . . ." Without words, she wrapped her sister in a hug. "Please don't be mad at me right now. I don't think I can take one more thing tonight."

Emma patted Rae's back and huffed. "Fine. If you'll tell me what's going on." Then her head shifted on Rae's shoulder. "Mrs. Mansur?" She pulled from the embrace and went to greet Arik's mother.

That left Rae to deal with Bryn. And her niece was a far tougher nut to crack.

"How about it?" Rae asked, doing her best to plead with her eyes.

"You'll spill it all? No more sneaking around and keeping us in the dark?"

"No more. Cross my heart." Rae made the sign with her finger and held out her arms.

Quirking her mouth to one side, Bryn reluctantly stepped closer. "I'm serious. I want to know."

Rae felt the tug of a grin as she took her niece in. So stubborn, just like her Aunt Rae.

But the moment they touched, Bryn leaped back with a cry of pain. "Oh! What is that?" Her hand flew to her neck. "Something's burning me."

When she faltered on her feet, Rae reached out to catch her. And as she did, she looked down at her niece's neck.

Right below and behind Bryn's ear, an angry red symbol marred the flesh.

"No, no." A pit opened in Rae's stomach. A deep hole of terror—deeper, darker, and more painful than she'd ever felt before. Because this was her Bryn. Sweet baby Bryn. "Not her. Please, no."

With horror rattling through her limbs and churning in her belly, Rae sat on the floor holding Bryn. Her precious niece.

And the second of the Watchtower Maidens.

29

Thunder boomed outside and Bryn's eyes opened. She stared blankly up at Rae before rising to a sitting position.

"Bryn, sweetie?" Rae asked, stroking her niece's dark, shoulder-length hair.

Blinking, Bryn climbed to her feet, shaking her head as if her ears were ringing.

"You're going to be fine." Rae jumped up after her. "I know it's scary, but it should stop hurting right away. How do you feel?"

Emma had joined them by this point. With worry etching her features, she reached for Bryn's shoulder. But she missed as Bryn walked toward the door, murmuring, "Can I use the bathroom?"

"Of course," Arik called to her. "Down the hall near the corner. You know where." His voice trailed off as he came to stand between Rae and Emma. Brow furrowed, he watched Bryn exit and rested his hand consolingly on Emma's shoulder. "She'll be fine."

Then to Rae, he added, "She's tough. If anyone can do this, you know she can."

"Do what?" Tears pooled in Emma's eyes. Frustration or fear, Rae couldn't tell.

Likely both, as she was suffering the same clash of emotions herself.

Another explosion of thunder rattled the windows. Dare

turned around, and then strode to look out to the sky.

Willyn sent him a quizzical look.

"No sign of rain," he said in a bemused tone.

"Rae!" Emma demanded, gripping Rae's arm hard enough to sting.

Overwhelmed and unsettled by what had happened to Bryn—what *she'd done* to Bryn—Rae glanced at the globe, to Marit, and then to Anna, who looked on apprehensively. Finally, her gaze locked with Arik's. "I don't know where to start."

"At the beginning," Marit said from her wheelchair. Sympathy in her eyes, she held out her hands and motioned for Emma. "Come here, honey. I know you're frightened. I'll explain everything."

After one last questioning glance at Rae, Emma relented, taking the chair nearest to Marit.

With her sister occupied, Rae all but collapsed into Arik's arms. "This can't be happening." She spoke into the crook of his neck, clutching his back. "I had barely begun to accept this for myself, but Bryn?" She choked down a sob. "It's not fair. It's not right."

Arik smoothed his palm down her hair again and again. "I know, but you'll be there for her, and so will I. And so will Emma, once she understands."

"An ancient evil?" She pulled back to look up at him. "The oldest evil? And now I've put my niece in its sights?"

"*But*," he stressed, "you've given her the power to fight it." Hardening his tone, he added, "You also have power, Rae, and I know you'll find it. You'll harness your magick and use it to defend all you hold dear, especially the people you love."

Rae nodded numbly. "I will." But white-hot fear lanced through her body, slicing her heart and stabbing at her gut. Her muscles ached, her head throbbed, and as she fell victim to her complete lack of control, her inability to alter destiny, a vision flashed in her head.

She saw herself crying and confused, broken and hollowed out. She pictured the day Arik had told her to go. The day he'd shattered her heart into a million pieces.

"I see now. I understand." As despair tried to rip her mended heart apart again, Rae released a shaking breath. "I know why you hurt me before. I *get it* now."

Arik only nodded.

"I would do whatever it took to get Bryn out of this." Clarity came with a rush of blood in her head. "But there's nothing I can do, because this will happen. It *has* happened."

That flow of blood heated her veins, thrumming with a new source of energy—Rae's determination to do exactly what Arik said. To harness the new gift she'd been given. To dig deep and discover her magick.

And use that magick to defend what she loved.

"I'd already decided to stay here in Savannah. To stay with you." Rolling her shoulders, she pushed back against the dread, though she knew it would be with her in the days to come.

"I'm still afraid," she admitted.

"I know." Arik's stare was fierce.

And Rae gave thanks for that. What she needed now was strength and support, not false words or empty assurances.

"But I won't run from this. I'll take it head on."

"That's my girl," he whispered, love burning alongside the ferocity in his gaze.

"And I will fight." Rae's hands balled into fists, almost of their own accord. "I will learn. I will study. I will practice." She waved her arm to the crowd of people. "Most of the coven didn't even know they were witches at first, and just look at what they accomplished. Together. As a team."

"You'll have yours as well," Arik said, brushing his thumb beneath her chin.

"I will." Rae curled her fingers around his wrist and held

his hand to her cheek. "After all, I've already got my very own warrior scribe."

"Your very own." He leaned down, kissed her lips. "Now and forever. Come what may."

"Come what may," she whispered against his mouth, sealing the promise with one more kiss.

Releasing his hold on her, Arik shifted his gaze to someone else, another who stood ready to fight beside Rae.

Anna drew closer and told her, "I remember something you said to me once, when I was filled with doubt and battling my own fears."

Swallowing a surge of emotion, Rae bit her lip. She listened.

"So now I'll throw your words back at you." Anna grinned. "You don't have power because you chose magick."

"Rae," Anna said, taking her hand. "You have power, because *magick chose you.*"

Vision blurring with a surge of tears, Rae pulled her friend into her arms. "Thank you. Thank you for everything."

Anna sniffled suspiciously and withdrew to wipe her eyes, just as Rae did the same. They shared a light laugh.

"Rae," Dare called from beside the window, the strain in his tone slashing through the tender moment. He tapped the glass with his finger. "Bryn's outside. She's leaving."

"What?" All the resolve Rae had just mustered was swamped by a resurgence of concern for her niece. She ran to the window and looked out. She knocked on the glass, hoping to get Bryn's attention.

In the sluggish, measured movements of a sleepwalker, Bryn halted and went absolutely still. Standing in the middle of the street, she rotated her head, slowly, so slowly. And as the wind kicked up her hair, Bryn's brown eyes—void of recognition—clashed with Rae's.

"Bryn!" Rae shouted and rapped the window again. "Bryn!"

Lethargically, her niece turned and continued her listless

march away from the house.

"What's wrong with her?" Emma was beside Rae, having raced over to peer outside. "She looks drugged."

Thunder cracked through the air, the glass trembling inches from Rae's nose. Like Dare had noticed before, there was no rain. Hardly any clouds.

Because it wasn't thunder.

She sensed a shift in the atmosphere, as if something had changed.

As if something had come.

Rae touched Emma's arm and backed away from the window, just as another noise filled the air. A loud howl sounding in the night.

"That was no animal." Shauni stood up in a fierce pose, just as Paige and Kylie leaped from their seats, mimicking her posture. Several other witches stood as well, arms loose by their sides and feet spread to shoulder-width.

One by one, the coven stood.

Each of them in a fighting stance.

Adrenaline flooded through Rae. It seared like gasoline and fueled her into action. "I've got to get out there. She's all alone."

Whirling, ignoring Emma's call, Rae bolted across the library, barely sparing a glance for Arik or Anna.

But she expected they knew what to do.

Arik turned to Joseph. "Stay with my mother?"

"I won't leave her side." Fulfilling his oath, Joseph went to Marit and stood behind her wheelchair.

"Rae!" Marit's voice, no longer frail or fragile with fatigue, lashed out to stop her in her tracks.

Hand on the doorway, she turned back to Arik's mother. To the matron Akasha.

"You have the power within you." Marit sat up straight, her gleaming stare reaching deep inside of Rae, as if by her will alone, she could ignite the fire of magick. "You are of the heart.

You are *the spirit* of the Maidens."

Rae inclined her head. Message received.

Then she ran down the corridor to go after her niece.

And to fight whatever was coming for Bryn, whatever was coming for them all.

And she would fight like hell.

The sound of others jostling into action registered to Rae's ears, but she just kept going. She was already on the front steps when Anna shouted for her to wait.

"I can't!" Rae yelled back. "Bryn's out of my sight!" Calling on a strength she never knew she had, Rae flew into the street. She stopped to scan the area, catching a glimpse of her niece as she turned the corner.

In the brief moment she paused, Anna and the other women caught up.

Viv was the last out of the house and ran straight up to Rae. "Sylvie and the men are going to stay here. To guard Marit and Emma."

"To hold Emma back, you mean." Lightning crackled in Kylie's palms. "Your sister's bold beneath the sweet. She'll do fine."

Rae nodded quickly and was about to ask about Arik when he burst out the door, sword in hand. He cleared the steps in one leap and sped past her. "Where?" he called out.

"She turned left." Directions given, Rae fell into a sprint behind Arik. His longer, stronger legs ate up the ground, but she pushed herself, pumping and driving, doing her best to stay with him.

He screeched to a halt at the end of the block and stared up at an enormous house. The sprawling home had once been majestic, but after years of neglect, cornflower-blue paint peeled from the wood siding and ivy had long ago staked its claim, trailing over the wrought-iron fence, the porch banisters, and around the windows.

"She went inside," Arik said, not even winded from the hard run.

Coming up next to him, Rae drew deep breaths, channeling every bit of her willpower to ignore any strain or discomfort. She had to concentrate on getting Bryn back to safety.

She chin-notched to the house. "This place has been empty for years."

"Exactly. So there's no good reason Bryn would have gone in there, especially now." Arik turned an intense stare on Rae. "We have to be prepared for anything."

Rae nodded and stepped toward the front gate, still standing open from Bryn's entry.

"Rae," Arik said sternly, catching her wrist. "Anything."

"I will be. I *am*." She slipped free but held his gaze. "But that's my niece, and I am going to protect her."

"So am I," he said. "But we're better off together."

"Truer words." Paige stood with her hands on her hips, looking as if she hadn't been affected by the run either.

That's right. Rae relaxed a fraction as she recalled Paige's special gift. *Super-speed. And super-strength.*

Rae turned back to the house with its dark, cracked windows. When this was over, she'd be sure to treat the coven girls to a day at the spa.

But first, she needed to kick some demon ass.

The howl she'd heard before burst from the sky, rolling from above and in from both sides. The vicious baying came from every direction.

But now the eerie sound was joined by others. A dark symphony of hellish screams—shrieks and moans, as if souls of the damned had been set free to roam the night.

And maybe they have, Rae thought, spreading her fingers and focusing on her palms, trying to summon power there as the coven women seemed to do.

The same women who circled around her now, gazing up at

the abandoned home where Bryn had disappeared.

"We're ready when you are," Anna told Rae.

"And we've got your back." This from the usually calm and serene Hayden.

But it was Willyn who spoke next, her uneasy stare aimed at the top of the house. "Bryn's standing in the window."

Rae jerked up her head. She found her niece looking down, staring blindly with a vacant expression.

But that wasn't why Rae's spine turned to ice.

Garnering her courage, she kept her eyes on the gloomy house. On Bryn. Her voice was tight and chilled by terror when she whispered, "And something is standing behind her."

30

Rae burst inside the house, raising a cloud of dust and the smell of mildew. A huge corridor veered off to the left and another to the right, while a third led straight ahead, beneath the hard angle of a wide staircase.

"Upstairs," Rae said. She was eager to get up to Bryn. And whatever dark shape had been looming over her shoulder.

Shadows darkened the large house, and cobwebs stretched across every corner. Rae kicked through a fallen chunk of plaster as Arik and Anna flanked her on both sides.

She moved toward the stairs, but startled when a shrill scream pierced down the right hallway. The fastest by far, Paige was gone in an instant, her speed leaving nothing but a blur in her wake.

Willyn and Lucia were right behind her, having entered and edged to that side of the foyer. The three of them stopped outside of a closed door.

"I'm coming," Rae said under her breath, ready to follow the three witches.

But another scream echoed from the opposite passage.

Rae whipped around. "That's Bryn's voice."

Another screech from straight ahead.

"It's a trick." Arik gripped Rae's arm. "But Bryn's here somewhere."

The scream turned to pleas, a tormented yell of, "No, no!"

Rae wanted to clap her hands over her ears. The sound of

her niece being tortured almost shut her down. But now was the time to govern her emotions, because she couldn't allow the evil to turn them against her.

"She's in here!" Lucia stood with Willyn at the end of the long hall, while Paige rammed her feet and fists at a closed door.

"Paige can't get in?" Claudia looked to Anna. "Even she can't break it down?" The red-haired witch called fire to her hands, a weapon at the ready.

"I don't think things are as they appear." Anna's chest heaved as she glanced around. "Be careful believing what you hear and see."

"Look out!" Viv yelled, before she tossed up her arms, using her telekinesis to catch a cement block that had fallen from above. She held the potentially lethal object in mid-air, and then eased it to within a foot of the floor.

She dropped it to shatter on the rotting wood, but the fragments of cement morphed into hundreds of huge gray moths that fluttered upward. They zoomed into everyone's faces, beating at their eyes and wiggling into their hair.

"They're not real." Shauni stood with her arms slack, not defending herself from the onslaught as the others were. "They have no voices. They don't exist."

As if her statement had broken through a glamour, the moths flickered and vanished.

"There are no ghosts here." Hayden touched her palm to a papered wall. Then drew back to dust her hands together. In confirmation of what they already suspected, she said, "The darkness here is too great. They've all fled."

Paige shouted, "What the hell is going on?" She gave one last kick to the seemingly impenetrable door.

"I saw Bryn in the third-floor window," Rae said firmly. "I know that was really her, or why else would that . . . *thing* have been hovering around her?" She turned her face towards the ceiling. "I know she's up there."

"Listen to your instincts," Anna said in full support. "The evil is trying to distract us, but mainly you." Blue eyes on Rae, she repeated a version of what Arik's mother had said. "You are the only one who can save Bryn. Our powers may work against the monsters, and we may be able to guard your back, but whatever has its hooks in your niece can only be driven out by you."

"You are spirit," Arik said. "You bind the Maidens together."

Bolstered by their faith, Rae tried again to summon her magick. And this time, she felt something stir. Not in her palms, not in her gut, but in a place nestled right below her heart. A warm twinge and then a soothing sigh.

She felt the power of spirit swirling, awakening to answer her call.

"I'm going to get Bryn." With that, she rushed to the stairs, taking them two at a time in her haste to find her niece.

The darkness responded, loosing a horde of beasts from within the shadows.

Something Rae couldn't see streaked by her head. Though invisible, the beast scratched the skin below her jaw as it passed.

Below her, an uproar sounded, a flurry of shouts as the coven began tossing warnings to each other or bellowing their rage as they fell into battle. Rae kept running, focused on reaching Bryn.

"Go!" Arik yelled from a few steps below her, Anna and Kylie not far behind.

By the time she reached the landing on the third level, her thighs burned and her breaths shuddered. She turned in a circle to get her bearings. "That way." She pointed in the direction she'd seen Bryn.

"Rae, help me," a plaintive voice sounded from behind her.

Kylie was closer, so she dashed to the closed door, Bryn's

plea still coming from the other side. One second there was a shadow on the ceiling. And the next it changed, taking shape and diving for the blonde-haired witch.

"Kylie!" Anna screamed, shooting off a blue ball of magick just as Kylie dropped to the floor on her back with lightning streaming upward from her fingertips.

Both attacks landed and the black form incinerated, dusting the air with ash.

"Rae, please!" Bryn's begging voice again, high and thin, as if she were suffering.

Kylie gained her feet, opened the door, and went through. Anna trailed after her. As soon as they were inside, the door slammed shut, trapping Anna and Kylie within.

The thumps of their banging fists rang out as they pummeled the wood.

Arik hurried to the door and tried to force it open. But like Paige, he had no luck.

"Raaaaaeeee."

A hundred needles pricked the back of Rae's neck as she slowly turned. This time, the call was different—deep and scratchy, soulless and cruel.

As Arik worked at the door, Rae pivoted on her heels and searched the halls. Until she found the owner of the abhorrent voice.

"Bryn," she said, her own voice cracking with horror. "I'm here now. I'm going to help you."

Head lolling grotesquely to one side, Bryn crooked her finger at Rae. Steps shuffling on the dirty floor, she backed into a room.

Without hesitation, Rae went after her, not at all surprised when the door closed with a *bam*! and locked behind her.

She tried to ignore the smell, a cloyingly sweet yet putrid odor.

Arik pounded on the door from outside. "Rae!"

"I'm here," she tossed back. "I'm with Bryn."

Controlled by the thing in her body, Bryn slid down the wall and huddled in the corner, wet, garbled laughter spewing from her lips. "With Bryn?" it taunted. "Liar, whore, bitch."

Bryn's forehead lowered, and the demon inside glared up from beneath creased brows. "When have you ever been *with* Bryn?"

"You're the liar," Rae said. "I've seen your tricks, your cowardly illusions." She stepped closer. "Get out of my niece's body. She belongs with me, with her family. And you can't have her."

"I've already got her." The thing grabbed a hunk of hair and ripped several thick strands from its own scalp. From Bryn's scalp.

Though the beast hunched inside, the resulting cry of pain belonged solely to Bryn.

"Bryn, sweetie. I'm here. Just look at me. Focus on me."

"Aunt Rae." Bryn's face collapsed, her brown eyes watered. "I'm so alone."

"No. I'm here. Come back to me. Shove the darkness out." She tried to rouse the magick she'd felt in her heart before, but the warm sensation had been doused by anguish. Drowned by the revulsion of seeing her niece possessed.

And the vile creature seemed to know she wavered. It gave her one malicious grin before her niece's voice changed again and she started to cry. The voice was a child's now, and it belonged to a much younger Bryn.

"Nobody loves me. They always leave." Bryn's tears streaked her face, leaving trails in the dust covering her cheeks. "My daddy didn't stay. He didn't care. And neither do you."

"Bryn, stop." Rae ached for her niece. Even if the words were forced, the pain beneath them was all too real. "I love you. Emma and Granddaddy love you." She crept closer to her niece. "And Arik has never stopped loving you. We'll all be together now, the big family like we used to talk about."

Rae licked her lips and advanced a bit more. "Come home with me." She tried to quiet her mind yet she wanted to scream.

"Home?" Bryn tilted her head. "You won't stay. You always leave."

"Not this time. I swear." She held out her hand. "Bryn, you're the fighter of this family. Now I need you to help me. Drive it out. You can do it."

"No, she can't." The beast was back, slapping at Rae's outstretched palm, its razor-sharp claws extending from Bryn's nails to slice out in fury. "And you can't either."

The thing growled, drool slipping from the corner of its mouth as its eyes—Bryn's eyes—flooded with pure black. "She's ours, and you've already lost."

"She is *mine!*" The love and fear Rae felt for her niece tangled up with a surge of rage. The mix of emotions set off a spark, just the tiniest flicker of the warm sensation from before. The power of spirit born in her heart.

Only this time, she latched on to the energy, allowing her gift to spring forth and gain control. Magick spread from her center and out to her limbs, coursing through her body with the strength of life.

With the purity of spirit.

As the sensation built, a pale purple mist floated up from her palms, a delicate haze she directed to Bryn.

When the mist curled around her niece, the thing inside her spit and cursed. It howled with a force that rattled the walls.

Growling, frothing at the mouth, it jerked its head in a fast circle. "Bitch. Whore. Bitch. Bitch."

Rae continued to surround Bryn with magick, as the demon inside slowly loosened its hold.

"We're not leaving. We're here to stay." The thing laughed again, though the cackle had lost its edge. "We are only the first wave. Those who've been here all along. Just waiting.

Waiting for you."

Rae ignored its threats and focused on Bryn.

"You woke us all. And we'll be back." The last words were hardly a whisper, as the monster finally seeped from Bryn's body.

Rae was certain the demon was gone when her niece dropped her head against the wall, wiped her hair from her dirty face and, staring boldly into Rae's eyes, uttered, "What the fuck?"

"Come on." Rae hooked her arms under Bryn's elbows. "We have to go."

"That monster was in my head. In my body." Bryn smacked her mouth as one did when trying to get rid of a bad taste.

"I know. But that's not the only monster we have to worry about." Rae grabbed the handle of the door, and to her surprise, it swung open without resistance.

She and Bryn rammed toe-to-toe with Arik. He made a move as if to pick Bryn up, but she swatted at him.

"I'm good, thanks. And no offense, but I'd rather be on my own feet in case one of those bastards tries to slip into my head again." She touched her neck. "The last thing I remember is the burn. After that, it's just bits and pieces of being held under murky black water."

Her description of demon possession caused Rae's stomach to turn over with nausea. "I'm not going to let that happen again." She patted Bryn's neck. "You have magick now. Real power. But I didn't find mine right away."

"So let's just focus on getting out of here for now." Arik looked quickly to the side. He then performed a deep lunge, some sort of pivot, and came up to slash his sword through a shadow streaking toward Rae and Bryn.

"They want you now," he called to Rae. "You and Bryn, while you're still only two of the five." Then he shouted, "Anna!" and pointed with his blade.

She whirled and fired in one smooth move, pulverizing

another of the shades.

That's how Rae thought of them. A shade or shadow, but one that had come to life and meant to drag her into its dark existence.

Putting Bryn between herself and Arik, Rae took the lead and strode back toward the stairs. "We're at a disadvantage here. We need to get out."

"They seem to be weakening, though," Kylie said, taking up position on one side of Bryn while Anna closed in on the other. As the only one without any power or any weapon other than her fists, Bryn needed to be shielded from attack.

They maintained this arrangement as they ran down the stairs, with Rae halting midway to fend off a shade.

She had no idea how her magick would work as a defense, but she released a mist toward the beast just as fire erupted in the demon's center.

With a strangled moan, it burned quickly to a brittle black crisp. "They're clearing out," Claudia called, the apparent thrower of flames. "Whatever you did up there had most of them running for the hills."

"Or slithering for the shadows," Kylie said. "Whatever their kind does."

"You guys okay?" Paige streaked up to stand next to Claudia. "Lucia, Willyn, and I were being attacked from every side, but then that door finally popped open, and the assault stopped."

"Your magick," Bryn said to Rae. "You released your power and drove out my demon. But that's also when the possession of . . ." She waved her hand as if searching for words.

"Of the house," Arik said. "I don't think the shadowy demons we saw were the only forces here. But when Rae released her power, they all weakened."

Doing a complicated swivel with his blade, he shot Rae a grin. "My Akasha." His eyes glowed as if he couldn't wait to get her alone and take another look at the symbol on her flesh.

"All right," Anna said, chuckling and holding up a hand as she started to walk down.

Sending a secret smile back to Arik, Rae formed a small puff of magick in her hand and blew a kiss through the pale purple mist. "There's more where that came from."

"And I'm out." Bryn shook her head and departed as well, leaving Kylie to descend with Rae and Arik.

The golden-haired Kylie beamed at them. "Go ahead and kiss. I don't mind." She bounced her way down the stairs, saying over her shoulder, "I've always been a romantic."

Settling for simply taking her hand, Arik went down with Rae and escorted her all the way outside. With the possessing demon and other dark forces departed, the abandoned home returned to a lifeless and empty shell.

Somewhat dust-covered but with a fairly bright disposition, the group trekked back down the street to Arik's house.

"Oh, thank God!" Emma's joyful cry streaked over the manicured lawn when Rae came into view, Bryn tucked under one arm.

Emma met them in the grass, taking hold of Bryn and Rae at the same time. "I was so scared. So scared." She patted their heads, their faces, and gave them a head-to-toe inspection.

"We aren't hurt," Bryn told her. "Although I do want a shower more than oxygen right now." She shivered and made a face of disgust. "I've got demon residue on me."

Emma slapped her heart. "Please, don't say that. I'm still getting used to the idea."

"Arik," Ian said from the porch, front door open and light spilling out from behind him. "You have a visitor." He glanced around the crowd and grinned. "Well, *another* visitor."

"And it's right happy I am that you all survived." Mahalia's form filled the doorway before she too walked down the steps.

Arik's home was one of the largest in the district, yet everyone seemed to want to stand outside.

"I've got it," she said, crossing the grass in the moonlight. "I know what my mother was trying to tell me." She put one hand on his shoulder and the other on Rae, as if confirming they were truly safe.

"What was it?" Arik asked, tugging Rae against his side. Physically and mentally exhausted, she absorbed his warmth and let him hold her up.

Mahalia handed him a piece of paper, etched with a symbol and a word. The symbol he and Rae both recognized. "This is the sign for the fifth element, the element of spirit." He kissed Rae on her forehead. "Also known as Akasha."

"Yes, your mother's been filling me in." Mahalia's smile was delighted when she said, "And I'm so happy for you both, you and your mother."

"Thank you." Arik said, his affection for Mahalia in his voice. "You started this whole thing with that early morning visit." He looked up at the moon. "But you don't usually come over at night."

"I had to come." Her eyes flicked between Arik and Rae, and she sighed. "You've just had a victory, and I'm glad for you. But there's something you need to know."

She tapped the paper he still held. "This word, I've heard it before. This word," she drew a breath, "it's going to be a problem."

"What does it mean?" Rae asked, leaning over to read the writing. The spelling was odd.

Anna moved closer to Rae and looked down at the paper. She read the word. "Mahalia's right. It's going to be trouble. This word refers to an affinity for dark entities, particularly demons. And I'm especially concerned about these demons and the ancient power behind them."

"What do you mean?" Arik asked her.

"Those from tonight, the ones we fought," Anna shook her head, "they aren't like any we've encountered before."

"Me either," Ethan chimed in, a concerning claim from a demonologist.

"But Aunt Rae beat them back." Bryn crossed her arms. "I was lost in the dark, cold and alone. Then all of a sudden, she was there. Her voice, her eyes, and the purple haze." She chuckled then. "But not the one from the song."

The laughter did Rae good and was likely more infectious because it was Bryn's. All Bryn's, without a hint of anything hiding beneath.

"And like Arik said," Bryn continued, "so far we're only two. There are three more Maidens out there we have to find."

Bryn snapped her fingers and pointed at Rae. "And I still have magick to tap into." In lieu of a happy dance, she performed an upper cut to the air.

Laughing at Bryn's antics, Anna hugged Rae, long and hard. "Listen to your niece, Rae. You have time to prepare and find yet more allies to join you in the fight."

She eased from the embrace and moved to Ian. "The globe, I'm sure, has much more to tell you. And as someone with just a bit of experience," she said with a teasing tone, "I think you did pretty well. For a newbie in her very first battle."

"Hey," Rae objected playfully.

But Arik came to her defense. "She was amazing." His hand circled on Rae's back. "And she didn't even have her Huktai there to protect her."

"Maybe I will be the one protecting you." Rae flicked the tip of his nose.

"Enough of that." Mahalia swatted playfully at Arik as he started to kiss Rae again. "Let's all get inside. I know you all have got to be hungry, and I've been dying for a chance to fire up that big ol' kitchen."

"I second the motion," Lucia said, thrusting her hand in the air like a pupil in class.

With the consensus that food was the right answer, the

witches paired up with their men and made their way into the house.

Only Anna hung back for a moment. "You know, there's been so much going on that I haven't had the chance to tell you something."

"What's that?" Rae asked, happier in this moment—post ancient-evil battle—than she would have expected.

With a gleam in her eye and a soft smile, Anna winked and said, "Welcome home."

Rae watched her oldest friend enter Arik's house. The house she believed she would one day share with him.

Laying her head on his shoulder, Rae closed her eyes as Arik stroked her hair. "I know it's only just begun, but the power that flowed through me . . ."

She turned and lifted her face to his, "And the love that still does, for Bryn, Emma, Anna." She lifted on her toes, lips curving as she added, "and for you. It's all come together perfectly, as if it had always been meant to be."

"It is meant to be." Arik beat her to the kiss, lowering his mouth to hers for a long, sweet moment beneath the shimmering moon.

Then he pressed his hand to her heart. "And this is where our magick will grow."

"Stronger together," she said. "Come what may."

As Arik took her lips again, she felt a hint of the magick he'd mentioned, just the first bloom. And she knew it was love.

Yes, the shadows would return, but with friends, love, and ~~~~~ on her side, Rae would stand and fight for her home. For ~~~~~ them all.

~~~~~ de her would rise again. Whenever needed.

EPILOGUE

She sat upright on the stone slab, filled with a new realization. New power. And new hate. The same hate the dark masters thrived on. The thirst for vengeance that fed their ancient and twisted souls.

And now she knew what they were. Now she was privileged to know their name.

DoSaa preSyajana. Their title spoken in the sacred language.

Yet she didn't miss the humor of the translation. In English, they were the servants of darkness. The *servants*.

The irony was too much.

Having both her memories and theirs shoved into her mind had been excruciating, but so very worth it. She now possessed a world of secrets.

She now possessed the *secrets of the world*.

Along with that came full comprehension of their language, so old and arcane. Power and force in the very words.

The *DoSaa*—the Darkness—as she thought of them, still surrounded the stone table. One of them stepped closer. "You understand why we allowed you to receive our gift."

"Yes," she said, newfound strength in her voice.

"You understand to whom you answer."

"Yes." When the reply stuck in her throat, she swall and repeated more clearly. "Yes."

She still belonged to them. They could still hurt h she'd yet to experience.

"Your corporeal body is long-dead and in the ground," the dark one continued. "You must seek out another and make it your own."

"Yes." She dropped her gaze in deference and respect. She was almost out of this abysmal place and would do nothing to reverse her newly elevated position. Her new role. One that would free her and endow her with unlimited freedom. Unlimited *life*.

Just the notion brought a cruel grin to her lips.

"Then leave us, but never forget . . . we can always reach you." The dark one stepped back to fall in line with his brethren. "We can always *touch* you."

Tightening her muscles to hide the shiver his warning induced, she nodded and closed her eyes.

The deep voices of the *DoSaa* rose up in unison, the weighty sound enfolding her in a delightfully sinful embrace.

The force—the *power*—of their words filled every particle of her body and consciousness, turning both into a singular energy. A singular entity. One that required no mass, no specification.

The whole of her being existed without time, place, or meaning. And there she floated, drifting in nothingness.

Until she found herself hovering in the air, above a noisy, riotous room filled with people. Brimming over with real, live humans.

The smile she conjured was sharp with malice. The laughter she released filled with anticipation.

For she too had become a master. A ruler who would dominate over the weak creatures who dwelled in this world.

But to harness the extent of her powers, she needed to acquire a new form. And the rowdy pub was packed full of young, strong, attractive bodies.

She homed in on a stunning blonde, tall and leggy. But passed her up when she noted the weakness of her arms, the slight bulge of her belly.

No. She would have the appropriate physique. One befitting the ruler—the warrior—she'd fought to become.

Ah, there. The interesting-looking girl wearing a sleeveless shirt and tight jeans, all in severe black. Toned, strong arms, a long, lean physique. And most importantly, a vibrancy in her eyes. A bright smile.

Both of which were about to be extinguished.

With nothing but the power of her thoughts, she willed the spirit of the girl to depart. Then she waited for her chosen one to get a dazed expression on her face. After which, the bold brunette soon slumped in her chair and fell forward onto the high-top table.

When the human passed on and her form went slack, the one who'd come to claim her body streamed into the now empty shell.

Instantly blood heated her veins. A heart beat—*ka-thump ka-thump*—pounded in her chest and echoed in her ears. The proof of resurrection brought her head back up with an unruly burst of laughter.

Across from her, a young man asked if she felt sick. In answer, she grabbed a beer mug and clinked it to his.

"Thought you'd blacked out," he said. "Maybe you should order some food."

"Oh, yes," she whispered seductively, easing out of her chair and around the table to trail a hand along his rugged jaw. "I definitely need to *eat.*"

As she nipped his neck and drew a tiny drop of blood, she sensed her former self, her *true self*, returning to take over the new body.

She pulled back from his tempting flesh and licked her lips.

"What the hell?" the guy asked in shock. Then again, louder, as he shoved away forcefully enough to topple his stool. "What the hell!"

an to look as he stumbled away. Eyes wide and
e stared at her in disbelief.

Crooking her head to one side, she popped her neck with a
loud *crack*! Then she glanced down at her arm, overjoyed to see
ink running in rivers through her skin.

"What's happening to you?" a girl shouted from nearby. "Oh
my God! Look at her eyes!"

The body's dark-brown hair had been close enough, but she
had both the desire and the ability to match the rest of her
appearance to her previous life. And so she did, right in the
middle of the few stunned bystanders who'd noticed the change.

While the rest of the bar partied on in ignorance.

She reveled in the transition. She could sense each tattoo
that appeared on her body, and could *feel* her eyes fade from
brown. Changing colors to one blue. And one black.

"What . . ." The young man held out trembling hands. "What
are you?"

In a lightning-fast move, she had her arms around his waist
and her tongue on his throat. But just before she took another
quick bite, she laughed low and spoke close to his ear.

"Call me Searenn."

Suza Kates writes both paranormal romance and romantic suspense. She lives in Savannah, Georgia with her family and four ridiculously spoiled cats.

For more on Suza and her books visit

www.suzakates.com